10/83

10/
10.84

The Lizard's Tail

LUISA VALENZUELA

The Lizard's Tail

A NOVEL

Translated from the Spanish by
GREGORY RABASSA

FARRAR · STRAUS · GIROUX

New York

Printed in the United States of America
Published simultaneously in Canada
by McGraw-Hill Ryerson Ltd., Toronto
Designed by Jack Harrison

Library of Congress Cataloging in Publication Data
Valenzuela, Luisa
The lizard's tail.
Translation of: El señor de Tacuru.
I. Title.
PQ7798.32.A48S413   1983   863   83–5507

The Lizard's Tail

The Prophecy

A river will flow
(I want to flow with it)
A river of blood will flow
(I shall open the sluice gates)
river of blood
(I am myself in that river)
of blood
(just what I like)
           and
     enough! Conjunctions revolt me

and Then Twenty Years of Peace Will Come

     —twenty years means nothing
     —what's coming can be postponed forever
     —I won't even mention peace. It's static, frozen. It
     doesn't concern me and doesn't consider me.

I will cut the old prophecy short and the river will
continue to flow through my work and my wit. A river of
blood will flow to the rhythm of my own instruments.

THE ONE

The accordion

Ever since my earliest childhood the accordion has awakened this kind of ant-crawling tickle in me and I lose my bearings but find some calm. Not the flute, though, the flute perks me up. And let's not mention drums, drums are something quite different and I'll go on beating drums through the length and breadth of my life—when I don't turn to the bass drum, when I don't turn to the bass drum, and that will really be magnificent.

Did I say length, did I say breadth, did I say *my* life? How stupid. One ends up using other people's clichés as if one were like them, as if one could deal in human dimensions when impregnated by the infinite, the eternal, the all-encompassing. I am the Immanent, I am the salt of life.

That's how it is and I won't justify myself. If I have never (another word I loathe) justified myself before, I don't see why I should do it now when we have succeeded at last—along with my sister Estrella, my sister who is in me—in fully accepting our greatness. It was like building ourselves out of sand: accepting greatness grain by grain until this our single body was formed. And now that we're made completely out of sand, out of pure greatness, time doesn't pass for us. The beard I have grown is a worthy beard, a prophet's beard—it's not a cover-up as has been insinuated by some of the chosen few who still have the enormous privilege of being able to contemplate our person.

They come to consult me.

They come to consult us, my sister and me, even though none of them knows the Secret. No one, never ever (tra-la-la, that tricky measure of time again, as if it mattered to us), has seen me without clothes on and that's why no one tra-la-la has seen Estrella. Except for that man, that one who recognized her and baptized her and gave her the kiss. That man, that so-called teacher, who luckily no longer belongs to the realm of the living. It was her/my only true kiss. The Kiss.

Others, quite different, were once my lovers. All those females who simultaneously paid me homage. Now I've eradicated them from my world that mimics theirs, but when I sail along on my island of reeds the winds sometimes drive me close to their territory and I observe them through my binoculars. I can't quite see them—tiny and red as they are—but I can see their dwellings, the anthills, the *tacurús*, tall castles with towers and battlements, dungeons and tiny cells. I learned something from these females, although they weren't worthy of my respect. Only one deserved such a distinction, and when I met her, she was already dead. So much the better. It saved me from falling into the temporality of love or desire.

The ants, on the other hand, knew about me in my life and recognized me. I was so young then, responding to music of the accordion at siesta time. They say my mother gave a double shriek when I was born and then died forever: there was nothing left for her to do in this world. They say that day was so like the others that nobody—not even my mother—sensed the omen, and with good reason: ever since my birth I've mastered the invaluable art of pretense and mimicry. That's why a little later my cradle was a fruit crate hanging from a bough and I became the Thousandmen flower for many a day.

4

Golden yellow with crimson spots, I was the Thousand-men flower while the unenlightened talked about measles and fed me potions.

Flour, water. My godmother made noodles, concocted a stew, gobbled it up, and digested it. Long, crushing siestas, during which I, barely two years old, used to sneak out, running away from the ever so sad sound of kitchen accordions, and went looking for laughter. The creaking, sun-dried earth cracked a smile for me, opened up in fits of laughter, led me to the anthills, those castles. Why did the ants, so tiny and red, have castles, while I didn't? I think it was my yet-unknown sister, the future Estrella, who made me do it: I felt the itching right where she dwells—between my legs—and to deal with the itch I got into the habit of climbing onto castles. I couldn't reach the highest castle yet, but I chose one that was just right for me and I sat down and crushed it. It was an anthill, but it was also my first castle, and the ants recognized me, of course, and covered me with their own sumptuous redness. I was resplendent and quivered in the sun. A robe of red ants, the most beautiful cloak I'd ever had, alive with pulsating antennae and festive thrills in each one of its folds and stitches. Later on, I tried to find another living robe, but everything that came to me was already dead, even though still warm. The robe of serpents someone suggested I rejected as slimy and unconstitutional. The other robe was one of love and respect: not one of those man-eating ants bit me. They revered me. They loved me.

In my puberty I'd also learned whom to love. When my testicles dropped for good and my sister Estrella complained for the first and only time, before finding warm comfort between the two of them.

"Manuel's got three balls, Manuel's got three balls," shrieked the idiot Eulogio in the midst of the marshes, the only words he ever uttered in his life. Since my name still wasn't Manuel in those days, it didn't bother me much. Rather, I experienced it as praise: what today I call Eulogio's Eulogy. The homage to Estrella from a mute idiot who only spoke to point her out. My first miracle.

I recounted it ever so many times to the Generalississimo, with a few alterations in the text, of course. Miracles can be elastic and the Generalississimo understood that, although in other matters he was a little obtuse (this stubbornness of his is what caused the failure of my last attempt with him and prevented me from bringing him back to life). But the Generalississimo is secondary, I'll talk about him sometime, when his turn comes. For now and forever it's my turn, I'll concede him a crumb when I feel like it or maybe when Estrella strongly demands it. She loved him, I think, even though she always had the delicacy to try to hide it.

Getting back to the miracle, I used to tell the Generalississimo that Eulogio had shouted—his only words, his only human emission:

"Manuel's got a halo, Manuel's got a halo,"

or

"Manuel is a saint, Manuel is a saint,"

or, closer to the truth (if there is such a thing),

"Manuel has three . . . marks on his forehead."

The Generalississimo didn't waste his time on unimportant interpretations: he was accustomed to taking words literally and accepting facts as they were presented to him.

Estrella, on the other hand, discusses everything, she analyzes, vivisects, and interprets. Metaphorically speaking, of course, as it should be, since she is the living metaphor.

Estrella. Discovered by the red ants. She was the

6

only one who got to know the dungeons of the ants, the secret tunnels where they suckle life. I sat on the ant castle and I destroyed the castle. She penetrated into its innards. I had taken all my clothes off during that visit to the world of *tacurús*, and without knowing it I already knew that my true clothing would be the living robe. Estrella managed thus to enter the collapsed realm of the ants and learn their secret and chat with the queen. Simple circumstances that led her to *be* the queen and make me, who subsumes her, her omnipotent god.

Now I know: ants are wise and at the same time bold, or maybe vice versa, or also vice versa. Precisely. Wisdom leads them to boldness, boldness to wisdom, in a cyclical, pendular way unknown to the majority of sad mortals, who are terrified by knowledge and refuse to risk their skins to attain it. Not ants. They know that in order to attain knowledge one must pay a price, and they are ready for anything. A lot of them are lost in the search, whole ant colonies go out of control and put together the oddest structures, beautiful, useless, and fatal. But ants are inferior beings: they need drugs. Ants have herds of aphids that they milk like cows, they suckle on the aphids and get drunk and know. I must have got drunk as well at the age of two, in an unmentionable way, and since then I have known. No. Quite the contrary. The ants sipped from me and that's why they didn't eat me alive. Ever since then, they've known. Thereafter, the anthills, the *tacurús*, have become more erect and majestic.

I am superior. I don't need any drugs, although at times I share those of others out of pure sociability, so as not to seem different. And to keep my business going: I produce drugs—no longer through my pores but in an industrial way, so others can attain, even if only in fleeting flashes, a little of the light that illuminates me.

For my personal use, I *am* the drug, the drug is I.

The ants sipped from my pores, from my most private crevices, that's why I feel I haven't stolen anything from them by building this subterranean castle of mine. The Tacurú. With tunnels and passageways, bridges and cat-walks, dungeons and cells, and these ventilators like little towers that, seen from the air, look like a field of anthills.

It might be that some daring ant, *in illo tempore*, made its home in my person in order to instruct me, so many years later, on the shape of the tunnels and the ventilators, so as to keep me out of sight of those who are hunting for me.

A field of anthills is what my castle looks like when seen from the ground up. From the ground up there is always so little to be seen.

Wise *tacurús*, tubes through which the wind comes to bring music throughout my labyrinthine castle. A sound more like a moaning accordion than like an organ. The accordion of nostalgic childhood siestas. Underground castle, Aeolian, a miracle that I often celebrate by drinking a glass of the choicest formic acid.

I've mentioned my floating island and I've mentioned my castle on land—underground. That's me, versatile. Master of all landscapes.

Why did I come back to my native soil? Ask the few who are allowed to see me, for they know the risks that my return entails. Because I am my native soil, I am—we are, I mustn't forget Estrella, even if I never mention her in public—made of this finest, purest sand. I am—we

8

are—like crystal: all of one piece, and I don't deceive myself.

The government people, who are supposed to be my enemies, can't act without me. They have to consult me. They use intermediaries, they beat around the bush, but nevertheless they consult me. I go along with their game: I play the part of one who doesn't know, who hides from official agents, I only let disguised emissaries find me. I transform myself, assuming the most complex personae, and pretend to hide. But I still let them find me and applaud the results. It's important for me to pull the strings even if my name never appears in the newspapers. I've erased my name, though from time to time someone thinks to call me Don Manuel. I don't encourage it at all; public opinion doesn't interest me in the least and I prefer to let them believe what they believe: that I've become invisible, that the earth has swallowed me up. Officially, no one can find me, not the police nor the gendarmerie, not Interpol nor the CIA nor the FBI nor the KGB nor any of those initials that were especially created not to find me.

I'm invisible for two reasons, one better than the other:

—I know how to camouflage myself under their very noses

—I've become indispensable to the ones who give the orders.

Capital. Night

"I tell you he's a dangerous fellow."

"Come, now. He's just a poor lunatic, he thinks he's that Minister of Well-being, so many years ago, remember? The Sorcerer."

"Does he only think it? Couldn't he really be him?"

"No. That man was liquidated by the military right after the coup. How could they let him come out of it alive? That fellow was a threat to them, he knew too much. And they're letting this one go on grazing peacefully, that's all, even allowing him the clownish pleasure of pretending to be hiding when everybody knows he's going around strutting through the Marshland. It seems there are people who worship him and bring him offerings."

"Government people, of course."

"You're exaggerating, woman. I agree that the military are animals, but they're more or less rational animals. They don't get involved in witchcraft."

"What's been going on lately is witchcraft pure and simple, you can't deny that."

"This unfortunate situation is repeated every so often in human history. It's called fascism."

"There wasn't any reason for its happening to us, a literate, accomplished, hardworking, peaceful people."

"It's the socioeconomic contingencies. We've got to

fight against them, not against nonexistent witchcraft."

"I think you would do well to take a little trip through the Marshland. You might be able to clear something up. What's the man's name?"

"They say it's Manuel, like the other fellow. A very common name. But they also call him the Papoose, Eulogio, the Sorcerer, Estrella, Sixfingers, the witchdoc, the Sawman, Red Ant."

The drums

No reason for concern, they're subnormal, that's all. I've always said so. Now they think they're going to find me in the Marshland. They'll find me if I want them to. I've got my own inner country, a country of the mind where I take refuge when I feel like it. I know they're talking about me again in the Capital and there've been some sharp ones who've got me pinpointed. Let them come.

I'm a submarine of the mind, I submerge at will, I watch them through my secret periscope and if they get close I can madden them with a drumroll.

A serious matter, the drums. They're the strength of the world that lies over the border. Drums, tambours, congas, snares, bongos, *tamborils*, *marugas*, *guaguas*, gourds, tambourines, *huehuetes*, *tablas*. Those. I get strength from the drums and I give strength back to the drums threefold. The drumhead of my skin resounds, Estrella pounds in wild pulsations, I flail about and vibrate as if the hands of ten black drummers were playing me. Twenty hands with cold blue palms stimulating me with the sweet intensity that only those hands can bring out.

I'll have to go back. I'm going to go back.

For three days with their nights he prepared for the trip and sent out his calls. Concentrating in front of his own altar, which was a large mirror, he gave off mental waves so they could come looking for him on the wrong day. He also gave off certain Hertzian waves on a private frequency and put on his white robe, waiting for the sunset.

At the indicated hour, a double row of false anthills were lighted up to mark the landing strip and the Beechcraft landed without any trouble.

"I'm going to take advantage of this extra trip and load the you-know-what," the pilot told him. "We're going to have to fly very high, here's the oxygen equipment if you need it."

"Don't worry. I *always* fly high."

The broad band of the river showed them the border, and after a few miles the pilot made out the other clandestine landing strip. An almost blind landing, and the plane took off again, leaving him alone in the jungle and at some distance from the sacred terrain for the *quimbanda*.

He was obliged to walk in the growing darkness, following the cut through the jungle. The white robe was becoming stained with red earth and the splotches of sweat turned into scabs. Perhaps that's why, or perhaps because of other more secret signs, when he reached the sacred terrain where the ceremony was taking place, he provoked the cry.

"Eshú! Eshú!" shouted the priestess, already possessed, contorting under the enormous white cloth the others held at chest level.

"Eshúuuuu!" was the general shout as he took his first step into the clearing, and even though it was more of a shout of terror, he puffed up with pleasure. The drumbeats changed, the call to Eshú began, frenetically, the priestess redoubled her convulsions, trying to get Oshalá out of her body. She had to make room for Eshú even though Eshú's turn had passed.

What pleasure for him, being recognized in his darkest, most diabolic aspect, being acclaimed like that even if it was out of fear, not welcome.

Drops of blood began to fall heavily on the white cloth and draw flowers on it. No one wonders where the drops might come from, the trance is slowly taking everybody over and men and women jump into the circle and begin writhing with the pain of the dance, moaning like women giving birth, quivering and shaking. And he, hieratic in the center of the circle of dancers, breathes deeply and feels himself elevated. The drums roar with fury and the hands of the drummers can no longer be seen and the *babalao* makes a halo about him with the pestilential smoke of his cigar. Someone hands him a bottle of cane liquor and he begins to spin on his heels and sprinkle the liquor on all the priestesses dancing around him, distortedly.

Shangó doesn't come down, Iemanjá doesn't come down, in spite of the calls. And the horses of the saints gallop, stamp, buck, with no spirit riding them because Eshú has taken over the festivities and he's unrestrainable.

Here I am and I elevate myself
I unfold myself
Something of me is elevated through the air while the dancers down below tear themselves to pieces

I'm not among them, I'm up there, a pinpoint of light that shines in condescension and twinkles to the rhythm of the drums

I am she, I am Estrella up there and down here I am I, above all others

> I squeeze them and bless them
> I tolerate them and love them
> I flood them and I SCREAM

I scream and no one hears me. I purify myself and live through the remotest times

With the weight of three balls, no one can drag himself along the earth without feeling different. The idiot Eulogio shouted, and thanks to that shout I was the Other One, the marked one. Who can reproach me in the marshes, at age thirteen, for having got undressed in front of an idiot and a little girl with extra fingers and toes? She was Sixfingers and that same day the raft dam split and Sixfingers drifted away from me. Eulogio lost his speech again and no one ever called me Threeballs, although everybody knew—I made sure—that I was different. Superior. Complete.

In order to avoid questions, he abandoned Eulogio on the desolation of the raft dam, and all alone he poled the boat to where he thought the dry land was. In the middle of the lagoon the pole wouldn't touch bottom and he had to row, though he didn't know how. He spun about a lot, he was his own whirlpool, he spent a whole night trying to get somewhere and in the morning reached the place where the marshes ended and he was able to walk, first with the water up to his knees, then splashing through the mud, and finally on dry land, oh so dry that after three days of walking he yearned for the water, the bright lagoon. When he reached the great river, he didn't even pay any attention to it. He only knew that he had to cross, and not by swimming either; he recognized its breath, its threat.

On the other side of the river, crossing the border, he finally came upon the one who seemed to be waiting for him.

The one who was to be teacher before seeing himself degraded to the humiliating status of pariah had a sign in his house that said *Suffer the children to come unto me* and he, who was a child at the time, considered himself called. He swears that he never noticed what was written underneath, in very small letters: *From the rear.*

He entered frontwards, head held high and his three balls, as one might say, in his hand. He put them on the table, as one might say, in order to inquire about the phenomenon.

The teacher knelt before him and kissed him on the supernumerary. Sister ball, he mumbled, sister, sister. And that was how our man came in contact with Estrella, through the teacher's kiss.

Estrella, his twin sister, the one who in the maternal womb chose to be incorporated in him, to remain forever under his cloak.

The teacher initiated him on the drums and gave her a name: Estrella de la Mañana, Morning Star. It was a baptism filled with emotion that wasn't limited to his privy parts but which in some way took over his whole body, flooding it with tremors.

The teacher, impressed by Eulogio's words, called him Manuel and invested him with his first white regalia, a robe embroidered with pearls and hemmed with lace.

"You look like a bride, Manuel," the teacher said to him, sighing, and he accepted the doubtful compliment, sensing that it was a matter of his own marriage to the recently baptized Estrella de la Mañana, for him Morning Star and Night Star, Star of Life. Let her guide you, he would repeat to himself over the years, and she would guide him along his intricate way through swamp and marsh. The teacher, without understanding too well that he was digging his own grave, was godfather to both: he kissed the groom, the bride, and also a little above and below.

That was how the initiation was initiated and the rituals begun, along with the slow apprenticeship in recipes: the preparation of propitiary perfumes, the soap of seven powers, talismans for and against the evil eye, herbs to make one fall in love, incenses for cleansing, and its opposite, the pestilential unguent for revenge.

A few recipes he learned too well, and others less so. Certain perfumes, like that of Venus, always turned out volatile and somewhat rancid on him. But he created completely new formulas that provided him with a seat of honor—somewhat shadowy, it is true, being obscure formulas—among initiates all over the world.

The formula for the essence that opens the doors of the accursed secret was his greatest specialty, and that was never transmitted to anyone. He kept it for his own private use and some few times obtained great satisfaction. That formula had given him very good results during the life of the Generalississimo, when not only esoteric but also earthly powers passed through his hands.

Now I don't want earthly powers, now I'm on a different search and I've come under the protection of the mystical egg, while Estrella rises up on her own and sparkles, translucent. Estrella, so much a woman, so much mine, twinkles only for me and only I can see her. For now we play the waiting game and work hard, but someday we'll obtain the fruit of our marriage and it will be such a very, very perfect fruit—our son—that there will be no need for any other being in this world. We won't need anybody, not even to play the drums. The drums are for now and not for when the time without measure comes when we will be three and one at the same time, as is fitting.

In the meantime, the drums are calling for a sacrifice and Estrella, so self-effacing, offers it herself. Her own menstrual blood, drop by drop, rhythmically, falling on the cloth of Oshalá which was so white before and can be seen coagulated with red-flowering now. This is her true sacrifice. Drops of a blood that renounces the son, not of that other vulgar, alien blood which, with limitless generosity, we went about spilling in order to calm the minor gods, the ones who interfere: a river of blood will flow.

The smoke becomes thicker and thicker, it masks everything now, and I can only see a few white shapes that go on and on, jerking to the ever more frantic sound of the drums, I can't see the drummers' hands as they fly over the drumheads, I can only hear the palms as they drum, the fingers, the fingertips, a succession of back, palm, a succession of fingers, palm, palm, changing the beat, and I imagine the movement in the dense smoke of the cigars that makes me invisible, and without moving I make myself part of the movement, I give myself over to the smoke. Estrella floating and I floating, too, in a different dimension. They're clouds. It's no longer cigar smoke, now it's clouds that dress me, enwrap me like veils, and I float without the ballast of Estrella and I go along unraveling in ecstasy.

That's why I'm so pure, that's why so beloved—by me.

From the white shapes below, beyond the clouds, one has broken away and is beginning to rise up. It's approaching me, floating through the air, and I can't help recognizing it with a shudder that almost brings me back to ground level. It's she, it's the Dead Woman, the dream of my life, the one I always wanted to meet face to face in movement and not, as always, protected by invulnerable rigor mortis. She, so transparent and blond, ever more radiant, approaches and her mouth quivers as if she were trying to talk to me, yes, she's going to talk to me no less, the chosen one, she doesn't appear to just anyone, she comes only to me, who has invoked her so much, her body almost entirely of pure air breathes deeply and fills up more with air, trembles, is on the point of transmitting her message to me, says:

"Come down, damn it. Come down and be a man."

I keep this phrase to myself in the most hidden part of my being, like a treasure. I haven't ever repeated it to anyone, because human evil might misinterpret it. I know its essence, its essence is this:

"We beg you to abandon your divine kingdom on high for one more time. Go back please to the mortals who still need you."

She's always been rather blunt in her messages, but no one can deny her immense store of tenderness. She's the honeycomb and I'm the bee who builds the comb, who nourishes itself from the honeycomb, multiplies itself in the honeycomb, and destroys it. Therefore, I graciously heeded her request, came down and made myself a man again. I ceased being a god for a while again. The drums fell silent and the smoke vanished.

The small plane—once its precious cargo had been delivered—came back to pick me up and return me to my side of the border.

"I'm sorry, sir, we had a little run-in with the bastards here. Every so often they attack us, to let their people see they're not in with us. There weren't any casualties, of course, but as you can see, a window got broken during the shooting. We're going to have to fly low. Please forgive me, sir."

"It's fine. It's just right for me, for now."

Capital. Day

"That man is up to his old tricks again. I think this time we're going to have to eliminate him."

"Is that an order, General, sir, Mr. President, or just a wish?"

"I'm afraid it's the latter. Until we find out where he hid those documents, we won't be able to touch him. But double the surveillance. I found out that he crossed the border again and had a secret meeting. Also, the Beechcraft he was traveling in, which was delivering the merchandise, was shot up."

"Do you think that he's turning information over to our neighbors, General?"

"No, it's impossible for him to have any new information other than what we feel like giving him. But, just the same, he's dangerous."

"For the country?"

"No, for us."

The flutes

There isn't always a wind in the lands of the Tacurú.
On a few drowsy, stifling middays, the false anthills instead of ventilating suck out the air of the tunnels and our
man can hear the flutes. The time has come for him to
emerge from his enclosure, but he knows he can't do it.
Humility then falls upon him like a mace and long hours
go by while waiting until the sun calms down and the
ground stops creaking. Maddening, frightful hours. He
then wanders through the long corridors, howling in tune
with the air-sucking flutes, sometimes kicking the walls.
His castle, the Tacurú, is a maternal womb full of twists
and turns and hiding places, and he kicks the walls and
tries to destroy the womb. Tries to kill the mother once
again. To bring on the collapse.

Estrella is in him to restrain him. When he draws
back his leg to launch it with all his might against one of
the columns, Estrella contracts with pain and leaves him
doubled up, rolling on the floor.

"Maidens, brave maidens," he howls, and the brave
Indian maidens run to him in their white tunics, saying
very softly: "Weep weep, gray owl," and cradle him in
their copper-colored arms.

Singular moments, these, when a touch of poetry is
permitted, a touch of tenderness. From the time he was
thirteen, Estrella has been the repository of tenderness for
both of them. Dear, plush Estrella. He strokes her as the

maidens cradle him, and sometimes, through a conduit that isn't at all alien to him, Estrella weeps on his hand: white, painful tears. He then holds out his hand for the young maidens to lick.

Brief beatific instants brought on by the lingering lament of the flutes. From which he usually recovers in no time. He then forgets the beatitude and returns to his alembics and retorts. He mustn't be distracted for more than a second, for now in his leisure time he is looking for a certain magical formula that will save the world. Overpopulation, thanks to him, will no longer be a problem; there will be food for all mouths because there will be fewer mouths, and war will once more be a thing of pleasure, not a necessity as in these pitiless times.

He has promised Estrella that the final compound will be a colorless, odorless, tasteless liquid. Inserted vaginally, it will dissolve the uterus without affecting the patient in any way. She might of course lose her sexual appetite, but that eventuality doesn't worry Estrella, rather it makes her happy.

So, pretending to be playing, he experiments with the different compounds on the Indian maidens and inserts liquids and sometimes his fingers into them until they feel an itching that isn't utterly disagreeable. But the uteri keep going and sometimes they produce an offspring, no one knows how or by whom. When he finds out (which doesn't usually happen, for there are those who roam secretly through the castle passageways—rather pale, it's true, but in good health), he demands that they be brought to his table, done to a turn and with an apple in the mouth.

Inevitably, the apple won't fit in the tiny mouth, newborn meat is too insipid, too white, and though he swallows it happily in the knowledge that he is master of lives and properties, the next morning he has stomach cramps. He doesn't care: a rite has been celebrated. One must take some part or other in human reproduction, and he finds himself at the other end of this assembly line: he incorporates the fruit of human reproduction into his own organism, assimilating it. He doesn't spend his precious energy in improbable partnerships.

Though, in the hope that the miracle of Sixfingers' birth might be repeated, he doesn't totally discourage reproduction under his roof. Sometimes he even allows emissaries from the Central Government, men who have reached his domains disguised as hoboes or furtive hunters or Indians or deserters or fugitives, to get lost in the meanderings of the Tacurú and have some fun fertilizing the maidens. For that same reason, he is not too upset by the long useless hours he spends in his laboratory searching for the precious liquid that will dissolve uteri like salt in water. He even thinks of abandoning the experiments in exchange for the birth someday of another like the one he loved in his childhood. Another Sixfingers will be born, and once more he will learn the names of birds.

First love: Sixfingers
Great love: Estrella
Veneration: the Dead Woman

In this trilogy Estrella comes out on top, for he knows he'll never be separated from her. Even if that were possible. The unnatural imbecile who suggested a surgical removal paid for it with his life. There will never be any scalpel or the shadow of a scalpel separating him from Estrella, flesh of his flesh.

The Dead Woman, too, accompanies him through his life, but only in memoriam and in the reality of her forefinger—her total identity. Estrella isn't jealous of the Dead Woman, she loves her too, in her way.

23

Sixfingers is only the warmth of a childhood memory and has ceased to count in matters of love.

And that's it. For he has better things to do.

Many females had tried to trap him. At one time he was a man of real power, a luscious mouthful. And women would offer him much to get their hands on him. But he was always so dignified, so distant. "Women? What do I need women for?" he would ask himself. "I come with a built-in woman, I'm complete. I've got no reason to go looking for myself in mirrors."

A few times he would condescend to explain: Whatever we renounce enriches us, and let me point out that I am renouncing sex, the greatest of renunciations. Just draw your conclusions."

And on some private occasions he had been heard to say: "I obey a superior being who dictates my behavior. I obey Myself."

Only one woman believed she had him and he let her think so for convenience. He called her the Intruder. When one fine day he had to start calling her Madam President, he decided to join forces with her and pretend he was caught in her trap. Keeping all his dignity intact, of course, never dropping his pants. Oh no. For very symbolic reasons, he condescended to explain to her one night (for reasons tribolic, he would secretly chuckle to himself).

He performed his sexual duties perfunctorily, but even so, he performed them for over a year, proud of fucking no other but that widow, and with the fringe benefits of knowing her sterile.

"Who wears the pants here?" he used to shout at her,

grabbing her by the hair, and she was forced to admit to the evidence, even though she occupied at that time the highest of civic positions.

No problem for him. He could easily handle Madam President. He felt absolutely secure in his seat of honor, even when she appeared on the balcony of Government House and the people who were gathered in the square supposedly to cheer her voiced their demands:

"Madam President, fight back, give the Sorcerer the sack!"

Nobody was going to give him the sack, and certainly not Madam President, who needed him for everything.

He made sure that Madam President would never betray him: he had her in the palm of his hand, and precisely for that reason, though not without a certain disgust, he sometimes made the effort of taking her in his arms. He smeared Madam President with his seed so she would always remember that the power she held over her people was actually a power that came from him, her Master.

(Maybe history would have been different had he known the Dead Woman in her lifetime.)

I am the Master, because love cannot master me.
I do not breed. I never scatter myself.

He had an only child and that child was himself. The only woman who deserved his genes was the one who had conceived him, and just for that purpose. With the simple act of being born of his own spermatozoon, he gained convincing proof of the primordiality of the egg: the hen has never been more than an intermediary, and once her mission is fulfilled, it is best to destroy her.

These ideas come to him when the flutes whine, during those crushing, air-sucking middays in his subterranean castle. His hatred for maternal cloisters grows then to exasperation, but his love for himself grows accordingly. He, who was his own father and who destroyed his cloister, is also the first woman, due to Estrella—without cloister or opening whatsoever, the pure egg.

The birds

Motherless and fatherless, on his own, the perfect orphan. At age two he became a threat and so was banned from his land of the anthills, condemned to live on an island.

Don Ciriaco passed by the kitchens one day riding a sorrel and agreed to get him out of that dried-up landscape, away from the ants.

"He's the son of Doña Eulalia, may she rest in peace. She knew all about herbs, a real saint. We can't let the papoose go around playing with poison, he'll turn the evil eye loose if he keeps on destroying anthills with his ass."

Don Ciriaco agreed to take him off, along with Doña Eulalia's herb collection and some unguents that he demanded as a bonus. He didn't mount him up on the horse's rump, for he was too small. He straddled him over the animal's withers, between his arms, putting him on the reins side.

Wrapped in the vapor of that horse's sweat, he had his first dream, which now he thinks of as prophetic. When he opened his eyes, he found himself in that confused and unknown region called the jungle, and the smell of wild jasmine, whose flower is transformed and changes color with the passage of time—from white to the most violent violet—intoxicated him to the point of making him see double: the landscape repeated upside down, sinking into the ground.

It was the edge of the marshlands, the first encroaching of water. Palm trees above and palm trees below, mirrored in the water through which the horse was sinking as it trod over a carpet of tender, treacherous green that gave way under its hoofs.

Maybe that's why he never liked green carpets. He always preferred red ones.

The first step into the kingdom of waters, the first lesson in learning how to read reflections.

Don Ciriaco dismounted where the water was already up to his knees and he pulled his boat out from among the reeds. He put Eulalia's herbs into the boat with great care and then he loaded Eulalia's son, just like another piece of cargo, placing him on top of the bags of flour and sugar. He took the halter of the sorrel, gave him a slap, so he'd go back to dry land and graze until he was called again. With his pants rolled up, Don Ciriaco began to push the boat through the barrier of water lilies that looked like sockets blooming with purple candles.

The last thing the papoose saw of that half-land, half-water was a black crane perched up on a palm tree croaking goodbye to him.

The initial path can be repeated forever.

In the boat, the two-year-old papoose lay among the bags and let himself be carried along the cut opened through the reeds—a narrow waterway that the boat poled by Don Ciriaco followed with some difficulty. Stick in the pole and push, on one side and then on the other, through the gallery of reeds that at times threatened to close in and swallow them.

Eulalia's son, Eulalito, whom everybody called the papoose for lack of a name of his own, didn't pay the least bit of attention to those parallel walls of high golden staffs that almost shut out the sky. What he discovered and loved along that strange route were the giant communal webs that the boat passed. Yards of dark webbing, a net of lace to catch flying fish, and the clump of spiders huddled peacefully in a corner, pretending to be napping, waiting for a good catch. Weaving the appropriate nets and going to sleep, wasn't that a most effective system?

Maybe so, in a world of tangles. But the reed barrier suddenly ended and the boat came out into the open water, where the ways of fishing are very different. Oh, wonder of the eternal lagoon! All visible space became water, with no horizon, and that water was black and transparent at the same time, with inner gardens like an emerald. In those days the papoose couldn't have known anything about emeralds, but he discovered then the deep gardens and was entrapped forever in the other face of the mirror. A mirror of black waters, the decomposition of the world.

Underneath the water were growths like forests of pine, with tiny yellow flowers that lost color as they went down deeper and farther from the surface, losing color but doubtless acquiring something unsuspected when they reached bottom.

On the surface of the lagoon, a vast expanse of polished dark crystal. On a horizontal plane the infinite, which is nothingness; but on the vertical plane—penetrating—the subaquatic world that emerged at times in a single floating leaf. The papoose sometimes grabbed it, discovering the long black strand that linked the leaf to the inscrutable bottom. And every so often they would pass a water hyacinth, a squat plant with inflated bladders like a frog. Then the papoose would dip a hand deep in the water and Don Ciriaco, looking like a gondolier as he poled along, would mutter from the stern of the boat: "The piranha," just like that, in the singular, because he was a man of very few words and because he wasn't referring to a type of fish but to a curse.

And though the papoose understood, even if he had no idea what piranhas were, he kept his hand in the water as if it didn't matter, because he already knew that he could ignore threats.

So, floating over woods and meadows, over fathomless black wells, avoiding wild creatures, heading toward a sun that blinded them and made those dark waters look white, they finally came to Don Ciriaco's island, where Doña Rosa received the papoose with the same indifferent expression with which she received the sugar and the flour. She had six children and was expecting another. What difference did one more spot make to the jaguar? she said to herself. She did like Doña Eulalia's herbs, though.

The papoose was small for his age, and pale. He became immediately popular with Amalia, the oldest daughter, who placed him in a large fruit crate, hanging from a bough, and played with him as if he were a doll.

The years spent on the island were cotton years, bland and even warm, and under their influence his life might have been quite different, had it not been marked from the very start. One certain day a piece of yellow cloth opened up over his cradle-hammock-fruit crate and it seemed to have a complex scarlet design printed on it, intricate grooves.

"It's the Thousandmen flower," Amalia said as she went about telling him the names of things. He identified so much with the flower fluttering over his head that he even fell ill.

Another day, while exploring the little jungle heart of the island, he saw something throbbing that looked like a small burlap bag hanging from a branch. The bag first sighed, then it shuddered all over, until there emerged a dark bird that seemed much larger than the bag. The bird immediately flew away, but he kept it in his memory. "It's an oriole," Amalia told him, and he identified with the oriole.

It's a tanager, a cardinal, a *tero*, an *aguapeazú* whose call is a danger signal, an owner-of-the-sun, a baker bird —Amalia went on pointing them out to him and he wanted to be all those birds, but it was easier to be the boa constrictor or the alligator that Don Ciriaco sometimes hunted for their skins.

A lot of time spent with Amalia learning from her, until Cora was born. Right under his nose. Hanging from his branch that was already starting to bend, in his nest that was getting too small for him, like the nest of the oriole, he saw. All curled up and fetus-like so as to fit into the fruit crate, pretending to be asleep, through the slats he spied on those open legs, that fierce hollow that was opening up as if to swallow him, until water began to pour out and then a hairy spider started to emerge, and emerge, taking shape as Cora's somewhat slimy form.

First they cut off the dark plant strand that joined Cora to the bottom of the dark lagoon, then they washed her and took him out forever from his nest and put her in. Wrapped in yellow cloth, her skin the red of the color print of the Thousandmen flower.

He couldn't hate her. He left her in his nest and called her Little Flower, and with the passage of years he went about teaching her the names of the birds and he learned to count with her fingers. That's why his measuring system was never decimal: because Little Flower, Cora, had six toes on each foot and little stubs on the edge of each hand, next to her pinky. She had other things, too, that he would begin to discover in time, but in earliest infancy only those little stubs, which he used to suck until he fell asleep.

He never caught a *dorado*, he never had that lively and struggling strength at the end of his line. He never hunted an alligator or a swamp deer. Don Ciriaco always left him on the very short stretch of solid ground that was the island, to help and watch over the women. He was too strange to be allowed to go into the terse silence of the marshes. Too white; he would attract evil glows.

When he was seven years of age, he began to understand what that business of helping and watching over the women was all about, and he wasn't interested at all. He was only interested in Sixfingers, because she was different. Around that time the rural police came to harass Doña Rosa and he didn't help her in the least; what could he have done, in any case?

The roar of an outboard motor grew louder in the distance and Sixfingers and he left their lair in the little jungle and ran toward the pier to see what kind of animal was approaching. Doña Rosa kept on washing and scrubbing the clothes on the rotten boards without paying any attention whatever to the death rattle that ended up frightening off the *siriri* ducks and made the *aguapeazú* call out from among the reeds.

They almost had to put a boot in her face, the rural police did, for her to lift up her questioning eyes. They weren't going to ask her anything, they never had any doubts: let her do the asking. But Doña Rosa remained unperturbed, mute.

"Tell us where you are hiding the fugitive or we'll beat you to a pulp."

"Fugitive?"

"Yes. Fugitive, bandit, outlaw, escapee, runaway. The guerrilla."

"I haven't seen any one of those."

"We are not asking you if you've seen him. We're ordering you to hand him over. Sing."

"Sing, sing!" they shouted again at Doña Rosa.

And the papoose and Cora, hidden among the reeds, were happy: they would finally find out what kind of bird Doña Rosa was, by her song.

More than a songbird, she turned out to be a croaking black crane. All that when the policemen began kicking her in the face and kicking and dragging her across the logs of the pier. Sing, they shouted at her, where have you hidden the man? And they made her kneel, twisting her arm behind her back, made her kiss the floor and rubbed her face against the rough wood. Doña Rosa sprawled out right there, her clothes in shreds. And the papoose and Sixfingers in the reeds, hugging each other tightly. Sixfingers kept her eyes shut, the papoose kept his wide open, and once more he saw the hollow, so dark, so persistent, and this time it was for him to know what could happen to the hollow from outside inward.

One policeman first, then the other one, dropped their pants and fell on top of Doña Rosa, letting her shriek all she wanted, because in the immensity of the lagoon, in the midst of the broad swamps that had no end, who would hear those shrieks and who would care?

The papoose didn't even try to do his duty: he couldn't watch over her or help her. He could only keep on staring and staring at that confused scene, till Doña Rosa was left stretched out there, like a broken doll.

The second policeman, as he pulled up his pants, warned her: "We gave you something no shitty guerrilla could ever give you, you ought to thank us. Now we are going out to look for him on the other islands, but don't worry, we'll be back."

Maybe not Doña Rosa. Almost surely not Doña Rosa. But the papoose, when they were alone on the island once more, dreamed that those vultures were coming back. It was an exciting dream.

Capital. Night

"Why won't he die, I ask myself, why won't he just nicely jump into the lake. If the dog dies, the rabies might be cured. If the man disappears, all our troubles are over."

"Let's not fall into the trap the government is setting for us. It's easy to use that fellow as a scapegoat and overlook what's going on around us. I think the troubles that afflict our poor country are based on elements infinitely more complex than the life or death of a single man, no matter how much of a sorcerer he might be. A man who might not even exist, a man who's like the personification of collective hysteria and its undefined fears: he makes me think of the Middle Ages, when during witch hunts, after a good session of torture, they all confessed to having attended the Black Mass. I think the same thing is happening here—from being so oppressed, people see the devil everywhere—and that could be just what the government wants."

"Oh no, I think that underestimating the strength of the enemy is the best way of giving the enemy strength. Somewhat like the devil, since you pointed it out. What's that business about the devil's best trick being his making us think he doesn't exist?"

"Atomizing the enemy is the best way to displace responsibilities. And making us believe in the existence of a distant enemy is the best way of obliging us to shift focus. These military are very, very skillful. They've calibrated to perfection this campaign of rumors about the longevity or resurrection or reincarnation of the Sorcerer in order to sink us in the swampy terrain of superstition and legend, where it isn't at all easy to get a footing. They offer it to us as the most perfect piece of information, if we are to accept Warren Weaver's definition as quoted by Umberto Ecco: 'The concept of information does not refer to only one message in particular, but to the statistical character of a group of messages; in such statistical terms, the words *information* and *uncertainty* are intimately inter-related.' The emphasis is mine. From this point of departure we should begin to analyze the official manipulation we are ourselves subject to with respect to the *uncertainty* of the material that comes to our attention. Apparently they're transmitting a message, but nothing obliges us to accept it as a truthful message. Quite the contrary. There's an excess of ambiguity in the information, and it's impossible to trace the source.

"I think we have to consider that business of the Marshland as a real metaphor. We should analyze the elements that have been offered us point by point and deconstruct the textuality inscribed in the para-official discourse. We should try to structure our basic coordinates on the dichotomy of that governmental position. It's a perfect specular play: with a repressive superego on the surface (the government) and its repressive inverted image underground (the Sorcerer). This double figure hampers our movement, denies us even the slightest interstitial freedom. It's Bateson's 'double bind.' The present power structures of the Central Government are put together, without a shadow of a doubt, with the cognizance of a labile ego on the part of the people, acquiring in that way a power of manipulation over the aforesaid people in accordance with the dark face of the reality presented to them. Awakening in them superstitious fear

and at the same time the vague promise of salvation by
magic; freezing them in that way in the realm of the
imaginary."

The song of the saw

With six fingers you can point out invisible space,
with six fingers it's worthwhile scratching your inner self.

And Sixfingers drifted away forever and left me stuck
to a fixed path that I will defend down to the final consequences. She went off in silence without looking back and
I stayed on more solid ground, ignoring that at that precise instant we were unfolding: she the flower and I thousand men, forever.

A thousand men I shall have at my feet. A thousand
and a thousand more times a thousand and a thousand
more times 28. Things like these are sensed or remembered in the vastness of the lagoons. Now I know, the
lagoons, one after another, threaded together by unsuspected passages among the reeds.

There are cuts that only I know, that I ordered
opened with saws. The mystery of the raft dams and the
floating islands I discovered in my own flesh at a very
early age: the raft dam split and Sixfingers went floating
away from me on a newly formed little island. I never
heard from her again. Now I look for her in my moments
of meditation, in my own liquid times. With her extra
finger she could have pointed out the way that can't be
seen in the water, she could have made me find her.

36

At the age of seven, after a certain incident I prefer not to mention, they left me a boat so that I could get around and warn of danger. I never warned anybody about anything, what's danger for some people might not be for others; instead, we began to go with Sixfingers to the edge of the lagoon, to the raft dams of reeds.

Natural occurrences that go along with their deceptions, making us believe what isn't and yet is. The roots of the reeds tangle under the water and form a cushion—the raft dam—where more reeds grow. Vast expanses of false plains that sometimes the wind breaks up and turns into floating islands at the mercy of the wind. These islands go about changing place, constantly transforming the look of the lagoons, which seem quite still, but never static.

That's why I can sail on my floating island now, because modifying landscapes has been and is the passion of my life.

Sixfingers and I would frolic here in other regions of time that were just right for us. We would get to play and she would open her legs just as on a certain occasion her mother, Doña Rosa, had opened herself up. Except that Sixfingers never cried out, instead she would laugh like crazy when I explored her with my finger. Two fingers, three fingers, four fingers, five, the whole hand. I regretted missing a finger that would have made her truly happy, but, no, true happiness has never ceased to flow from my hands when I've wanted it to.

It's strange that I should be the one seeking her in this new cycle and not she going about the lagoons calling for my hand. Holy hand.

On certain nights, however, I can hear her. Papoose, papoose, she calls me, like the quack of a duck. Sixfingers changed into a duck, web-footed as she was. Waterproof. One of these nights when I feel inspired I'll make some incantations and have her come back and I'll introduce her to Estrella. Only a sixth finger can touch Estrella, only something out of other worlds. Sixfingers I suspect was the daughter of her own brother, she deserves the high honor of knowing my Estrella.

I limit myself now to seeking her on physical terrain and I have them open the cuts. When I know that the consultors won't be coming to consult me for a while, I go off and float through the lagoons in search of an appropriate place. I take the sawmen along with me and I show them the spot. And so we discover new lagoons and explore the expanse of this swamp world. With their saws my men go about opening paths, cutting through the raft dam of reeds as if it were made of wood. I feel like Columbus every time we reach another water mirror, coming out of the poisonous world of reed clumps, once again into the transparency of another lagoon. The raft dam is a Pandora's box. Once a sawman was bitten by a pit viper and we had to saw off his foot so the poison wouldn't spread. I had to fire the man for being careless, but I've kept the foot in my private museum as a trophy.

That night, the sawmen went into mourning and sang as never before. That's the charm of my sawmen, that's why I don't get rid of them all. They're virtuosos on that ever so delicate instrument that is the saw, and when they finish opening a cut, they perform the most moving musical pieces. I hide amid the tranquil reeds of my floating island and listen to them with unction. Sometimes I weep.

A time for meditating, for mingling with nature. Perhaps there in the Tacurú important emissaries are waiting for new consultations, but in this state of mind I prefer floating on my island and cradling my memories. Not because the time for action has passed and I'm now in a mood for pure reflection. Nothing of the sort. I'm more like a tiger crouching in wait, ready to leap. I'm the swamp tiger. The lurker.

38

During my meditations I wonder if in this business of making cuts, in this sailing along on an island that's a floating clump of reeds, I'm going off in search of Six-fingers, or if in reality the one I'd like to find is Eulogio. Eulogio knew and for that very reason he must already be—should be—dead. Thinking him alive means doubting my own willpower. I awarded him a voice and I took it away from him again forever, a means like any other of getting it back for Estrella. Eulogio's ex-voice is now the quiet voice that Estrella only uses to communicate with me, that is to say with the rest of her/my person.

Sometimes Estrella wakes me up with her weeping and I caress her until we both go back to sleep, calmer now. Sometimes she demands certain sacrifices: finding Eulogio, anointing him with honey in order to sweeten that ever so harsh voice with which he accused her—insulted her, really, calling her a ball—and leaving him on top of a *tacurú* at the mercy of the ants.

Why did I go swimming naked in the lagoon in front of the cretin? Since when does a person hide from idiots, who's ever ashamed in front of them? But all of a sudden Eulogio's eyes lighted up; he had a glimmer of intelligence when he shouted, "Manuel has Three Balls." And she was discovered, discovered by me too, although at that moment I couldn't understand it.

The doctor who suggested an operation, telling me it was a cyst, paid dearly for his boldness. Every so often, Eulogio pays in someone else's skin, through an intermediary, a power of attorney, one might say. When Estrella demands vengeance, any victim will do, and more than one Eulogio has been anointed with honey and planted in the middle of an anthill to serve as fodder for my friends.

That's how the present government came to recognize me, when word got around about these sacred sacrifices. People wanted to put me on trial, but the government, rather more intelligently, decided to name me its adviser in arcane matters of repression.

Now there are those who venerate me. They call me Brother, they call me Father. I get away from them on my island, accompanied by the sweet music of the saws. The sawmen play with very delicate Viennese violin bows that I ordered especially for them. On the consultors' small plane I'm accustomed to receive exquisite items, and not just to make my taste buds quiver. Old tool catalogues arrive, for example, and I dream aloud about the most refined methods of torture. Aloud, because I know they've installed a plague of hidden microphones in my castle and I amuse myself that way, hinting at what might happen to them if they get too smart. *Juntas líquidas, tableros dieléctricos* of cemented asbestos, bronze axle shafts, winches, piston valves, instruments ever so useful if you know how to apply them properly.

Personally, I never talk about revenge; I'm too much of a gentleman, almost a lady: no threat will ever blossom on my lips. But they know quite well what awaits them if anything bad should happen to me, that's why they take such good care of my person. They may not have much imagination, but they're no fools, and I never leave them much room for fantasy, I prefer to sin by being over-explicit.

I note all this, not in order to leave the evidence out in the open, but simply because I'm writing a novel. Not when I'm floating along on my island, no. When I'm float-ing along, I fish for elements to enrich it: an electric eel, a ray, piranhas, anacondas, those lethal beings from the depths of these black transparent waters that no one dares enter. Only my sawmen get off the island and sink their feet into the swamp. I send them off in the boat and keep my distance, because it's one thing to know about de-composition—I like that—and something else again to feel it in your own pituitary. The most translucent water with its bottom vegetation becomes foggy and gives off its miasmas when one of them stirs up the bottom. Putrid vapors that I smell from a distance with delight but which could asphyxiate me close by.

I learned about this spongy warm mud as a papoose. You try to set foot on it and you sink in up to your knees. There's no solid bottom, there's something marshy about it, and its fascinations are irresistible to a child. Not so much for a grownup, even less so after the drowned men.

I'm sure they threw them to me as a way of saying indirectly that they'd identified me. As if I cared. Sir, sir, the sawmen called, something that surprised me very much because I've forbidden them to speak to me. Sir, sir, and I knew it was an emergency.

(Did I say I'm writing a novel? I lied. Actually, I'm putting together an intimate diary so that the present day will take place in all times. Even though these labels are unworthy. My life and therefore my diary combine to form a great novel. *The* novel. The Bible.)

I went over. Sir, sir, sir; like a vocative. And I managed to catch sight of the drowned men, their skin all earthen and swollen. I recognized my old suggestion: take them up in a helicopter and throw them into the river, I had ordered back then when they asked me what to do with those who'd been damaged in excess during interrogations. Into the river, I was quite clear, never in my lagoons. Never in my lagoons.

For that very reason and for the last time, I sank into the mud and I turned the heads of the drowned men, who have the modest habit of floating face down. I didn't seem to recognize any one of the three, although that event couldn't have bothered me very much. I gave the order for my sawmen to saw off their heads, and that night the saws sang as never before. I also hummed a tune when,

41

well packed now, the three heads were turned over to the emissaries who had come to consult me disguised as Indians. And I told them:

"Here's a gift for the great white chief. Nothing too important, the great white chief shouldn't even bother thanking me. Just a memento."

An aide-mémoire, rather. Yes. Something to remind him of my power.

Capital. Day

"Colonel, get General Durañona immediately."

"Yes, Mr. President."

The colonel withdraws when General Durañona enters, and the president comes straight to the point.

"General Durañona, that man has got to be eliminated."

"You know very well, General, that for the moment we can't take that risk. Besides, he's an excellent adviser."

"As an adviser he hasn't got any better ideas than the ones we'd have ourselves if we put a little time into thinking."

"Precisely, but he has at his command weapons that we military men still haven't focused on. Don't look at me that way, Mr. President, I'm not referring to intelligence, I'm referring to weapons of the spirit. We mustn't forget that the man is a wizard, he knows the occult sciences."

"For that very reason he's a threat."

"For that very reason, Mr. President, General, sir, the fact is he would represent a greater threat to us dead than alive. Because of his knowledge of the occult and because of what-we-already-know. On the other hand, for our enemies . . ."

"I don't think we have any enemies left, we've eliminated them all."

"Thanks to that man, as you call him, we keep on discovering enemies even among the most irreproachable of our citizens. That strengthens the regime and justifies the repression that's our means of self-expression, our only *raison d'être*."

"I still have serious doubts about that man."

"General, sir. We can't wipe out our theoretician with a stroke of the pen. I could almost say our theologian— we're men of action, and he knows how to create the action when we need it."

In the Tacurú

"What's this business of addressing me with your hat on? Are you unaware, perhaps, that everybody is to come before my venerable person with his hat in his hand, humble, head bowed?"

"It's a uniform morion, sir. I suspect that not many men in uniform have come before your presence lately. Our morion is a sign of respect, sir. We have higher orders always to wear our uniforms crisp and complete, sir, and this has been a very long trip and very tiring, but here I am, as if just out of the cleaner's, not a single wrinkle. It's the least you can expect of your faithful grenadier."

"Decidedly the least. As for the rest, I'm quite sure everything can be expected of you. It can be seen in such noble bearing, in your alert look."

"Thank you very much, sir. You flatter me."

"You deserve it, son, you deserve it. Plus a few other rewards I'll give you at the proper time if you tell me now everything you have to tell me. Tell me how things are going back there in the distant Capital, and more specifically in the place you came from."

"Confused, sir."

And he told one about the conversation between the president and General Durañona almost as if he'd been there. Verbatim. That's why, when the latest consultant

45

arrived, I knew how to handle the delicate situation and signed the decree.

"Doubt," I almost accused him personally, "doubt is going to lead our country to ruin. Everyone who has doubts must be torn out by the roots, we can't let him draw a single breath. We've fashioned a perfect plan and we're not going to depart from it no matter who falls or who perishes. Because only that plan is over our heads. This is the great lesson history has given us and the one we never remember when the moment arrives. So many governments have fallen in a clatter, so many noble projects have failed because of the simple fact that the Plan wasn't followed, from trying to modify the direction while in full swing. That's how people fall victims to storms and list to port, if you take my meaning. The majority of great political shipwrecks have come about from not sticking to the initial plan. We're not going to allow that to happen. We're going to keep on sailing against wind and tide on the exact course that we mapped out when we weighed anchor. We'll crush anyone who gets in our way, friend or foe, and if it becomes necessary we'll change pilots—but our plan is one and it's ours. National Reconstruction demands it that way. The guidelines are centralization—apparent—and cohesion, with hierarchy and efficiency, with the military apparatus finely calibrated to the service of a project that can only be implemented by force. This is an ideological viewpoint that permeates the bases put together by us and by the military High Commands with the firm intention of passing on the discipline of martial values to the whole body of state agencies so as to channel the authoritarian tradition toward objectives of social and economic progress. The way our first communiqué has set it forth. That's it. By which one can infer: we will impose our model on the world and will continue going along swiftly at full sail against wind and tide through the stormy seas of history."

"Very good, Captain, sir."

"And if the Commanding General has any doubts, then let him be overthrown, defeated, defenestrated, replaced, annihilated, disappeared, diluted, exploded, swallowed, petrified, erased, dissolved, mashed. But not kept in the Highest Office any longer. It's unhealthy for the Nation. Doubt has to be eradicated by decree. There's no room for doubt in history."

And then they consulted me about the possible war with our neighbor to the west. It's going on twenty-five years that they've been coming to me with the same question, indirectly. And I always answer them: Declare it! Buy the most modern weapons, collect new taxes to buy more weapons, and declare it. There has to be some pleasure in life.

The idea fascinates them. Every time they buy some new weapons they're like kids with new toys, they're all full of giggles and excitement, and then they have their doubts, at the last moment they doubt. That's why I mention the business about the decree, but also, for that same reason, I profess the love of a father for them. They're so fickle.

Capital. Night

"I think we should analyze one by one every link in the chain of signifiers that has been presented to us, and if possible, fetter the government with it.

"For example: what more obvious metaphor than that of the Marshland? Our so-called Sorcerer has been situated in the Marshland, a zone that is transparent and fetid at the same time, a place that looks like a crystalline paradise and is in reality a swamp, formed of decomposing plants, bogs, poisonous flowers, and all manner of vermin. Could you find a better representation than this of the human unconscious? The clarities that conceal, the putrid smells that surface with each step. We accept it as a real place because that's the way we are in the darkest regions of our being. That's why I insist that the Marshland is a symbolic location. As is symbolic that purported Sorcerer who lives underground and sails about on an island. As is all of his recollection of a quite distant past, which, by being past and distant, appears nostalgic. Our duty now consists in dismantling these symbols and interpreting the unconscious discourse of the government, what it's transmitting to us in spite of itself."

The Egret

How very delightful. My novel is working out marvelously. In order to have a strong protagonist, is it not necessary to have an antagonist of steel? It's certainly not worth mentioning that I am the protagonist, that point has been made only too clear, but now I'm also my antagonist and I'm growing bigger every day. Gigantism doesn't frighten me. My castle, the Tacurú, which used to be a convent, has been turned into a real anthill now. And that's no joke: neither person nor place can avoid fulfilling its destiny. Little ants, little ants; teams of masons, that is, go along opening new tunnels and enlarging the old ones. They cut, dig, model, and, above all, they raise the height of the ceilings because my new stature requires more space. When people take you for a symbol, your size becomes immeasurable.

Luckily, with this limestone earth, it isn't necessary to shore up the tunnels. It would be horrible for me to feel I was inside a mine, I detest anything that has to do with extractions.

"Pardon me, there, Mr. Master, but a messenger from the Outer Lands has arrived."

"Frisk him thoroughly for me, as usual. Don't miss a single nook or cranny. And once he's disarmed, have him come in."

"It's degrading," one of them dared say. One who naturally never set foot in these latitudes again (or in any others, I'm afraid). "Degrading, humiliating, letting yourself be felt up by women."

Degrading? Humiliating? He was crazy. It's the only free fun I offer those who have the high honor of appearing before me. Because, as far as the other fun is concerned, I charge for it. Not this: my Indian maidens come dressed in their white Indian tunics and first they frisk the stranger up and down, on all sides. Then they pull his clothes off and stick their fingers where they can and press what has to be pressed in case he's hiding some dangerous item in some natural conduit or under the skin. They feel him up well, they search him deeply. Many strangers come back to visit me just for the pleasure of being frisked for weapons in that way and many times the maidens bite a little when they suspect something or scratch, as if by accident but with full cruelty, retaining pieces of skin under their nails. That's why sometimes I watch them through my one-way mirror, and when some stranger shows a scratch on his face, I recognize him as blessed. Branded with my brand. Not with fire, no, not with a red-hot iron. Branded in blood, as is fitting.

Everybody has the livestock he deserves and I have my herd of men.

Not a flock, like the other one's. Neither troop nor team (although at times . . .). A pack of hungry wolves, a herd of young buffalo, who, if they've been marked on the face by my Indian maidens, will obey me blindly.

My maidens choose them to perfection. They know that only those with the tightest sphincters and the hardest balls can join my herd. The incorruptible ones. The whitest ones with the sharpest teeth. They're the flower of manhood and that's why I can count on only so few for the time being. When the herd reaches a thousand men, it will be a regular army. The men of my flower, the Thousandmen flower. And we'll raise the golden-yellow banner, streaked with blood, and go out to conquer the world.

I still need quite a few. With luck, and if this messenger who's now being frisked appears with the sign on his face, it will be 99—but I'm in no hurry: I want the choice to be perfect, and I've got all the time in the world. It will be these warriors or their sons or the sons of their sons who will inherit the brands.

The new messenger came in unmarked, but I think there are grounds for appeal. He has a very good bearing, fine features, a faintly ironic smile beneath a small golden mustache, and I think I like his eyes. He comes to attention like a god.

"At your orders, sir."

"You can call me your Master, that's all."

"My Master."

"Fine. If I can master you, you may come closer. Come, let me feel those biceps a little, that smoothness. Take off your dark glasses . . . such blue eyes . . . take off your cap . . . such blond hair, curly. Take off your pants, such . . . come, come closer. I'm not going to bite you. Get up on that stool."

I didn't let him leave, notwithstanding the fact that he was to carry an important message. On the contrary, I put on my parade uniform (oh yes) and I made him my aide-de-camp. This is a government in internal exile, ruled by its own laws.

I punished the Indian maidens for not having pointed him out. I punished them through an intermediary, that is, I gave him my personal whip, the Lizard's Tail, made of the finest leathers, designed not for animals but for people. And he knew how to use it. Naked, the maidens howled under the blows and I recorded those howls, which completely covered my discreet moans of pleasure, controlled, like everything about me. Now I use that recording as background music when visitors come. It gives a certain austere character to my castle, and the visitors feel more at home.

I cleansed my new aide-de-camp of his name and now he is called the Egret, being so white and graceful. I should have called him Nightingale and sometimes I do: he has such a marvelous voice. Especially fine. Estrella doesn't like him, even though we complement each other: he doesn't have any balls—he says he lost them in a street fight when he was very small, and sometimes I make him reenact the events. I'm the attacker and I keep his supposed testicles between my teeth and then I put them where it can't be imagined. He doesn't like that game, he says it makes him suffer. I insist that it's like a psychodrama, therapeutic.

Therapeutic for me of course, that's what's important. It might help me consummate my marriage to Estrella.

A son of Estrella's and mine, the purest and most perfect combination. For which I don't disdain the co-operation of the Egret. And since he can't distinguish any anomaly whatever in my scrotum—he's only known his own empty one—from time to time I let him lend his tongue and his saliva to the most noble of procreative causes.

Certain nights I spend awake, pondering. I picture the great moment and ask myself, not without a certain anxiety, how Estrella will get through the pregnancy. She's so consistent, so small, so round, so placid. Will I have to carry her in a wheelbarrow? Will she puff up so much that she'll hinder my movements? Will I have to anoint her with sweet-smelling pomades so her skin won't crack and streak? Will the pregnancy last nine months? And what will the birth be like, and through where? I can help with that. I have my own openings.

Sometimes I hold a general rehearsal and my aide covers me with sandalwood oil, and as it runs over my skin his hand is so soft that I'm afraid I'll get used to it. I give him a good lashing, then, and off I go to weep in a corner of the room.

Luckily, much more demanding tasks claim my attention and stop me from growing soft with lust. In my hands is the fate of the country, maybe the entire world, and I mustn't forget it. The pleasures of the flesh are accessories compared to the pleasures of power. They alone matter.

I order my aide to get dressed and attend to the new consultants who are arriving more and more often. He gives them my blessing and passes my word to them. The verb. Which is to act, to act. Not to let the situation get stagnant, not to let softness get the upper hand with them, act harshly, tightening the noose.

Fortunately, we have no problems on the economic side. Ministers change but systems last, and the inflationary process is glowing now in all its splendor. The people are more and more undernourished, lacking even the strength to revolt.

Sometimes I'm disgusted by a people with no rebellion in them. It makes you want to see them rise up just a little, raise their heads; I'm going to have to send them some stimuli, I'm going to have to motivate them. Let's see if you can wake up, folks, let's see if you can call a few little strikes here and there and show your discontent at long last. That way, we can squash you with greater pleasure. Cockroaches.

For mushrooms

My Master is heaven. It's also heaven when we go boating like this and I stand up in the stern of the ever so long boat, erect like the egret, untouched by the sun under a darling parasol, and I push this sort of gondola along with the drive pole (which is a long, interesting rod) and we simply make no noise at all through the dead lagoon.

The Master lies at the bottom of the vessel, his noble white beard more radiant than all the fine lace in the world. I have woven cloaks of *ñandutí* lace for him to cover himself with when the breezes rise up. I am the egret, my nest is *ñandutí*, I can weave at will, and the Master appreciates me more this way, naked, than wearing a harsh fatigue uniform.

We go gliding over the black water and my biceps shimmer as I lean on the pole and the Master admires me. I admire myself. It's divine. My Master's head almost at my feet and I naked, and my Master lying at my feet goes and opens his mouth, slowly, greedily he goes and opens his mouth, and I can't hold back any longer and I let the stream loose on him. I aim well and it's like a thread of gold that flows out of me into my Master's mouth; and the Master laughs, laughs, twists, and drinks it eagerly.

"You pissed on me!"

"You liked it, Master!"

"What do you care if I liked it or not! That's no business of yours. You're going to get your punishment. Goddamnit, you're going to get your punishment. Now let's get going, and put on your tunic, come on, right now. I don't want to see you all tan, turned into a shitty nigger. That's all I need: pissed on by a nigger."

I'm going to turn this cretinous son of a bitch who pissed on me into a dog. I'm glad you liked it, Master, the castrated imbecile says with his little fluty voice. And of course I liked it, you fool. If not, I would have broken your ass right there with a swift kick, I didn't learn *capoeira* foot-fighting for nothing. And don't think I haven't thought about abandoning you in the middle of the lagoon. But who would row me back, eh?

On all fours, you wretch! No, don't you straighten up again. On all fours. And bark, I tell you, and lick my hand. Let's see. Make those barks louder. And now whine a little . . . Woof . . . Let's hear it. Woof . . . like this. That's the way I like it. I like it . . . Come, let me put your

54

collar on, doggie. Nice doggie. Let's see, do peepee against the wall. Peepee, I say, that's why I took you out for a walk. Pee, that's your mission in the world now. A canine Manneken-Pis. Lift that leg up high! That's the way. And more piss for me, eh, not just a few little drops.

And bark for me, woof, woof woof. And whine for me. That's the way I like it. Yes. I'm a dog, too. A police dog. Come, don't run away from me, what do dogs do among themselves? They smell their behinds. Smell my behind, that's the way, doggie, that's the way, more as if you liked it. Let's see that little tongue, that big dog tongue. Harder, deeper. And now mount me, the way dogs mount. Mount me and stick it in me! Stick it in me, I say! You can't? All right, don't cry, don't cry, do what you can.

Calm down, come here, let's fix up a pretty little kennel for you, do you like it? And this chain, look, it's nice and long, you'll have plenty of room to move around, but don't pull too hard, not that, never that, never, never pull too hard, because the collar's bad, the collar has spikes that will stick into your pretty, long, hound neck. If you pull, the spikes will stick you and tear that pretty neck, doggie, the only stiff thing you've got, the only thing erect.

It's not a thoroughbred I want, I want a dog that's good and male, with fierce potency in reserve. I'll try to get you a veterinarian who can fix your problem, let's see if they can give you a graft or something, I want a dog who's heady, ready, a real horny dog.

That's what I tell him and while he whines in his corner I think about possible solutions for this disheartening contretemps. Inflate it like a balloon? The air would escape through the pores: disinflated when I need it most.

55

Insert a rod into it? That wouldn't enrich the volume. So what can I do? The ex-teacher might have had an answer to that question, matters like this were vitally important to him, they're only secondary to me and that's why I can't hit the right key and find the quickest solution. I've got other things to think about, I can't waste my time being distracted by trivialities. Trivialities, the dog's prick? Without doubt, especially now. Nothing is irreplaceable, there are ever so many substitutes. It's just that leaving something unfinished, a desire unsatisfied, a string untied, throws the meticulous order of my feelings out of kilter! The precise network of my feelings demands that my desires be fulfilled, my slightest requirements, my smallest whims, my wishes, my urges, my necessity, my libido! Nothing loose, nothing left to chance, this spayed dog could just as well turn against me, could just as well bite the hand that feeds him if I don't succeed in straightening things out! I know what will help: the mushrooms!!!

By simple phallic association, he knows that the mushrooms will provide the necessary solution. So now he is marching down the tortuous corridors of the castle, retracing a long-forgotten path to return to the source.

He wears the Grand Master's robe with the embroidered eye and holds high the golden candelabrum that once belonged to the treasure of the Dead Woman. The candles are obligatory, for the kingdom of the mushrooms is not one to be viewed under direct light.

During his first glorious identification with the ants,

he had cultivated the mushrooms in the confines of the Tacurú, but of late they have given him no gratification. So the mushrooms had been relegated to oblivion until that moment. Forgotten ever since the government had installed the cocaine-processing plant in his domain.

Still, mushrooms possess their own powers. With mushrooms, one can travel in time, see past and future, know all knowledge in the blink of a moment, increase one's already measureless powers of divination. For that reason he never tried to commercialize the mushrooms. He concentrated on the cocaine—such a perfunctory, unintelligent drug. Ideal for those who seek euphoria and refuse to look inward. Cocaine is the religion of the people, and that's for the best: it makes it easy for him to keep them happy and to fill his pockets.

All this he ponders as he walks cautiously ahead through the chambers of his labyrinth. He advances with the golden candelabrum held high, and the embroidered eye winks. It is not too ostentatious a robe, though; it is the same old one he puts on when he wants to make it rain.

(In his observatory, out in the palm forest, he keeps the machines for bombarding the clouds, and that other, so much more modern machine for fabricating clouds. But, in order to bring on the pluvial phenomenon, he relies above all on his psalms and on his imprecations.)

The same old modest robe, even if rain is the least of his worries as he advances toward the cavern of natural dampness where the mushrooms grow. All the way, he simply prepares himself to receive the mushrooms and for the mushrooms to illuminate him. They will certainly have the answer to his problem, not only by affinity but by sympathy, symbiosis, mimesis. He has to tread a long way to reach them. Vast tunnels with twists and turns and crannies meant to pacify the mind, to quiet the soul. He passes through galleries with the circumvolutions of the brain, and with the brain's spongy texture. Through spiraling corridors that become vague under the candle-light, he drifts as in a dream in search of the source. Deeper and deeper he sinks into the womb of the earth. Old Pachamama, old mother earth with such rocky, sterile innards that are neither warm nor receptive nor cushiony.

Solid-rock bowels through which he travels, feeling totally at home. He is made of that same granite, he is unmovable but as corrupted as the womb of the earth. The womb of the earth, its guts that at certain points are covered with mildew, the slippery clay-like mucous membrane of the earth, its momentary silk touch, the co-agulated liver-red with the throbbing of a heart, it all reaches him and moves him.

Moves him forward, that is, pushes him on. It's not viscosities he is searching for. He is in search of the pre-ternatural rigidity that will allow his aide—the dog—to catapult him—the Master—to the heights of ecstasy.

So this viscosity has to be left behind, other passages have to be traversed in order to reach the purest of humidities.

Suddenly, at one curve along the way, he comes upon the unexpected dry tears of the earth: a vast cavern of white stalactites falling in very thin threads like frozen rain. Tongue to tongue with the stalagmites that are born from the floor and weep upward.

Ever so white stalagtites of salt, brittle. Breakable. Shaping a paradise of incorruptible and fragile purity. The salt burns everything, it won't allow even a drop of life, which is future corruption. The world of things rotten has been left behind—swamps, lagoons. Now he has to open his way through the tunnel of salt that has never seen a presence. He advances stiffly, holding the candelabrum high, and goes along cracking the stalactites and the stalagmites, which thunder with the dry sound of broken bones.

Opening his way through the solid rain, he feels pure, sublime (who would have thought so), thanks to the purity of the salt, the great protectress. The most clean. Radiant. The light of the candles mingles with the salt and bathes him with iridescent reflections. All the curses bestowed upon him drop away from his body as the stalactites brush him while they fall, cracking at his feet. Bongos, *guacharacas, güiros*, and the beating of the soft drums, the sound of his feet breaking the crystals of salt, creaky. For a timeless period, immeasurable, he opens his path of salt until he finally reaches the milestone. The great stalagmite of fleshy colors that signals the entrance.

When he used to frequent those grottoes of mystery, at the beginning of the cultivation of the mushrooms, the stalagmite was his altar. He would spend long hours dreaming before it after having ingested the mushrooms by twos, as established by the ritual. Then, the stalagmite was the Virgin of Salt and under the petrous covering the crystallized body of the maiden was quite evident. That happened long ago, when he used to dream of forcing the clearest and purest of maidens to remain completely motionless as the drops of salt water rained down from the ceiling and became petrified over her body, ever so slowly, over decades, during which he tirelessly contemplated the motionless maiden becoming the living statue. The statue of salt with eternal inner life. Sometimes he could feel her throbbing under the coarse salt blanket, sometimes amid the vivid purples and reds of living, bleeding flesh the face of the Dead Woman would appear to him and he could allow himself the luxury of a few salty tears. The consubstantiation with weeping had nothing to do with any weakness.

All of that in times gone by, when lesser dreams found room in his destiny. Not now. Now he finally grasps the truth of the statue of salt and understands its sublime form. And he perceives the phallus, the unmistakable phallus that will clarify so many doubts for him and allow him so many others. A gigantic phallus with a pink droplet spouting out of the glans. A promise.

So he entered into the chamber of the mushrooms with hopeful step and for the first time was dazzled by its beauty. He saw the enormous vaulted cathedral with walls like precious stones of transparent crystal that had interior gardens like the water of his lagoon, completely mineral this time, static. He saw outpourings of liquid sapphires, coagulated emeralds. And vast pink walls of quartz, hematite. All from the play of the ever so transparent salt and its mineral drippings. Copper and iron oxides detained there for centuries, sulfates waiting for him, for him who arrived impoverished, holding a golden candelabrum.

And the mushrooms were in the center of that cathedral of transparencies, inmersed in their own watery glow.

With just the stump of the candles left, he takes a few steps toward the radiant clarity of the mushrooms, the clarity that will be his after their ingestion. The brightest of clarities? No. Right there, in the far end, something even more radiant than the mushrooms themselves glows with mushroom color, with a more disquieting greenish light. The light seems to be calling him and he goes forward, perhaps in search of himself, in the hope of seeing himself in a radiant mirror, something that will give him back his dazzling image.

What is it that shines with such intensity? Is it a golden mirror in the depths of that bejeweled natural palace that no human mind is capable of conceiving? No. Is it a divine glimmer, like a quiet lake that reflects itself? No. It's only the incomprehensible glow of a pile of rags. Of talking rags.

"Yes, sir, my son, although I well know that I should call you son of someone rather less virtuous than I. Yes. Here I am, in spite of your neglect, surviving after all these years just to teach you a lesson in humility. I am the Machi, yes. You brought me from my southern lands with promises much brighter than these cursed mushrooms. Radiant promises. And I didn't believe you, that's why I came, just to disconcert you. How could it have occurred to you that the Machi, the mother, the teacher, the witch could fall into such a coarse trap, a clumsy net woven with promises? I am the only promise, I'm the one who has the gift of prophecy in which the prophecy is fulfilled. Everything else outside of me is empty, I once told you, do you remember? And I don't care if you've forgotten completely, my words are still there, they have the power to make the stifled memory become flesh in you. Because of those words, of what I told you that day, you left and never came back, you disappeared with the idea of wiping me out of your life and out of the world of the living. What poor judgment, eh? What a lack of deep knowledge in spite of all you think you know. I, on the other hand, don't need to have you before my eyes to know that you're still sowing evil out there, scattering through the world the cruelties for which you weren't born."

"Of course I was, you old witch. The first memory of my life is the shriek of the black bird, and then the black cave of the woman that opened to expel the monstrous being with six fingers on each hand. No one, as far as I know, has received so many omens from the kingdom of darkness, no one better than I, nor so predestined."

"Those were simple manifestations of the superior forces to which we are all submitted."

"Shitty old Machi, all rags, I can't see what superior manifestations of forces you can talk about, thrown into a corner, turned into a rag on the floor, without shape now, nothing but bones, giving off a light of green putrefaction."

"You never did have a good disposition, but you're getting sourer with age. Take care. The tea from certain little mushrooms would be just right for you, it would restore your calm."

"Little mushroom tea! Little mushroom tea! I came to find big mushrooms, the ones that will give me power through another, the potent ones. I don't need tea of any kind. If it's a question of drinking anything, I'll have Machi soup, just so you'll know. You're nothing but bones, old witch, not even good for jerked beef and jerked beef's the driest thing you can think of on earth. I'm going to have some soup made with your bones and drink it as a downer at night."

"It will be mushroom soup, I tell you. I haven't eaten anything else since you saw fit to forget me. And it's a known fact that mushroom soup is no good at night, it gives bad dreams, old witches appear to you and unload on you all the curses you've earned throughout your life, which is saying a lot."

"Shut up, old soup bone. I've got a dog who . . ."

"Don't interrupt, will you. I radiate light and therefore I irradiate the word and you're nothing but a vile
reflection of me, rather ill-born, and if on a certain day
you went away from me it was because I allowed it and if
you've come back now like the unremembering fool you
are it is because I planned it that way, I called you before
me. I've got something to tell you and you're going to
hear me or burst."

I did both, I heard her and I burst. In fury. But I
didn't listen to her for her sake, cheap old witch, I lis-
tened to her because Estrella had begun to writhe around
in her skin and I felt very uncomfortable while I was
telling the Machi a few truths. That's why I fell silent, for
my sister, because the Machi had been able to recognize
her a thousand years ago and called her Little Morning
Star, and Estrella is grateful for that, and doesn't forget
flattery, feminine as she is, mawkish as she is. It has to
be accepted: Estrella happy, me happy, therefore at that
time I took the Machi away from her ridiculous
Araucanian shrine, an ordinary hut, and I brought her
home to assume the sublime duties of guardian of the
mushrooms. All for Estrella, and now Estrella obliges me
to listen to her, weighing heavily on me, forcing me to
kneel on the ground in order to accommodate her and
calm her. And the Machi talks and talks, taking advantage of it to spit in my face everything I haven't let her
express all these years. She talks and talks and I'm peaceful because she forgets in the meantime to reclaim the
sacred *trapalacucha* pectoral from me. Though I haven't
the remotest intention of giving it back to her. It probably
was her ritual object or whatever, but now it's come under
my aegis, it's mine alone. It's true that these ceremonies of
cold Indians aren't very interesting, they lack passion,

63

nothing like the hot magic of blacks, loaded with energy, but the sacred *trapalacucha* is something else: thick silver, it has force. With the sacred *trapalacucha* hanging from my neck I feel sovereign, above all during the festivities of the Waning Moon. I listen to the Machi so she won't take the pectoral away from me, or from a distance call back its powers. She's quite capable of doing a bitchy thing like that to me, the shitty old woman. She can also deny me a little of the green phosphorescence that she's gathered for herself and send me off through these galleries escorted only by bats.

"You should trust them, son, they would guide you with all necessary precision. They're quite a bit more perfect in matters of radar than somebody I know."

Old devouring witch, the things she kept on telling me, accusing me as if she had the right to. I don't intend to repeat them, so as not to bore anyone, pure lies, stories invented by that perverted mind of hers. Filthy-minded old crone, there in the solitude of her grotto imagining things that I, well, maybe, no?, but which she had no reason to go letting out.

I allowed her to talk, and while she talked—so she wouldn't cancel my powers—I repeated once more the ancient incantation:

> *Mirror am I. Look into me. The transparency*
> *will be found in my image which is*
> *in the purity of one who suspects and is.*
> *Illusory, beguiling, guileful I am.*
> *Earth is my flatus, and the heavens*
> *and the seas my lessened palpitations.*
> *I am the fathermother neuron.*

And I carried off my good harvest of green-light mushrooms even though she tried to stop me. This is my house from top to bottom, and everything that grows here and breathes here is mine. The green light more than anything, even though the old rag had sparkled with it.

I'm the fathermother neuron, no one is going to come on shining more than us, right, Estrellita?

Who can shine more than the Sorcerer? Even less now that he's appropriated phosphorescence. That's why in the Capital, at night, secluded behind closed doors, this voice can be heard:

"One tries not to be trapped in the greasy web of superstitions, but these are sticky, dark times, and superstition is impregnating everything with its fetid smell of backwaters and swamps. Ideas are decomposing, noble precepts are slowly rotting, and the smell of decomposition reaches us in waves, suffocates us. The sirens of police cars break the rotten air at times, and the muddy look of soldiers who, morning, noon, and night, aim their machine guns at us. We can no longer walk through the streets of the city without being pushed against a wall and frisked for weapons. They manhandle us, they transfer to our bodies the swamp smell of rotting plants. The rains don't wash us, the floods either, quite the contrary. Now it rains unseasonably and in the wrong place, deserts are flooded and meadows become barren. As if someone were playing with the clouds.

"And on top of this, and on top of this: Superstition

is slowly hemming us in. Superstition that goes by the name of fear. Now the so-called evil lights twinkle in the north and we don't know where they come from. A greenish glint appears at dusk and only dies out with the dawn. Possibly it's still there, permanently, appeased by day. It's the light of rottenness, the clarity of horror.

"At least, if it went away with the day, if during the day we could walk along the streets and perform our tasks with no one bothering us, without fear. But every so often a mysterious car with four men inside springs out of nowhere and carries off one of us, hooded, and we never hear from him again. What keeps us from acting, from defending ourselves, what paralyzes us? Superstition. The uselessness of all this. The terror. The disgust. The weariness. The need to believe in something. The dreams. The nightmares."

Maneuvers of the Sorcerer

I must clarify here that Brigadier General Mastrotti has been overthrown. He has been replaced at the head of government by General Durañona, a hard-liner. As it should be. And it cannot be said that these little hands of mine have not done their meddling in such a happy—for me—occurrence. One more good thing I have done for my country: I have given them a firm and decisive leader. General Mastrotti had turned out to be a little bland for us, not very practical, imprecise, consumed by doubt, which is the worst of consumptions. I laugh, because now in Military Headquarters No. 8, Barracks 7—his old regiment—he must be enjoying the benefits of his relaxation of discipline. The master torturers are no longer the great artists of pain that they were in my day. Now they're a bunch of bunglers, with no skill at all. Any poor devil can torture today, there's no more respect for specialists, those who calibrate their art with the utmost precision.

When I was able to impart personal instructions, torture in this country was a fine and true embroidery. We knew up to what point we could squeeze, we knew how to carry the subject to the very edge of the unbearable without letting him slip out of our hands. No master of torture can bear the great failure when the subject peacefully leaves for the other world where no one can catch him. You have to know exactly how much the body can take, you have to know the limits; destroying it doesn't mean destroying it totally, it means this: bending it, breaking it, undoing it and, you should know, carrying it to the depths of pain in full consciousness.

We practiced a lot to reach perfection, I'm proud to say, we experimented rigorously. My men couldn't be accused of sloppy amateurism.

Today they no longer consult me, they think they know everything, and they're a bunch of bunglers. They've read my manuals, I have to admit, but reading's not enough: technical advances have to be put to use properly. Too bad about poor General Mastrotti, Ret.: it's possible that he won't live to be turned into a martyr.

And to think that they planned to send him here to me, to my Free Territory, no less. Sacred bullshit! They would have contaminated it! A leathery general, what do I want him for? I could have given him as a plaything to the Indian maidens, of course, but I've got no reason to be discourteous to my poor girls and give them so unstimulating a toy. The poor things have never hurt anyone, although they haven't done anyone too much good either, that's for sure.

Luckily, welfare won't be the coin of the realm with General Durañona in charge; things are going to get much more amusing. This general respects my ideas as if they were his own, and he applies them right down to the last consequence. He's an upright man, a true leader. He doesn't have a somewhat softish hand like the other one, no sir; he does his name honor. I suggested to him the creation of a paramilitary corps to reinforce the repression. It's no longer enough with the parapolice, which gave me great satisfaction, especially in the days when I moved happily among them.

We need people, Durañona has communicated to me, and I can impart my usual advice, as if they didn't know it, as if they needed my endorsement for those chores. Well. Take them from the jails, I tell them, it's from the jails that you get the best personnel, not only the most suitable but also the most devoted, the ones who are grateful. They're capable of anything, they're even capable of loyalty, it's incredible.

Umbanda

"Like you people, the so-called Sorcerer, the witch-doc, also dresses in white and says he's religious."

"Yes. But with the opposite sign, turned around. He's on the dark side, and that's not a secret to anyone. If his attire bothers you, we can try to make him wear black, or red. His white robes or whatever, dyed with the blood of his victims."

"I didn't mean that. What difference does the color of the clothes make, we're not staging a play, we're trying to fight a reality that's hard to get hold of, with aspects that reason can't grasp. I don't know if you'll be able to do anything, but please don't waste your efforts on aesthetic considerations."

"I find you very Cartesian, my friend. Colors don't matter, what matters is the symbol, it's on this level that we have to operate, not on a visible level."

"Fine, fine. I've already thought it out, *similia similibus curantur*; if they attack us on the side of irrationality, we counterattack on the same flank. One must never underestimate the enemy. But let it be stated that this isn't our usual way of acting. You may now proceed."

And proceed they would, now, in relative calm, because they had found the ideal site: the old mansion at the end of some almost completely run-down streets, where the urban zone begins to blend into the unknown and streetlights throw off the palest of beams. In the back of a poorly planted but well-walled lot, with good watchdogs, an apparent placidity hid broad cellars that in the past century had been, alternately, a prison, the refuge and storeroom of smugglers, and a prison again, finally to be condemned by some more or less contemporary inhabitant who tried to get away from those two dense ghosts. But one day the old woman who lived in the house now heard the voice of the ghosts and stumbled on the cellars. She ran to get the Umbanda priests, who could still meet clandestinely, and begged them to come to her house and cleanse it of evil spirits.

"The cellars are full of voices and I don't know what they're trying to tell me."

"Don't worry, we're going to help you. Just get the necessary materials ready, and don't forget to have three bottles of cane liquor."

Not for drinking, the liquor: just to try to pacify the forces.

So, when the small group of dissidents headed by Alfredo Navoni went to ask them for their unlikely help, the Umbanda people didn't hesitate to point out the place: the former prison that would open its doors wide to free them.

Where does that shout of triumph come from? Who dares disturb the majesty of my dream? Guard! Bring me the dog.

Dog, aide, lick my feet, rub me with your damp snout, lick me, dog, I can't sleep and today is Friday, dog, and a full moon, someone is trying to hurt me. You should turn into a wolf, not into a faggot dog, a lapdog.

70

Into a wolf, I said. I'm going to change you into a wolf. Now it's my turn to piss on you, but mine is sacred piss that's going to give you back hatred, cursed Egret, fucking fairy; turn into a wolf, I said, howl at the moon, loud, I say, loud so it calms down and stops screwing me. With my inner eyes I can see it, reflected on the black lagoons, and it's laughing at me, the whorish moon, the moonish whore, it's laughing at me, reflected one, two, twenty times, one for each lagoon, and they're *my* lagoons, I'm not going to allow it. Fifty, a hundred, and in every reflection it's laughing at me, the great bitch, in every one except one. We've got to get to that single reflection, there where the moon isn't laughing, where it's quite serious, trying to annihilate me. Howl, wolf, come let me put these fangs on you and this skin to your back. Howl, hairy, cursed one; you may not have balls, but you've got more than enough fierceness, imbecile. You deserve this kick. Take that. And don't slaver, don't whine. Up, wolf. Howl.

Men and women in white in the dark cellar, shaken by violent fits, fighting to the death against invisible powers. Many laughing, sometimes, laughing in great bursts, their faces like moons.

They shudder, sing, and laugh, and sometimes a too intense spasm shakes their bodies and they give out a shriek of horror that has something of triumph about it. At times, someone doubles over and moans, taken with total pain, then the others lift him up in their arms, stand him up, and run their hands over his body, from head to foot, their hands open wide, as if sweeping him, getting the evil off him, and then they shake their hands in the air to cast off the invisible, the ungraspable and viscous. A negative force has penetrated the Sphere, it is necessary to drive it off, destroy it, and to do this they draw a circle of gunpowder around the possessed one and light the powder. The flames rise up high, blue, and the smoke and smell of the powder invade the environment. The dense blue and acrid smoke of gunpowder, transfiguring the scene, and the men in white now on another plane, writhing in the flames.

From the other side of the wooden grating that separates them from the Sphere, the magical space, Navoni and his people let themselves be trapped by what is *not* happening, by everything that those acts imply and reveal. The battle is without quarter, and they know it even though no one says so, the battle has been joined, and the opponent is five hundred miles away. It is possible that the gunpowder will reach him, the glow of the blue flames over which the men in white roll, singeing their hair and at times their eyebrows. Purification.

Bring me the morphine, they're destroying me, shouts the other one there in the north, under *his* earth, and the Indian maidens run to prepare the injections when they see him writhing on the floor. It's as if they were ripping out my guts, the obsidian knife penetrates me, sinks into me, I can't be, no, not me, the victim, I'm always the priest, not the propitiatory victim, no, not the scapegoat. Release me, I tell you. Release me.

And the Indian maidens, who haven't touched him— no one has touched him—look at him in terror, the syringe ready in their hands. The Indian maidens don't know what to do, and he goes on demanding his dose and shrieking for them to release him when nobody in fact is holding him.

Finally, one manages to stick the needle in an ankle,

in the hope of hitting a vein, and he begins to calm down a little, panting.

Lying in a corner, on the floor, the Aide can't help howling softly.

Go on, you shitty wolf, go on, you fairy, howl, that's the way I like it, howl, wolf, howl out for me what I hold back, go on, I need it, you're my voice, no, you're not my voice, my voice is my own, unique, I won't give it to you or lend it to you or let you have it, you're the voice, one that I recognize as if it had always been blowing in my ear. Speak out, Aide, dog, wolf, fag, shit. Howl, Aide. Howl, I tell you. That voice is a very special voice and I don't want to lose it.

"Can one know, after such a squandering of energy, if you have any effect?"

"No. Or maybe yes. We can feel it in our skin. But don't expect any immediate results, I'm afraid it's going to be a long and very difficult struggle. It's not an ordinary enemy, this man is evil incarnate. Don't be surprised if reprisals shower down on us."

"Do you mean that you've awakened the sleeping dog?"

"That dog never sleeps, as such. But if he really has powers, and I'm afraid he does, at this very moment he's probably planning revenge. Things can become very serious."

"And how can we get in touch with you people again, in case you learn something? With smoke signals?"

"Please, Navoni, we're in no mood for jokes. You know quite well that you can find me in my office when you need me. And don't forget: we've risked our necks on this project, too. We above all."

Ceremonies of revenge

Revenge. All my blood calls out for revenge. They've been practicing witchcraft against me, I will throw the forces of my force upon them, I will annihilate them, I will tear them to shreds, I alone, I'm not going across the border for help. I alone, with all my power, will make mincemeat of them. I've sent out orders that no stone be left unturned. They're dangerous people, they know how to manipulate the powers of the mind, and there's only one way to avoid that: destroy the mind. My people in the Capital have been well trained in that, they use their instruments to perfection, but the others have to be found first. I've set up an operational dragnet and now my men are combing the Capital, even though it's not easy to identify such a volatile enemy. Lots of innocent people are paying, they say; so what? Innocents, if you please. Who, in some way or another, would not like to do me in?

The Central Government doesn't want to be identified with this extermination campaign of mine. They claim that they have to fight a more tangible enemy. Enemies of the government, the real enemies of the government, are those who aim at me, knowing that only through my person can they destroy the concept of government. So what, I'm invulnerable. But I'm not going to let them pull my leg.

For that reason, rather than to protect myself, I've ordered the pyramid built. A squat pyramid with sides that face the four points of the compass. If I was the propitiatory victim yesterday, today I shall be the priest, with no more ado I'll be the Supreme Pontiff, I'll be, as I have always been, the Lord High Executioner, the Abominable One.

I want them to bring my enemies in alive and I will wrench out their bowels with my own hands. Every one of those who celebrated rites against my person. And people won't be able to say—as they've never been able to say even if they wanted to—that my hands are stained with blood. No sir. That's what rubber gloves were invented for.

Hurry up, slaves, lackeys, animals, hurry up, animals all of you, even if I'm the one wearing the mask.

That's how I like it, a bit ritualistic and a touch Egyptian. Not completely, I have my own convictions, I always personalize myself and defend myself against foreignizing cults. I'll never let myself be indoctrinated or dragged along, I simply incorporate what's useful to me, I adopt it and adapt it. I'm the great syncretizer, the great ecumenist, the totalizer, the Sublime One. That's why I've put on this mask of Anubis, with whom I sometimes identify. That's why the pyramid they're building for me is a double pyramid, a pyramid that's double-faced and single-faced at the same time, unique. Unity symbolizes and divides me. Like my pyramid, which will be Aztec on the outside—squat, that is—and completely pyramidal, Egyptian, on the inside.

But Aztec as seen by all for the great sacrifice. They attack me underground and I elevate myself. My pyramid will be built of adobe: stone is hard to find in these parts and I need my pyramid *now*, without the slightest delay. Even though it's made of adobe. Adobe? So much the better. I'll be directly linked to the earth and will resist all tremors.

I tell my slaves to hurry. In this dry climate, adobe almost makes itself, and I need my pyramid as quickly as possible. My hidden enemy is about to attack me again and I have to be prepared. Those unknown white witches who made me twist with pain during the last full moon are going to attack again. I wouldn't want to repeat the experience.

I can't even drift through my lagoons or write my novel anymore. I take notes, yes, and I successfully prepare my revenge.

I have to put on the red robe of great vengeances and I'm almost ready. To think that my inept men in the Capital report that they can't find the tricksters, that there are no such white witches or the like. I've felt them in my insides and I shall make them come out of their lairs with a howl from the wolf. Howl. Aide, wolf, howl a little more, howl, I can recognize that voice. Not like the sirens of my dear patrolman's voices *in illo tempore*. Howl, not with that whistle voice, with a worthy, rarefied voice, howl, I can hear Her behind the high notes, yes, it's my Dead Woman, no less, my Dead Woman brought to life again in that deballed voice of yours, goddamnit! I should give you one of my balls in exchange for this miracle, except maybe not, it wouldn't be the same anymore, you'd go back to being just another ballocked one and not the Dead Woman. The receptacle of the Dead Woman's voice. Do it a little more, like that, with a sad little howl behind the words, that's it! Her voice, coming back to send messages to her people. Messages of vengeance. Extermination.

My dear people, my dearest ones, repeat with me. My beloved, come out to search for those sons of bitches, those tricksters who are out to destroy me. Vengeance, my dear people, my dear companions.

I need you, come out and blast them, come out, rise up, protect me. Let the white witches who hate me be blasted. The people will hear you, wolf. They will hear Her. Give out, talk, relax. You're very calm, extra calm, you can't feel your body, that hand is dead, you're going to feel very sleepy, sleepy, you're very sleepy now, how nice, you're sleeping, you can't keep your eyes open. Your eyelids are heavy. Heavy. You're going to sleep now. You're asleep now.

Speak now, my Dead Woman! Speak, I'm recording you. And tell them to blast them all, turn them to mush.

"My dear proletarians, hear me. I've come back to you. Today you need me more than ever. You need my unselfish and ever-loving protection, but forces of evil are out to destroy me. Don't let them, my dear people. If they destroy my cult, then nobody will look after you, no one will come from the Beyond to reach out a hand to you. And the attack is being perpetrated against my High Priest. A certain evil sect is celebrating black masses to annihilate him. It must be destroyed, the sect that meets underground in some cellar must be found, found and wiped out, and I count on you for that, my dear people, my beloved proletarians. I will ask my High Priest, my Lord, to pray for you. He will know how to thank you if you fulfill your mission."

No, stop. Erase the last phrase. I have no reason to thank anyone for anything. They will be doing their duty and that's the highest happiness any follower can aspire to. They should thank me: it's enough that I show them the way and give them certain directions.

The Peoplists

"If it weren't that she was a saint, I'd say it smacks of black Mandingo stuff. Messages from beyond the grave keep reaching us and it's Her voice, there's no doubt about it, it's Her voice that curls about the music or behind the voice of the announcer who is trying to tell us just the opposite. I think the time has come to act, we can't go on like this in the shadows. She's asking us to."

"We have to be alert, companion. It could well be Her enemies who are trying to mobilize us for their own ends. It seems to be Her voice, that's true, but a voice can be imitated. I propose we wait for further proof before taking clandestine action."

"I agree. In any case, I'm calling a meeting for Sunday. The voice promised to send new proof, proof that leaves no room for objection. Meantime, I've given orders for the companions in the west to be prepared, ready to be mobilized and to reopen the Secret Sanctuary. It has to be aired out after so many years, we have to see that everything is in order and whether anyone has discovered it or violated it so as to obtain the proofs they're telling us about."

"They should proceed with the utmost prudence."

"Absolutely. Today more than ever, we have to take precautions."

To the Altar, to the Altar

The High Priest, with his noble white beard, and his gilded acolyte approach the mysterious Altar of the Finger. Observe, ladies and gentlemen, the steps of almost divine majesty, not walking almost, almost levitated. With crimson robes—the wedding gowns have been immersed in secret tinctures—they advance solemnly toward the center of the earth, to the altar where the Finger gleams, alone and admonitory as always.

It's an infinite obelisk. It's a beam of light that perforates the clouds.

It can be seen for a thousand miles, although nobody perceives it, because nobody pays attention to these calls.

It is the Sacred Finger that will finally fulfill its noble mission on earth.

The High Priest and his acolyte advance with solemn step. One foot, almost dragging, makes a brief pause halfway along and then lands in front of the other. And the other foot slips along with the sadness of having to break away from the nurturing earth for a fraction of an inch. The High Priest goes along mumbling his prayers; and he asks forgiveness for the first time, humbly, because he knows that the Finger, as it points, also points at him, at him more than anyone—he's everywhere—and accuses him, ignoring the fact that it is at last about to fulfill its sacred assignment.

Mea culpa, mother, lover, *mea culpa*, this is my work

and no one, not even the Generaliss himself, ever suspected. Because I loved you more than anyone in the world and I knew about your lasting beyond death and I've helped to keep you alive beyond your mystical aura and your legend. You will always be here among us because of this forefinger that some people mutter I stole, because there's never a lack of ne'er-do-wells.

In the pomp of his march to the altar the High Priest relives the scene with such intensity that he can't help falling to his knees. His golden acolyte, three steps behind, doesn't react in time, trips over the prostrate figure of his Master, and falls in a confused tangle of arms and legs and then of saliva and other more secret secretions that stain the red robes with mud, the coagulants of passion that the Finger deserves.

The scene

The scene that he evoked took place when after so many, many years they finally managed to get her back. They had taken her away and hidden her far from their reach, but one fine day they restored her to the Generaliss, to him, and to the other woman, the Intruder.

And the three together proceeded to uncover her. After so many years. But he held them back.

We can't do it like this, so crudely, with a screwdriver and chisel, that would profane her. She's a Saint, we owe her the high honor of a ceremony on opening her sarcophagus.

Perhaps by raising the lid through the simple power of the spirit, perhaps something even less ambitious but equally filled with feeling. He began to intone the chants, the Generaliss and the Intruder joined in, timidly at first, then with fervor, and finally with an impatience that burst when the Generaliss took the hammer and chisel and began to pound furiously on the lid of the coffin.

"They've kept us apart for twenty years, I won't wait any longer. I want to see her!"

He managed to pop off the wooden lid, and another of resplendent crystal appeared, and in the depths of that ever so quiet water the embalmed body of the Dead Woman.

Here you are, here you are, the Generalississimo shouted, trying to embrace her. And, indeed, there she was, more beautiful than ever, more transparent and alive, and that was why the Intruder suffered an attack of hysteria and began to shriek like a madwoman. The Sorcerer almost had a dizzy spell. Snap out of it, don't be silly, he said to himself; this Sleeping Beauty will be yours if you can just stay calm.

He went to get the finest of fine diamonds in all Government House to cut through the glass, and the Generaliss let him do it and allowed him to organize the elaborate ritual in spite of his impatience. First it was necessary to purify the air in the room—the mortuary chamber—with incense and incantations. Then they shoved the Intruder out, for both men wanted to be alone with the Dead Woman.

Cutting through the glass took more than two hours because it was a task that called for the precision of a surgeon and the love of a mother. And finally there she was, uncovered, so perfect and glowing that neither of them dared touch her. The Generalississimo only passed his fingertips gently across her face, afraid that it would disintegrate with the slightest pressure, and then they embraced, the General and the Sorcerer, and they sobbed for a long time, the one on the shoulder of the other, each imagining it was she he was holding in his arms.

Meanwhile, the Intruder had not lost any time. She'd called together the entire High Command so they could be witness to such a magnificent event and had called the Hierarchy so they could reopen the canonization process (it was better for her to have a saint as a rival than just any old embalmed corpse).

The generals, the colonels, the bishop, the two vice admirals, the brigadiers, the chaplain, other high military dignitaries began to arrive. And they invaded the sacrosanct precincts, the mortuary chamber, which very soon, with the glow of torches and medals, began to look like a ballroom.

A lot of sparkle, yes, but, all the same, they all were dazzled by the beauty of the Dead Woman, a spiritual beauty that went beyond coarse matter, as the bishop, also dazzled, took care to point out. And once more they began to mull over plans for building a shrine for her in the streets. "In the most active downtown area, surrounded by parks and gardens." "That's it. We'll expropriate a few blocks around, knock down the buildings, let's say for about four blocks, and open up a broad *rond-point* with the mausoleum in the center, a real sanctuary."

"We could build a monument of solid gold, in keeping with her worth."

"We could stud it with diamonds."

"Carve the top from one single gigantic diamond."

"We could do that."

"Just a moment. I agree that we should give the people the inalienable right to venerate her. But to venerate *her*, the only one, the irreplaceable one, the one who is alive in the heart of us all. Because they could well have switched her on us. Who can be sure that this beautiful dead woman is anything more than a skillful imitation, or a woman made of wax? Or, worse yet, someone else's corpse prepared by a highly skilled artist to look like Her."

"Monsignor! Do you doubt my honesty in something so personal, so delicate?"

"Of course not, Mr. President, of course not. But you could be a victim of the trick, too."

"That's impossible! I would recognize her among all women. My blood recognizes her. Alive or dead. And venerates her."

"I have no doubt, General, sir. And I respect and admire you for that, God save me from wishing to offend you. But you must understand that in such a delicate situation we must be absolutely sure. Many, ever so many years have passed, and it seems impossible to me that she could have kept so intact. It would be a miracle. The best proof of her sainthood. And, as you are aware, the Church has as its prime mission to mistrust miracles until there is proof to the contrary."

"Excuse me, Mr. President, but Monsignor might be right. What do you suggest, Monsignor?"

"I think that it would be wise to call in a forensic physician to investigate the case."

"I'm a military surgeon, Monsignor, I think I'm capable of discharging those duties."

"Very well, Colonel Doctor. What procedure do you propose?"

"Analyzing the condition of the teeth would be too traumatic, we would damage that suggestive half-smile. Besides, I'm afraid the dentist who attended the Lady has probably died and the records haven't been preserved. Also, it wouldn't be right to let the matter out into the open, this investigation must remain strictly among ourselves. I think that the most sensible thing would be to examine the fingerprints. If there's no objection."

"I agree," the Generalississimo warned, half regretful already, "just as long as the finger is well cleaned off afterwards."

"The fact is, I don't know how to explain it, General sir, Generalissimo sir, Generalississimo sir . . . The Lady's finger is completely dehydrated. It would have to be amputated, put in liquid for a few hours so it would regain the necessary humidity, the impression made, and it would then be sewn back on with the greatest of care. And nothing would be different. I can promise you. It will be as good as new."

"Get this monster out of my sight!" roared the Generalississimo. "And don't ever let him into this place again," the Generaliss warned. "His idea is ghastly, irreverent. Sadistic."

I had to intervene at that precise moment to calm my Generaliss sir. No one but I could get close to him when he was enraged, and at that moment he was out of his mind, snorting through his teeth and even wailing a little. Nobody was moved. Those jackals and hyenas crowded around him, demanding the finger, that pound of flesh.

"The doctor is surgeon for the whole High Command, his sutures are invisible, he can't do any damage," one of the hyenas in back dared murmur. And I thought he was right, and that it would be best to get them all out of there and proceed at once.

"You don't have to watch the operation," I warned them. "It's enough to see the finger and compare fingerprints."

There was nothing for them but to move out, reluctantly, missing the amputation spectacle that had got them so worked up. They gathered in the main salon on the first floor and sent for some refreshments to ease their wait.

O General sir, O most beloved, O lord of shadows—
even if I don't call you that—O ashen eminence, eminent
ash who soon will drift away from us leaving me to care
for the Dead Woman alone and watch over this finger, O
man among men and lord of many men although never
all. O replaceable irreplaceable one, O little brother, un-
wary. I take charge of this ceremony, I wash away blame
while the chief surgeon of the State cuts off the Finger.

All that I don't say and you know, all you know even
if I don't say it, all you will never suspect—and who
cares, for your days are numbered, numbered by the fingers of a few hands and not the chosen hands of Sixfingers. Numbered by the fingers minus one, the same
one that the head surgeon with all the delicacy of his
sublime craft is now slowly slicing off, letting his love
flow through the scalpel and drooling a little. Only a small
avid thread of spittle that runs out of the corners of his
mouth slips down along his chin. Vampirish. I like it so.
The thread of drivel: the river of blood which I carefully
calibrate.

Always

In memory of that supreme moment and today too,
always calibrating them.

The absence of blood is important. That body so
dead, so forever dead, did not shed a drop. With all the

blood women use, all they overflow, squander, waste! That's why I look down on them—because they don't appreciate the sacred liquid, because they're not impressed by its scarlet presence. They say that my mother menstruated all through her pregnancy, I didn't give her a moment's respite. That blood so thick, unstimulating. I didn't want to keep it in my abode.

The water in which the finger will finally be submerged is blessed by me. Water completely purified of sin, water without vibrations so that the finger can charge it—I shall drink it afterwards when no one can see me, so as to learn the truths of the finger. I have already committed the truths of the water to memory, that's why I erased them, annulled them with my exorcisms. With this water, what has never circulated before will now circulate throughout my organism. I shall have the essence of the only woman who matters to me, and Estrella will receive the benefits of a digital femininity that will show her the way. It will be a breath of fresh air for Estrella, a stimulation that will drive her forward and make her mature; Estrella, like a ripe fruit waiting for the harvest. This finger juice will be the irrigation. The finger will be the plow and will open the furrow for me.

Where to stick the finger? Where, I wonder, can the wound be, the finger in the wound, my most intimate aspiration? Stick it in and keep it there and twist it around as much as one can, leaving no scar. Scars are sclerotic, dead. Only the wound is alive, alive in suppuration.

In those days I had no thoughts of the wound. Limiting oneself in those days to seeking another finger to replace the Finger, the great twister, the finger that will always poke about in the wound. Let's not be confused, let's keep our ideas straight. Looking for the replacement. Where can Sixfingers be wandering? She could have given me one of hers without feeling the loss, offering me just one of her leftover fingers that, for just such reason, had been so sweetly born on those hands of hers. Giving me a sixth finger, as an offering, so I could keep the true one. The foremost Forefinger.

All the time. The immeasurable quantity of time required to come in contact with oneself and grasp the marrow. The muddle. Luckily, I have all the time in the world before me, for behind me all I have is my center of pleasure and an occasional memory. A memory of that day, of the moment of the finger (and the Finger was never, never used, as suspicious people suspect), the Finger was never used by me with ulterior motives. Nothing ulterior or posterior as regards the Finger. Just posterity. That's it. Posterity.

And a wound remained, perhaps even a keloid scar. So what.

I understood my mission from the very beginning. The idea took shape as I was martially descending the steps of Government House with the Finger in a flask held on high. (The Generaliss wouldn't have thought to leave the side of his dead woman, *our* dead woman. If they had cut off a finger, he would stay with her to be her finger, her right arm, her whole body, her soul. Soul. What they both really lacked.)

I, then, alone, descending the marble staircase with the flask held high and my lucidity at its sharpest. I left the finger with the senior ecclesiastic and military officials—the jackals. Let them watch it macerate while I dive into other waters. I had three hours. Three hours are more than enough to perpetrate any substitution.

With what devotion I sought it! And, in the end, with what desperation. I used both my official prerogatives and my natural gifts. Everything, so as to procure another right forefinger from another beauty in her thirties. Said like that, it sounds like what it wasn't: easy. Holy shit! I had to keep the embalmer in tow in order to get the job done swiftly. I didn't find her in the women's jail or in any penitentiary—it would have been less discourteous. A double, a rather light blonde with very thin hands and a sharp forefinger, where would I find her in this indifferent, shitty city, in this morass of rather ambiguous, surreptitious beings? In a café, finally. Sitting quietly. Reading. Exhibiting her hands as she put sugar in her cup, stirring it a little. It was necessary to cut the nail and take off the polish. All that before proceeding, and she asking why, and what had she done. The guardians of public order who arrested her were people of few words; they obeyed my instructions and had no reason to go about making comments. Neither at that moment nor at any moment; I would take care of that, and they knew it well. So, complete silence and the bewildered blonde. She fainted at the climax. Let that information serve as one more note of human cowardice. I was left with not only the finger but the ring, too. As a keepsake. I let the boys have the damaged blonde—as a keepsake. They would know how to keep her in the shadows for as long as necessary. Until her finger grew back, maybe, or until it was erased from her memory.

I returned to the place of my vigil; with the false finger I went back to where the true Finger awaited me. And all were ready now to witness the solemn proof. The Generalississimo then came down from his aerie and in plain sight of everyone withdrew the Finger from the flask with devotion and with devotion held it in his hands for a long time. He seemed to be praying.

I prepared the small cushion and the glass slide. The Generalississimo, as if it were his own, inked that Finger and quickly pressed it down on the glass. There was a most complete darkness and in the total removal of light we projected the slide onto the white screen. A second later the beam of light that would unveil the mystery came from the other projector. Beside our fingerprint the other flowered: the old fingerprint registered a long time ago of Her whom we all know.

What a chill ran through the room! What a tremor of excitement when it was proved that the prints were identical. A single fingerprint, a single person at two different stages in time, two stages of the body. That finger drying there in cotton and the one—the same!—that so many years ago had made its mark of its own volition.

The Generaliss broke into sobs and I had to accompany him to his quarters, help him get undressed, and begin to calm him. Not for long, no. I left him with his aide and reentered the room where the Finger rested triumphantly on the cotton, surrounded by those reverent jackals. Reverent imbeciles, beclouded by an immanence that was really in me, not in this finger that would come to be mine.

I took the cotton nest and raised the Finger high. I went up the stairway and, around the corner, I made the substitution. The Dead Woman's finger finally rested against my chest, throbbing with me.

I'm all heart. Me. All heart. This is what I am right now, on my way to the altar, given over to my recollections. These memories are a lagoon of quiet, thick waters. They throb in me wholeheartedly, while my aide the Egret, the little golden child, tries to calm me in his arms. What can the poor creature know of my designs?

She is no longer she, buried again in a secret place. That body, as beautiful as it is and as undecaying, has lost all identity. She is only this finger by which she was once recognized, and this finger is mine now, now and forever mine. I built an altar to it, I preserved it for years, I suckled it with my own secretions, I can now do what I feel like with the finger, manipulate it according to my every whim. This finger can be, as I have said, my plow and my corncob. I have no need for any stupid eunuch aide embracing me now and thinking it will calm my palpitations. I don't need him for anything, at least not for anything effective, although I do have use for him in other duties. He has the voice, I have the Finger and I have my brain. We will be unbeatable.

Earth is my flatus, and the heavens and the seas my lessened palpitations. Wishing to calm them is only mad-ness. Mirror I am, look into me. I am illusory. I am the fathermother neuron.

I am also my eminent destiny as pointed out to me by the Finger. The Finger is all I need to fulfill myself, it's what is lacking in my aide.

The sworn followers

My dear companions. We are gathered today in the greatest secrecy by order of the Central Council. We have been entrusted with a mission that I would not hesitate to describe as historic, and for that very reason I wanted to share this sublime moment with all of you, without omitting a single companion.

Only a few details are of interest when it is a question of such a monumental mission, and I don't plan to continue holding you in suspense. Esteemed companions, friends rather. Brothers and sisters: If all is confirmed, the order will soon be ratified for us to penetrate the Secret Sanctuary, breaking the seals. Light will shine once more in those chambers, even if only for the time necessary to make a rapid inspection and give them a dusting. We must return them to their former glow and prove that everything is as it was then.

Yes, it's just as you hear, and I can understand the murmurs of surprise and even the shudder. But the password has come to us from the Central Council and we must be prepared to receive the order to march. And more than anything, we must be proud of having deserved such a great distinction. Let us, one more time, then, swear fidelity to the cause and know how to respect our vow of silence to the death.

I cannot hide from you the fact that this will be the most remarkable of missions. Also the most noble and the least bloody. For the time being. But every companion who agrees to accompany us must be prepared for possible dangers and fully assume the risks.

Before going into details, I should like to state a proviso that must be made perfectly clear: whoever does not feel capable of following instructions to the letter can withdraw from this room without any recriminations whatsoever. They will be properly excused and no questions asked. Free of blame or guilt, they can still work within our ranks. Provided they leave this room in time. Because once instructions have been given and the details of the mission laid out, it will be too late to step back. There will be no consideration then, and all deserters will be adjudged traitors.

We must also count on the cyanide capsule that was given to each of us when we went underground. Once we undertake this operation, we will never be parted from that capsule and we will be ready to swallow it if for some reason we're caught. Keep in mind:

A Peoplist doesn't surrender or betray; death is the only way.

Therefore, those who are not prepared to face the consequences should withdraw in time and remain in ignorance; we will bear them no rancor and we will not question their motives.

This will be an exceedingly delicate mission and we can undertake it only if we are pure of heart. Since our venerated Dead Woman has chosen to manifest herself among us, it is now our duty to break the seals of the Sanctuary and see that everything is in order. I only ask now that you deliberate and take a tally so we will know how many sworn followers we can count on in the end.

Small groups are formed. Deliberations, debates. Finally, the spokesman of the largest group:

"I think that a diversification of forces should be ar-

93

ranged. As they say, let's not put all our eggs in one basket. For that very reason, the group I now represent has decided to sacrifice itself by remaining outside of the secret. We choose ignorance for the benefit of our Cause. We will be the Venerators of the Dead Woman from the shadows. Thus, if, God forbid, one of you should fall into the hands of the armed forces and through negligence drag down the rest, we can be counted on to hold high the banner of our devotion. For this reason, if you will permit, we shall withdraw from the room, not without a most understandable regret."

To which the chief replied with a nod of the head and an effort to keep his eyes down so as not to show his feelings. Finally he said:

"With great joy I see that the majority of the younger Peoplists have stayed with us. I hope that their perilous decision hasn't been made out of simple curiosity but rather that they are imbued with the nobility of the cause that will be entrusted to them. Curiosity is the mother of many foolish acts. Therefore, we must satisfy it immediately, so it won't besmirch the solemnity of the plan.

"Let us listen to the instructions from our faithful Narrator. She will offer us words of wisdom. We must be fully prepared when the Moment comes."

The legend

Many, many years ago now, this land was ours and we lived in good fortune, thanks to an exceptional woman, a goddess. We called her simply Lady Captain and she expected nothing more from us, only to guide us along paths of well-being and happiness. She was always humble and always on the side of the humble and the unprotected. She was our light, our guide. Our Lady Captain. A mother to all of us. I can well say it, I, all wrinkles now, who was so very young then. She stroked my head one day and it was as if heaven had opened up for me.

She had come to our poor slum to lay the first stone for the installation of twelve new water taps, and I was in the front row since the night before, waiting to merit the blessing of her stroke. She was golden like the sun, and fair, and little by little she was giving us everything we needed, she was bathing us with gifts. Day and night, tirelessly, she would attend to very long lines of poor people who waited to ask her for some favor, or just to see her in her radiant beauty. She fought for the workers and never sold out to the bosses, she shook up the Generalissimo—her revered husband—so he, too, would fight in defense of the oppressed. "Be a man, goddamnit," she would say, jabbing him in the presence of others. She knew what it was to be a man, for there are some burdened down with testicles who can be cowards, while others, like this woman, are real warriors. She was our warrior, our shield, she fought in our name and defended us from the exploiters.

Until one day she left us, angelically. She wasn't with us anymore, off to heaven she went, taking all her courage with her. Not that she had chosen to, no. The Lord took her away because she belonged more on High than in this dirty swamp we call life. But she couldn't abandon us, no; she left her most beautiful body with us, properly embalmed, and we worshipped her in her glass coffin and for a few years we did not feel alone in the least.

Until a dirty military coup overthrew the Generalississimo and the Generalississimo had to leave without saying goodbye and she was taken away from us all without warning. We searched for her for years, we looked for her throughout the whole world without respite but without success. Almost twenty years passed before the Generalississimo was able to keep his promise to return. And he came back to us, in triumph as was fitting, and in a short time our Dead Woman was restored to us, truly restored, and there she appeared, as beautiful and as unpolluted as ever, untouched, and again we could worship her as in the old days.

Beside the glass case there was always the other man, the unknown one, the Sorcerer. Who got to be a cabinet minister. He was something like a father to her, and on a certain day that man spoke to us. The Generalississimo had just died and we had buried him with great pomp, when that man spoke. He told us about the Dead Woman's miracles, which we already knew about, in a way. So we began to ask her for things and to offer her things in exchange: votives candles, reliquaries, what we could; a wedding dress when she got us a husband, the crutches when she cured our lameness, flowers, candles, money, all our jewels. What we could. What we had.

That man built her a temple and we would leave our gifts there and pray. Until a new catastrophe came down on us, another coup, after which the cult was forbidden. But this time we were quicker and we were able to hide her before they took her from us again. We hid her with her treasures and all in this secret place that soon, after another twenty years have passed, we will visit again, but more stealthily, and only to renew the air she doesn't breathe, to shake the dust off her and show her our gratitude and the emotion we feel on finding that she has deigned to manifest herself among us once more.

In the other world, in the other memory, she hasn't forgotten us. We will dress her in her finest raiment, and once more, in her presence, we will repeat the oath to obey her unto death, and beyond death, too. She is our savior, we depend on her for the realization of the ancient prophecy. A river of blood will flow, Don Bosco said; the river is already flowing. A river of blood will flow and we will have twenty years of peace. If she has deigned to return among us, it must be to bring us the peace that we need so badly.

Hail to the Dead Woman! Hail to the Virgin!
Hail!

The Finger

Daddy's darling little finger, smack, smack, come to Daddy here and he'll give you another kissy and sorry sorry pretty little finger for taking you out of your comfortable little formaldehyde cradle, washing you nicely nicely with all that clean sweet water under the tap, all that sweet water to get rid of the poisonous formaldehyde smell, hydrated little finger; darling little finger, see how I care for you, embalmed as you are, and even so I preserve you in formaldehyde, just in case, and I wash you and wash you under the tap with fresh sweet water and you have to be appreciative about it, for there's a water shortage in these latitudes.

Divine little finger is going to be turned into the Great Avenging Finger, look, look how, point to the south, like that, pointing, that's why you're an index finger, point the south out for me, not like that stupid finger that always points to the west, the other finger is bronze, look at it, stuck eternally onto a statue, how banal, how unnatural, not like this beautiful little finger that's flesh and blood and nicely free, on its own, preserved by the miracle of science and of miracles.

Great Avenging Finger that will also give me other satisfactions when the moment arrives, Daddy's little finger, and now come here and pardon my pressing you on this ugly little pillow, but that's life: there will always be someone powerful like me to press others and ink them and use them for his very noble ends. Or for his dirty maneuvers. Whichever.

Who will doubt now that the Dead Woman is alive, that she's returned to the earth to demand revenge? Now I do have power over life and death, I can revive her whenever I want, I can cover their buttocks with the fingerprints of the Dead Woman. It will be something never seen before, I have to get ready. Identify myself fully with her. To think they say I failed in my resurrections. Rather, in the great resurrection when I made the Attempt. By Satan, I never fail in anything, it's just that sometimes I postpone my triumphs for a while.

Twenty years are nothing, as we rightly say. I didn't get to bring him back to life that time because of his lack of drive. Her, yes, I'm bringing her back to life because she deserves it, and because I deserve it, too. This deed, which will earn me my reward, is in itself my reward.

The attempt

He was praying in the private chapel he had at that time in the very heart of Government House. And the order had been given: Do not disturb His Excellency's prayers, except in a case of extreme emergency. And this was a case of extreme emergency and the messenger had no remorse whatever in pulling the Minister out of his concentration to give him the news. The Minister had been trying to blow new strength into the Generalississimo's image, in the center of the sacred pentacle, clouded in incense.

"It's too late, Your Excellency," the messenger mumbled, grief-stricken, "our Generalississimo has just breathed his last sigh. We have to be resigned. He's passed on to a better life."

"What better life, you wretch! What are you talking about? What life can be waiting for this man that's better than the one in this world where he had everything, absolutely everything, surrounded by the affection of his people, enjoying the ineffable privilege of having me by his side, with all the material benefits anyone could ever expect and more, with his spirit in peace after having had the great revenge of returning in triumph to this country that he had once left in defeat, what more can a man ask for but the enormous satisfaction of making his enemy pay, every one of his innumerable enemies, making them pay a tooth for a tooth and an eye for an eye for all the evil they had done him? A better life, you animal, can there be a better life for him than this life that let him carry out his plans?"

"Forgive me, Minister, sir."

"Master. From here on, I will be your Master, everybody's Master. He wanted it that way, he just communicated the fact to me in spirit. I was the one who took care of his revenge, and this is my reward. I will be the boss, the Master. With my head held high, I will take on the responsibility and I will know how to keep his name alive. And not just his name, something else too."

"Yeah, all right, master."

"With a capital letter!"

"With a Capital Letter."

"And now bring before my person those quacks who were responsible for the Great Catastrophe, for the Enormous Grief that Overwhelms the Entire Nation. I want them here instantly."

When he was alone, he felt a pressure in his chest that was really indignation over the abandonment. You can't do this to me, damn you, he shouted at the image of the Generaliss, knowing that it was too late. Now he would have to blow new strength into himself, because he had more than enough reason to suspect that with the death of the Generalississimo—General, really, why keep up the deception now—with the death of that man, his possibilities of reaching power were probably seriously reduced. Even if the Intruder succeeded the Generaliss. The Intruder? No one would ever place in her the hopes of salvation that the people had placed in their dead Generaliss. Although, who knows? That woman, well advised, tutored.

Nor was it a question of getting so far ahead of events. Several important things still remained to be done —and in that respect he was strictest with himself. He could well disguise reality for others. As to his inner law, it was never to deceive himself, to take events as they come, but to make them fit his needs. In this case in particular: to find a scapegoat. The doctors. When he had them before him, the first thing he did was order them to bring the Generalississimo back to life.

"Impossible, Mr. Minister. We've tried everything, as you can well imagine. Cardiac massage, oxygen, mouth-to-mouth resuscitation, drugs, everything. It's impossible to go against the designs of nature."

"Why not? Guard! Put these men in custody until you get further orders."

"Sir, you can't do this to us. Our other patients are waiting for us."

"Blast them! If He's dead, other patients in this country have no right to live."

A phrase that remained engraved in the collective memory as a synthesis of devotion and firmness.

The collective memory also registers an attempt at resurrection—never established with absolute certainty—which redounds to the benefit of the legend of the Sorcerer.

What is certain is that our man headed toward the chambers with a more martial, more ministerial step than ever. Enlarged already.

The Intruder had been left alone with her dead husband. Out of respect for her mourning. And the poor thing was weeping unconsolably. It was the only thing that had occurred to her to do in such historic circumstances. A weak woman, that one, who let herself be overwhelmed by events. Not like the other one, not at all like the other one, who was lying there a few steps away, still placid in her coffin beside the Generalississimo's bed, motionless. Solemn, as circumstances demanded of her. A queen.

I shook the Intruder a little to bring her to her senses and I decided then and there to turn her into my ally. Together we locked the doors and covered the face of the Dead Woman with an embroidered cloth. Don't let the poor thing see that we're stealing him away from her, I explained to the live one.

And I set in motion the ceremony where I revealed the best of my occult knowledge. I was young then, however, and the Generaliss leathery. I think I recited the incantations to perfection, the spells came out of me in one unbroken string. I had been rehearsing them for months, I couldn't have made a mistake. When I had no words whatever left, I pulled desperately at his feet, repeatedly, and I called him three times by his full name.

Summon your spirit and come, summon your spirit and come, I invoked, as in rituals of calling. And the Generaliss, unmoved. Hardheaded as usual. More and more hardheaded, hard, all of him hard, turning rigid before our eyes as we tried to soften him with the rites. Suddenly his jaw dropped, openmouthed with fright and quite dead. He was going to stay like that for eternity unless we did something fast. I had to tie up his lower jaw with a handkerchief, as with any ordinary corpse, and, though it was an acknowledgment of the end, we still refused to accept it.

"He looks like he's got a toothache," the Intruder said, and the idea was of some consolation.

I called him General Cavities, I called him General Toothache, knowing that matters of pain are matters for the living. And he, as if nothing had happened. Refusing to listen to me. Playing at not understanding, at being dead. Just to go against me, not to give me satisfaction, once more. It was the last time he had his own way, that goes without saying.

The colonels wouldn't let us go on with our incantations. They forced the door and burst into the room, to render—so they said—posthumous homage. Archbishop and all. I had to give up my post at the head of the bed to the Archbishop, but I remained there in spirit. Always at the head.

Now I can really do some reviving and no one will be able to interrupt me. Because I am reviving no one less than Her. Reviving in my own way, of course. She'll never stop being the Dead Woman, the Departed One, the Deceased. That's her most enviable condition. But I will manage to bring her back among us, all the same. I've already given orders that seem to have originated from Her and they're orders that are already beginning to be carried out.

She, revived by me, is speaking through my mouth. Or, rather, through the mouth of the unballed one, and now she makes her mark with her finger that's nothing but a stamp in my hands.

COMPANION: THE BEST ENEMY IS A DEAD ENEMY
A certain secret sect is trying to put an end to my memory

Destroy them
Venerate me

and I put her fingerprint here so they will have no moment of doubt. In that way I can be sure they will seek
out the members of that cursed sect who are trying to put
an end to me. They will destroy them so as to venerate
me. As is proper.

Commander in Chief

"Plot, that's the word. It would seem that our man
was right, after all. A plot is being organized against the
government. I've given orders to activate the search for
the subversive, unpatriotic elements, in that way con-
tributing firmly and energetically to the norms of the
process of National Reconstruction which we are embarked upon. We must prevent and repress this act we
could describe as a mystical crime, a true menace to the
purification of the State, but we also have to tread carefully and carry out an inconspicuous operation. On my
way to Government House yesterday I thought I caught a
strange effervescence among the people. They looked like
ants getting ready for some suspicious activity. Let's re-
double our efforts but let them not be noticed. Our image
has to be one of confidence, peace, and happy expecta-
tion, so the people will see that thanks to us the country
will once more find the destiny of greatness that ration-
ally and reasonably corresponds to it."

"It will all be done as you say, Air Marshal, but don't
go all poetic, it's not healthy."

The 20,000-man pyramid

A metaphor I am now turning into reality, because that's how the pendulum of history wants it as it goes from fact to symbol and from symbol to fact in the blink of an eye, with a flip of the fingers—of the Finger. The pendulum for those who, like me, make history, inside and out, living it and telling it, justifying it and/or modifying it. People who, like me, hold power—and there are so few!—are the only ones who can allow themselves this incomparable luxury: turning dreams into reality, passing from word to deed with complete impunity. Not from the word itself, which would be too simple. Passing to the deed from the uncertain basis of a popular word, a cliché, a metaphor, as I have shown above.

Therefore, I am ascending physically now, placing myself at the head of everything, dignifying myself, making an altar for myself, rising on top of the pyramid that I have ordered built. Without spending a cent, in exchange only for the spiritual good that I offer my serfs. My flock, my most devoted followers.

"We are building the Great Temple," I exhort them. And they drink in my words and, luckily, ignore the fact that over the centuries the builders of temples have never been the beneficiaries of temples. The blood of workers has always served to firm the mortar that holds up the temple, and I can't see why these must be an exception, no matter how bloodless and undernourished they may look.

"If you sacrifice them all, O Master, you'll be left without adorers, without a flock. And, on top of it all, with the temple unfinished," my aide, now my acolyte, dares whisper, and I let him have those infrequent outbursts of impertinence because I am magnanimous and sometimes I can recognize the relative good sense even if it comes out of the mouth of a eunuch.

Even Estrella has taken the side of moderation, and she makes me more indignant than anyone. Estrellita, Estrellita, try to understand that we're not talking about those practical things that are the private concern of women, we're talking about great, virile acts. Don't be like the castrato, think about the show. Think about the eternal glory of our name if we decide upon the great sacrifice. Marco Polo reports, I make clear for her in case she doesn't know, although she knows everything, that twenty thousand people were executed during the funeral procession of the Mogul Khan so that they might serve him in death.

"Nobody has died here," Estrellita specifies from the depths of my being and, luckily, only I can hear her. "This isn't any funeral procession, you're no Mogul or whatever, or anything like it, and there's no reason to believe Marco Polo, who was a seven-soled liar."

"Estrellita, you always have your feet on the ground . . . without your taking it as any reference to your shortcomings, of course."

I let a day or two pass and then I latch on to an irrefutable argument: during the inauguration of the Great Temple of Tenochtitlán, Aztec priests sacrificed twenty thousand men in a single day. They had them form columns of five thousand, each marking a cardinal point, and, crack-crack, they went along pulling out their hearts one by one as they climbed up. Like an assembly line. Disassembly, rather, just imagine what a sublime spectacle, such beauty, all that blood staining the stairs, a carpet of blood like a gigantic cloak of red ants, a living cloak of blood, radiant, shining, ant-like, hot. Four sublime tributaries of my river of blood.

Ughhhhh!

Estrellita, the traitress, had a stomach cramp and I had to double over, almost kneel down, almost begging her forgiveness, but none of that. I recovered immediately, and grabbing my balls in my hands, I called the guard to bring the Machi, the mushroom witch, to me. She would understand. After seeing so much green, so much moldy glow, she certainly must be thirsty to see a red bath of blood.

Ragbag came staggering in. Damn, I said to myself, she's gone blind, she won't be able to admire the splendor of my pyramid, I won't be able to explain anything about anything to her.

"You're wrong, son, you don't have to look at me with that expression of disgust that's so very much your own. I've lost a thousand things, but I've kept my senses intact. But what's this business of dragging me out into the sunlight after years and years in darkness? Everything dazzles me now, even your brute presence dazzles me, just imagine."

"Crone, Machi, I didn't bring you here for us to discuss personal matters. I brought you here to support my plan."

"And since when have you ever needed my support?"

"You're old and you don't understand a thing. Don't ask questions, limit yourself to answering when I ask you questions. And answer yes. For now, all you're allowed to do is be surprised and applaud. Listen well:

"That mound you see there, if your weak eyes can

107

distinguish anything and your weak brain can grasp anything, in a very short time will be a splendid pyramid. And not just any pyramid, no, it's going to be hollow and Egyptian on the inside and terraced and squat on the outside, an Aztec pyramid. I am the great syncretizer, as you already know. I am the High Priest no matter how much it bothers you. And my pyramid must be baptized formally because it will be my temple, because it will serve to raise me above all mortals in a literal sense. I was telling that poor acolyte of mine, who never understands anything, and the small person annexed to my person that for the death of the Mogul Khan twenty thousand men were sacrificed as a means of providing him with company, and for the inauguration of the main temple of Tenochtitlán another twenty thousand went under the obsidian knife. Don't you find it an interesting figure?"

"Twenty thousand men? A little overblown, don't you think? In these parts, that would nearly mean one per thousand of the total population of the country. Not an overly inhabited place, don't forget."

"Well, my idea was to have it as a symbol. My figure is a thousand really, a highly meaningful figure for me. A thousand men, that is. Like the pyramid's being the color of the earth, an almost golden ocher, that is, glimmering, and when the threads of blood begin to flow down over the steps and cross and merge, an enormous, most beautiful, gigantic, voluminous Thousandmen flower will be formed and it will be like a carnivorous flower. My emblem."

"Delightful. And everything will be transformed into revolting scum, with a smell that . . . well. And it will be all covered with flies. Green flies, that's for sure, to add a little more to the color combination. And just try to imagine the last two hundred men, let's say, trying to climb up the steps with the blood flowing, as they slip and fall on their asses, giving a spectacle that won't be at all edifying or grand, a real embarrassment, in fact. Look, as far as human sacrifice is concerned, I think you've already gone well over your quota. It would be better now to stick to something allegorical, wouldn't it? A single animal that sums it all up."

"Maybe a female animal. Maybe the Machi is all I need. Let me think about it."

"What blood will flow out of me? I'm pure mushroom."

"Look, I can always have you accompanied by a few fresh Indian maidens, beautiful girls with hot blood. But the main thing will be getting rid of you, you contradict me too much."

"No, I'm just insisting that something smaller would be better for you. Maybe a ringdove, so your evil instincts will be made perfectly clear. After all, you're making a pyramid, not a blood sausage."

That last phrase sealed the Machi's fate. Making fun of me? It was the first time anyone had tried, and it was also the last. I had her put in the stocks and her mouth filled with rags so she wouldn't shriek. After more mature reflection, I had them take out the gag so they could stuff her with nice red meat. No ordinary mushroom juice at the hour of the great sacrifice. She had done well to alert me.

The building of the pyramid is advancing swiftly and that's without much use of the Lizard's Tail whip.

Secretly, I have a much more ambitious project and I've had them bring me some rhinoceros-horn powder, which is an incentive to love. It's the most expensive thing you can buy today, and precisely for that reason it's indispensable to me. The inner pyramid will be my chamber of love. In this place my real wedding with Estrella will take place, once we've conquered the enemy. In order to consummate this ever so unique union, I will need all the help I can get: rhinoceros horn, Spanish fly, belladonna, henbane, any aid to stimulation. It will be worth the trouble, yes, it will be worth the trouble because we will succeed in engendering a son of god who will be god, pure and radiant. First, though, I have to go about clearing the terrain—the country, that is—of evil vibrations. Those who oppose our designs will be crushed without mercy. A son of Estrella's and mine, a son of my person, cannot be born where dissidence is rampant. Our son, my son, will require complete acquiescence, and for that reason, right now, I shall order the sacrifice of the Machi, that blabbermouth. It will be the high point of the ceremonies of revenge.

Capital. Day

"We have to act immediately to avoid playing into the hands of the subversives. The foreign press is printing lies about our beloved country again. Look at these clippings, just take a look. They say that over the past few weeks we've made more than two hundred people disappear, that we torture babies in front of their parents to make the parents confess, that we beat pregnant women until they miscarry. The usual routine, what else is new! Fortunately, we've given orders to bar these foreign newspapers, which have sold out to an international conspiracy. The less printed matter that circulates here, the better. But just the same, we're getting a bad image abroad. And that can't be tolerated. Our image has to be clean at all costs."

"What do you suggest, General, sir—that we ease up?"

"Absolutely not! What are you talking about? I'm going to replace you as Press Secretary if these are your brilliant ideas. No sir. We've got to organize a counteroffensive. We're going to defend our model at any price. We have to be prepared to crush anybody who stands in our way. National Reconstruction requires it, and we're not going to let them go around calling us fascists. We won't allow them to try to confront us with so-called human rights, such an unreal concept. Our image must remain as pure as our intentions, and that's your responsibility."

"Yes, Mr. President." The Press Secretary came to attention, clicking his heels.

As if I had nothing else to do, as if I spent the whole day here scratching my balls (I beg your pardon, Estrellita), yesterday no less a person than the secretary in charge of the press and information for the country came to visit me. I had to give him about five of my invaluable hours, because you must admit it's a tricky matter. We talked about the rumors and I explained to him how to manipulate information so that our countrymen—even when ignorant of what is being said—will be convinced that the assertions of the foreign press have no basis in fact and are the reflection of a dirty campaign of vilification. There's nothing like stirring up self-esteem to make the public react the way it should. When the government is criticized, they should know; the country is being criticized, nothing less; and when the country is criticized, the ones really being criticized are its inhabitants.

In addition, we drew up the following:

PRESS RELEASE
In order to complete the process of National Reconstruction, we must support a strong government, and not one that is one in name only, a solid government, not one that is helpless and deficient. It must be strong, because we do not know when this aggression will cease. For that end, we need integrated action

in families, schools, and universities, which will provide the norms of behavior that mold young people. There is no such thing as partial responsibility, responsibility is for everyone, even children, and, above all, it reaches right to the organs of communication, because the ideological struggle is directed at people's minds, and we are not going to restrict the freedom of the organs of communication, because by doing that we would be fighting in the way our powerful enemy wants us to. What we demand is responsibility in the media and in the people who direct them, so as not to give rise to psychological insecurity, which is exactly what the subversives are seeking.

Our own journalists will understand quite well that this means shutting their mouths and not echoing slander. But, oh, how boring, by Jove! having to clarify all that for the Press Secretary. They become more stupid every day, wasting their time on trivialities instead of concentrating on what really matters: finding my enemy and destroying him. As quick as possible, goddamnit! There's less than a week to the full moon, and I'm sure they're going to attack me again if we don't succeed in stopping them. The Peoplists, yes, seem to have begun to fight, but they tell me that, before anything else, they are going to the sanctuary of the Dead Woman to express their devotion. Pissing and missing the pot. As usual. You can't count on the people, so shortsighted, so tied to convention. Let them leap the wall and rush to the attack without asking anybody's permission! I give them permission, and I'm the only one who counts. Attack! Attack! was my message, but they want to respect the old verticalism and they go to Her, goddamnit, as if she weren't the most horizontal of all. Dead as she is, parallel to the ground. Verticalism. What a bore.

And the full moon only a few nights off and the pyramid that will never be finished and that imbecile of a Press Secretary asking me about the ABC's of his responsibilities, wasting my time.

I've decided to kill two birds with one stone. I'll give the moron instructions and take care of my own interests with one stroke of the pen. It used to be much more fun under General Mastrotti, when I acted under cover. Now I have to play with the cards on the table and am not allowed certain pranks. Anyway, I manage to get my little pleasures. And I say to the secretary:

"My dear sir: At your request and that of General Durañona, my worthy and distinguished colleague, I have offered all the information you need to handle this delicate matter. But as you will no doubt well understand, precautionary measures are never enough when we are standing up against a multifaceted and sibylline enemy. International public opinion has a thousand faces, it puts on all manner of disguise. We were attacked on all flanks, and we must defend ourselves on all flanks. The enemy who manipulates international opinion is ubiquitous, he's everywhere, in our high seats of learning, too, and especially right under our own floor, in our basements. It's a prolific, dark enemy, with hidden winding passageways, and only I know how to do battle against it. That's why I suggest you withdraw to rest for a time, while we—my acolyte and I—organize the details of a ceremony that I am going to arrange for you, Mister Press Sec., to confront the contingencies that might turn up in your very noble and very complex campaign against the campaign of vilification."

Later on, I suggested to him:

"A masked ceremony seems the most appropriate for

you, all sacred masks, all prepared. They will be like your own skin and enable you to assume an infinity of faces and forms. You will need them all if you want to concentrate on misinformation."

How tedious, how boring. The unspeakable monotony of having to advise utterly unimaginative men. A different cock, quite a different one, would have crowed during the life of the Generalississimo. He would have manipulated these minor strategies to perfection without any need of me wasting my invaluable time. In cases like this, I was only there to give the final touch, the master stroke, my contribution to the show, to everything that called for splendor. Because we have to admit that the Generaliss, in minor instances, always found the exact word without waiting for me to tell him.

And to think that now I have to prepare the ceremony for the boob. A few nights away from the full moon, as if I could afford such distractions.

It would be amusing to have him attend the sacrifice of the Machi, I'm sure that the crazy witch is going to give off a beam of green light when I open up her stomach. She might put a scare into our Press Chief and force him to believe in my powers. But no, I'm saving the Machi for a more succulent occasion. We might have a little fun now with the Indian maidens. I've been letting them lounge around the Palace for some time now, it's counterproductive. My pyramid must be much more radiant than the full moon. If I can manage to darken the moon, all the evil curses that the white witches in the Capital are trying to lay on me will turn on them and I'll be able to wipe them out, blast them like the dirty old toads they are. Old, useless toads.

I'd like to take the Press Chief to visit my pyramid, but it brings bad luck to show it off before it's finished. And more than one person will ask: If He doesn't know how to ward off bad luck, who does, then? I wonder who? It's just that I'm terribly busy these days, and even the simplest spell requires time and dedication. I prefer to limit myself for now to what can't be put off, and concentrate all my powers on the counterattack. That's my real process of Personal Reconstruction, the only one that counts. It's not because of worry over what might happen to me; as the whole world knows, I'm indestructible, but if I conquer my hidden enemy I'll be taking a giant step in defense of the plan of fathermotherhood that I'm committed to. Then the country will be all mine, the world will be mine, and no one will be able to stop me.

I'm filing my nails in the meantime, I'm practicing, the way a pianist plays scales. Little by little I'm laying the bases for my Kingdom of the Black Lagoon, and I've already ordered the minting of coins with my effigy. I now pay the builders of the pyramid with those coins, more a gift than real wages, and they can only spend them at the general store on my property. In that way, they always come back to me, the coins do, and I don't have to mint great quantities. The merchandise I sell them costs me very little money, or nothing, to be quite frank, because I exchange it for a few ounces of the product of my plants. My processing plants, of course, you mustn't think that I've become a farmer or any other such base thing.

Although I do fall into certain cultivational temptations now and then. With the hallucinatory mushrooms, for example, or with that other more secret crop of poisonous mushrooms that I like for their admirable coloration and their surprising shapes. Not to mention my favorite garden, to which I offer the most delicate of butterflies: the garden of carnivorous plants where I get my inspiration.

The Sanctuary

At last we have received the order to open the secret Sanctuary. We can now be certain that the messages we have been receiving this last month, the ones that reach us subliminally through regular radio programs, come from Her. This is corroborated by the written messages that are beyond question; the fingerprints have been meticulously compared and there is no doubt, they are Hers. It is our Dead Woman who calls us, She has come back from the kingdom of eternal light to offer us this radiant spark. A true miracle. A period of great glory is approaching and we must be worthy of this grace. She, the Saint, has come to save us. Let us go, then, with all nobility, to restore the brilliance of the Sanctuary. We are the chosen. Let us put into play all the unction, all the devotion, that we owe Her.

She is our Sacred Mother, the only one who remembers us. We will raise on high the banner of our love for Her and we will not let it be tied to any conquering chariot. We will be the worthy representatives of the people, we will all come to Her to show Her our reverence and our fervor.

We will march to Her with our heads held high, facing the enemy wherever he may be crouching and trying to stop us. We will cross the river of blood that the ancient prophecy speaks of, we will wait by Her side for the peace we deserve. We will go with our heads held high, yes, but inside we will be most humble, our eyes will be downcast because She will have lighted our way with Her radiant presence.

We know that presence of Hers very well, all of its divine glow, and we will not permit any representative of this government that is not a government of the people to stop us from fulfilling our commitment.

Superstition, heresy, some exclaimed as soon as they came to power, and with those words, those insults, they forbid us to venerate Her. We had to go underground, sanctuary and all, and little by little they squeezed our cult until we had to close Her shrine and hide the relics and the offerings. But now, after so many years, my co-religionists, brothers and sisters, we will finally tear down the wall. We will bring Her relics out into the light of day and from those relics we will draw the strength to fight the enemy as She has asked us to. And She will return to reign among us.

We must arrive before the full moon. Before it is too late, we will have to liquidate Her enemy as best we can. If we can.

I have finally got the people on the march. Now I can let myself be distracted by my new priorities:

MEMORANDUM
1. Of my new Kingdom of the Black Lagoon I shall speak later. For some time I've been working on the idea and I've already set in motion the first part of the project,

but I prefer not to mention it, so the idea won't be stolen from me. These government guys are suckling from me, they want to gobble up my brains so they can fill my privileged seat of honor. Do they think maybe I haven't noticed it? I'm quite sure they're watching me, studying my every step and even my tiniest sighs (my vital emanation, my prana). But I take my precautions, and, for example, I'm writing this vade mecum in invisible ink so no spy can microfilm it. Words of mine that are erased when I want them to be and that only I can bring back to life when I need them.

2. Buy Estrellita a little present to seduce her. To entice her.

3. Train the snipers and post them at the borders of my domains. No one is to enter without a pass, but, above all, no one is to leave. No one is to go out into the world and spread the good news before it's time. The Kingdom is already on its way, but the Savior has still not been gestated. (It will be my son. Personally I don't dream about saving anyone. I'm above it all.)

4. Get several gross of candles.

5. Complete the preparations for the Grand Ball of the Full Moon.

6. Expedite the most urgent invitations.

Is a charter flight from the Capital okay?

This has been my last idea of genius and I don't see why I shouldn't turn loose all my efforts to put it into practice. A masked ceremony for the Press Secretary, yes, a public one with me as Hierophant. I shall invite high government officials, the top journalists, all the noteworthy people in the country, and we will put on a grand ball for the full moon.

It really will disconcert my hidden enemy and it will

disconcert the full moon. My enemy expects me to react seriously, performing some countermagic to which they would know how to respond. And I, as usual, will have gone off on a tangent. I'm going to give a party. When they think they are attacking me and making me double over with pain, I shall be dancing to the sound of my drums. But no sacred *atabaques* or ceremonial beats. None of that. Drums for the *merecumbé*, the samba. I'll drive them all mad with dancing and laughter. A river of blood will flow, yes, but this time it will flow with laughter. A gallop of red laughter. Let's see if my enemy will recognize me in this my new disposition of spirit.

TOo

I, Luisa Valenzuela, swear by these writings that I will try to do something about all this, become involved as much as possible, plunge in head-first, aware of how little can be done but with a desire to handle at least a small thread and assume responsibility for the story. Not the story of humanity, but this minimal story of the so-called Sorcerer that is slipping from my hands, taken over by him, who had been the papoose from Trym Lagoon, a very precise and well-mapped place, now transformed into the diffuse and undiscoverable Kingdom of the Black Lagoon with him, a mere witchdoc, as Lord and Master. He's already expanding its borders and hopes to invade all of us after having invaded me in *my* kingdom, the imaginary one. I know now that he, too, is writing a novel that superimposes itself on this one and is capable of nullifying it.

A psychopath, a messianic madman who holds us in suspense. And a scoundrel of the first order; I've just received an invitation to his masked ball of the Full Moon (Come as you are, we will provide the disguise at the foot of the Pyramid). Masquerade to inaugurate a pyramid, what an idea. He has no inventiveness, he repeats clichés, and to cap it all, he's the most destructive being imaginable.

To the point of occupying my thoughts completely. I

can't even do my work now, or write either, or keep up my contacts with a certain ambassador so as to get asylum for a few people at least. I should have to busy myself only with that, a work more to my measure, with no pretensions of saving the country, but simply and more realistically a few who run the risk of death. I, too, was planning a party, at the embassy, so more people could get in and request asylum, and now I get this invitation and it throws me off. Although a masked ball . . . it isn't such a bad idea.

I can see that there are minor elements that bring us close (?) together. There's an affinity in the voice as I narrate him, sometimes our pages are indistinguishable. I try to see the witchdoc as he sees himself, but not too much; I try to capture his tone, but at times he changes it on me, sharpens it, and it sounds invented. How am I going to be able to invent someone so merciless? I tell his story so his existence won't go unnoticed. A country of ostriches, this, conduct we tend to imitate by sticking our heads in the sand, denying any danger.

And now this invitation drops down on me. It goes beyond all limits, it breaks all the barriers. I have to find Navoni and show it to him, to see what he thinks. Something has to be done.

I called Navoni's office, where he almost never is, of course, and I left a message: tell Dr. Estévez (any doctor mentioned there is of course Navoni) that I'll meet him at the Café de la Flor at seven-thirty. He'll understand. That's why I'm here now at the Café La Opera, it's five forty-five. Navoni should have arrived fifteen minutes ago and the invitation is burning in my handbag. If there's a police raid they'll find a compromising document on me and you won't hear any more from me. What will I tell the cops, that I'm writing the Sorcerer's biography and that's why he's trying to get on my good side and has invited me to his party? We don't know what position the cops take or pretend to take with respect to the witchdoc. Besides, if they go and ransack my place and find this manuscript, I've had it, I don't think they'd approve at all.

I look at my watch and know that I can wait only five more minutes. It's the rule and we follow it to the letter, largely out of prudence—the one expected might have run into an ambush and confessed where and with whom he really had a meeting—and in part because we want the lead role.

Not I. Some time ago I made a serious discovery, which I adhere to: if you can't be the protagonist of the story, then it's best to be the author/ess of the story. Except that now this firm separation weakens as I find myself getting mixed up in the story that I'm putting together.

Thank God, there comes Navoni. It's a relief to see people arrive these days, confirming the fact that they're still alive. It's also a relief, unfortunate, but a relief, to find out they're dead. The other possibility is the most intolerable one.

I know I'm to call him Alberto even though his name is Alfredo, and things like these sometimes amuse me and I don't take them as seriously as I should. We have to release tensions, I tell myself, keep our sense of humor even under the most terrifying of circumstances. Alberto, Alberto, I shout to him, all excited then, and he doesn't like that. "Don't attract attention" is the byword, and I, as usual, am out of step.

A crisp hello and he talks about other things and I know that it's to gain time and let people forget us, leaving us a modicum of freedom to communicate elliptically. Alberto/Alfredo lights a cigarette, orders a cup of coffee, which is the least conspicuous thing you can ask for in a place like this, looks at me.

I like the way he looks at people. It's an intelligent look, alert. I trust him and I know that this alertness keeps us alive in more than one sense: it reminds us of the imminence of danger and obliges us not to lower our guard even for a second. We can't be inattentive.

Finally, when he feels everything has returned to the seeming calm of downtown cafés where the nothing-ever-happens-here functions best, Navoni raises his eyebrows as if to question me. I hand him a copy of the well-known weekly *God, Country, and Home*, practically the only publication we can read without fear, and he takes it with curiosity. He knows that this is one of my inoffensive touches of humor, he knows that the information will be in that magazine, contaminating it.

Navoni thumbs through *God, Country, and Home* as if interested, comes upon the large card sent by the witch-doc, hesitates for only a few seconds, continues on with his concern with such illuminating articles, folds the magazine, puts it casually in his jacket pocket, goes on chatting.

"You're looking very well, are you thinking about traveling these days? I know that you were feeling rather lunatic, but I don't think a trip of this kind would be good for you; no, decidedly not, quite the contrary."

"I wouldn't dream of going, of course, I just wanted to tell you. It's very strange. I don't know why he invited me; he shouldn't even know that I exist. That worries me."

"Maybe what he's really after is for you to know very clearly that he himself exists. It's the only thing that interests him. A megalomaniac of the 'I don't care what they say about me as long as they say something' type. That's the kind of person he is, if you can call him a person."

"But I'm afraid now. What shall I do? Shall I give up the biography? You know I've got more important things to do in any case."

"Don't even think about it. If we're going to let them neutralize us to the point of not being able to write—I don't say publish—it would be better if we killed ourselves. No. You keep right on with what you're doing. With *everything* you're doing. I'm going to give you back your own advice. Once you sent us to deal with a certain figure; you said it's like in homeopathic medicine: *Similia similibus curantur*, like is cured by like, you said, and now I say to you that I'm beginning to believe that. Or I'm beginning to believe that these formulas are good for those who believe. We can't reject them, we can't allow ourselves to reject any possibility. Come and see it with your own eyes. There isn't much time left till the great night. I don't know if they'll let you be present, but I'll be in touch. So long, beautiful. Do a lot of writing."

A lot of writing, yes sir, that's terrific advice, as if you could get into someone else's skin just like that when your own has become so uncertain. You're kind of naked, with nothing to say, suddenly gasping for a little air. I should have gone to the masked ball, you have to honor invitations when they rain down from above, and not stay as I did, expectant, waiting for the okay to attend the counterparty.

A novelist is not in the world to do good but to try to know and transmit what is known; or is it to invent and transmit what is intuited? As it is, I'm not going, and maybe the masked ball I will describe will be more exact than the real thing, or maybe the Sorcerer will decide to write his own story of the party, or we will find out through some unsuspected source what really will happen and maybe that will turn out to be the least informative of all.

Every guest, as he arrives, will be given a terra-cotta mask with the face of an animal, something halfway between revulsion and beauty. A satanic parade. And later, much later, the actual orgy will take place. Then clubs will be distributed among the guests, and to the rhythm of kettledrums the dance will begin. Not an ordinary dance, no: a dance of destruction. The guests will all have to break at least one mask with their clubs, as if it were a clay jar, and since the mask is placed over the face of the other person, who knows who is breaking whose mask and, with luck, face, and reprisals will immediately ensue.

Still several nights to go before the appearance of the round moon and I can already imagine that dance of the furies while the masks are on. After they've been broken, there remains not only the great unmasking but the implicit promise of vengeance.

I'm being led into wicked imaginings, blown up most certainly by the Sorcerer, while I await the other invitation to the counterceremony of my Umbanda people.

One more deception won't kill the Peoplists, it might even strengthen them. That was so in this case, when, after the arduous work of taking down stone after stone, with the healthy intention of putting everything back in place and not leaving any tracks (as if anyone would see tracks there on that little forest path so far from the main road), they finally uncovered the Dead Woman's sanctuary, which, in reality, was a grotto. An almost bare grotto as they discovered to the horror of the oldest among them, those who knew about the treasures previously amassed there. Over the long period of clandestine seclusion, the sanctuary had lost all its adornments. The crutches were all there, certainly, piled in the corners. Also, there were casts of those with fractures whom the Dead Woman had miraculously healed, and there were the brass votive offerings and a few bridal bouquets almost turned to dust, but what about the gowns? The beautiful bridal gowns embroidered with pearls, the robes, the cloaks, the tiaras, the diadems? The finest of candlesticks, the votive lamps? All gone, everything that had given luster to the grotto, everything that had made it sumptuous and sacred. Gone.

There was a long consultation. The youngest proposed alerting the people and calling for a general uprising. The council of old members that was formed for the emergency calmed everyone's spirits:

"We can't deal with these matters of the soul by demanding that our people shed their blood. We must find other solutions. The enemy is multifaceted and much more subtle than we can ever imagine. He isn't always part of the government. Sometimes he attacks on his own and is just as ferocious. From here on in, let the Sanctuary rise to the surface. No more keeping it in the dark, let us bring it back into the light where it belongs. We will carry these few relics to a church, to the Basilica close to the Capital if possible, so we can give the cult of our Dead Woman back to the world. Thinking that this will keep us calm, the government won't oppose our project. We can also come to an agreement with the Church, as always. We'll symbolically donate the relics to the Virgin and we'll say that we're coming to adore the Virgin. They themselves do things like that, they call it syncretism."

"Unanimously approved. After all, She was always our own true Virgin."

"And this maneuver will upset the enemy and we'll be able to take him by surprise."

"Except that She has called on us for immediate action."

"Groups of activists are already looking for the secret sect of magical destruction. Let that part of the mission remain in their hands. We'll get the other part started, the less chancy one."

"Well spoken. I propose that we form a solemn procession with the relics that are left. We'll carry them to the Basilica. We'll pick up people along the way, it will be a glorious pilgrimage. Let us declare this day the Day of the Saint. Today She has come back to the light, She is no longer alive just in the soul of her people. She will live again in the memory of the world. It's a pity that we don't have her lovely embalmed body."

"They say they cremated it and threw the ashes to the wind."

"I don't believe it. But in that case they'd be sacred ashes and I'm sure they'd come and alight on the cupola of the Basilica."

"Come, then, to the Basilica. To offer her our whole-hearted and ever-constant devotion."

Days of waiting, but finally the real invitation arrives. Navoni lets me know that I can go, that's all; we'll meet on such and such a corner at ten in the evening. They'll pick me up without too much explanation, as is customary, even though it was I who put them in touch with the *babalao* Caboclo de Mar, the priest who had agreed to intercept the witchdoc's magic, short-circuiting it. I gave them the idea, but now they've taken it over, as always, and are carrying it out scientifically and I'll have to be content with the crumbs. And I know what I'm talking about, I was in love with Navoni years back, I know what to expect of him and to what extent I can admire him.

On this night with a moon that's about to emerge—full, I believe, or hope—I walk through the streets with my senses alert and weighed with memories of Navoni, of the one he used to be, the less mature chap who still retained a touch of humor in the face of danger—and danger would be kind to him and it wouldn't hover over him as it hovers over him now, cornering him so often, rendering him inaccessible. To me at least. Except that for me, too, now some danger is hovering and I, too—now —should have to learn to become inaccessible, at least to the guys who, perhaps, one never knows, are following me in order to grab Navoni. A trap? Using me as bait? I'm going straight to where the greatest of possible preys will be waiting for me, and that's why I'm careful. I'm careful because of him, too, especially because of him, and that business about going straight there is only a figure of speech, for here I go, on foot to avoid witnesses, toward the meeting place, taking all kinds of detours, going down side streets, abandoning the *diritta via*, looking for one-way streets so as to walk against the traffic, facing the vehicles, knowing at least that they're not following me by car. If they're following me on foot, I'll find out in some unexpected turn at a corner I haven't fore-seen. And I use the godforsaken darkness of these streets for my own benefit and I think about the Navoni of the good old days, when we would stroll along streets like this holding hands under the trees. Where have those hands gone, where are those tranquil streets? The streets have a different density of shadows now, and the hands only serve to cover the mouth and try to ward off a blow, as if it were possible to avoid blows in times like these. Five to ten, no moon yet, one more turn, I don't think anyone is following me, no one has paid any attention to me at all, but still, I'd rather not stand on the designated corner, or lean against the mailbox. One more turn around the block, I used to do it so often with Navoni, when it was so hard for us to part. Now, almost without saying goodbye, we've parted, we turn, and if I saw you I don't remember, because if I remembered, it could be lethal for the other. The mailbox reappears at the end of the block, the moon must be about to come out somewhere on that clogged urban horizon, and the car approaches me very slowly and I recognize it and I get in with a casual air, cursing between my teeth.

I would have liked another kind of date with Navoni, something a little more—how would you say?—tender.

They're getting ready for the Umbanda ceremony, all dressed in white, barefoot. With a certain devotion, I stay in the back of the room, trying to retain what I see. They're praying at the altar to Saint George, they sing

Saint Anthony, all of gold, open up the doors for us, we are about to start. Then one of them leaps back and seems to fall . . . Other men and women follow him, until they are all in a trance, and then no one can cross the mystical line, the "line of the old black man." We know that the battle is going to be arduous and no one moves in our corner, no one even takes a deep breath. If those who saw you then could only see you now, Navoni, making fun of me some time back because of this magic business, you said, as when I put ashes in your pocket to protect you, and you, of course, playing the wise guy, saying sure, of course, the ashes make me invisible, just imagine, watch me go into the police station there just like that, after all, I've got ashes in my pocket and I'm invisible. We have to see if cops believe in those things, what a bad break it would be if I ran into some kind of atheist who doesn't believe in magic, somebody pure, like that kid who recognizes that the emperor hasn't got any clothes on. And, boom, I'd hate to tell you the tale!

You are the disbeliever, I said to him back then, and now I don't know if I should repeat it, you're the disbeliever who doesn't understand subtleties, who has to take everything literally. Being invisible also means being inconspicuous, and that can only be achieved with a lot of trust in yourself. If you believe in the ashes, then the ashes will give you the trust you lack, right?

The subtle threads of the unconscious plot that I think I know how to weave but which I'm weaving little or nothing of. The fringe, that's all. It's pointed out to me by a sweet guide, a girl in white who comes over to me with a frail step and puts her hand on my head. Ho-ho, she laughs, I had black hair and curls, too, once, when I was a young man. I had curls just like yours. Now I'm a bald-headed old black man, but now I know. And the voice comes out broken, smelling of cane liquor, and I don't discuss that transvestism of souls but follow her along the hall and down the stairs to the zone called the Sphere, that dusty cellar with a brick floor and a heavy air.

"You are very subdued, my child, your aura has gone out. I see you dark, very dark inside, why? Have you been sticking your nose where you shouldn't? Are you poking around in mysteries? I see you so dark."

Of course, in the midst of all that darkness, amid gigantic shadows. Me dark? How else? I'm crouching at the feet of my guide, who has sat down on a fruit crate, and I curl up, hunch over, and deny it all; my aura out? who would ever have thought of something so silly? and my guide laughs in that broken old man's voice, so out of place coming from that soft mouth. Very dark, she repeats.

Out of the corner of my eye, as in a dream, I see the others coming down the rickety stairs that lead to the Sphere and going past the wooden railings. The gunpowder ritual is beginning for them, inside circles of fire, amid flames, to cleanse themselves of all the evil they've absorbed up above on their unprotected battlefield.

Separated from them by the wooden barrier, I contort with them and I feel the crackle of the flames in my hair and on my skin. The fire that purifies them doesn't seem to be reaching me, however, only that irritating smell of burnt gunpowder and the blue smoke that smothers all of us equally.

"The thickness of evil is great, my child. It has to be fought off on all possible flanks. Tremendous things are happening now and you mustn't even approach the cause of the evil, you mustn't contaminate yourself. There are devils."

"There are devils, but they're small, inoffensive, most pleasant devils. Especially one that comes from Agua dos Meninos, the market in Bahia, he's made of iron, with his trident and lance in his hands, his long legs, and a splendid smile on his iron mouth."

"Eshú!"

"Yes, the messenger of the spirits."

"No, the devil. All according to how you see him. One should never enter into possession of those elements, they always come loaded down. Never touch objects of evil. Don't approach them. You have to break away from everything that means witchcraft, and see, my child, you have all kinds of knickknacks. Get rid of them all, I'll tell you how."

And I listen, and the smoke from the gunpowder envelops me and protects me perhaps. It cleanses me. *Similia similibus curantur.*

The guests have left now, in a rush, some with feelings of guilt even. Have you ever seen anything like it? Although quite a few weren't there, and not as many private planes as expected landed on the formerly clandestine, now private strip. There weren't too many representatives of the government, but that didn't seem to bother our man. In any case, once the party had begun, everyone with his mask and his cloak on, anyone could think that he had the General President in person in front of him without suspecting that, in reality, it was a question of one more manifestation of the Lord of These Lands, Master of the Black Lagoon and very soon of the world. Under another embodiment that could have been that of any one of his guests.

He'd arranged things well, the Sorcerer; not a detail escaped him. The pyramid had been completed on the outside, and if the final touches were missing inside, that was unimportant. The squat pyramid looked perfect at first sight, with oil lamps lighting all its terraced sides, the Machi already sacrificed and boiling with greens in the great sacred caldron, and—a touch of genius—terra-cotta masks with the effigy of the Master for all the guests, men and women alike. And an identical black cape for all, in a mad cloning of Lords of the Tacurú, while the One and Only played pontiff atop his pyramid, dressed in a crimson iridescent robe and the mask of an ant.

He had thought it out well. A mask of feathers and an eagle outfit would have fed his vanity better and would have been more in keeping with his spirit, but the ants deserved this tardy homage and he would now assume with lordliness this new aspect of his rich personality. He would no longer be in his own incarnation, anyway. He would be in each and every one of his guests who wore his mask. His face. With eyes the exact tone of gray of his own eyes, and tiny holes in the pupils so the guests could look through those eyes. His eyes. Then nothing of what they were to see or what they saw would be offensive to them.

The guests climbed up the steep steps of the pyramid until they reached him on his radiant seat of honor on high. Beside the Master bubbled a caldron that gave off an aroma of humidity and herbs. The Indian maidens served the most ferocious alcoholic beverages and the Master gave each one a steaming bowl with broth from the caldron.

He went on serving it solemnly with a large silver

ladle, and as he greeted each guest, he held out the bowl as if offering communion.

"Machi bouillon," he said by way of greeting, and they all drank reverently, without understanding the enormity of the homage.

Details so well thought out! Around the neck of each of them, hanging on a small chain, a thin tubing of white metal through which they could sip the drinks and the broth without taking off their masks. A kind of maté sipper, so homey.

"I won't let them chew you," he had promised the Machi before doing her in.

And she had answered him: "Even if you let them, even if you want it, you're not going to change me into shit. I'm going to be where I'm not, and in other places, too: you're going to remember me."

So, as he held out the bowls to his guests, he added: "It's a one-course dinner, but what a dish. Pure wisdom, you'll remember me everywhere. It will nourish you forever. It will bring you infinite well-being."

Well-being, what one might call well-being, was probably what the others experienced. As for him, the darned Machi bouillon upset his stomach badly, and at the height of the party, when they were all quite drunk and happy and the pyramid was glowing in all its splendor and the drummers were drumming like madmen, drowning out the music from the accordions—because that's what they had been hired for, brought over from the other bank of the river, from the other side of the border, for no other reason but to cover up the accordions and condemn them to inaudibility. After the crop-dusting plane had circled the pyramid and the immediate area five times, spraying the white powder obtained at the local processing plants, with the Sorcerer shouting from on top through a megaphone: "It's pure, it's the most natural there is. Breathe deeply"—when the party was at its best, the people dancing howling fornicating and chasing each other in the light of an enormous full moon that hung over their heads, when the frolic had reached its apex, he fell into a strange swoon. He sat rigid on his throne, unable to utter another word, and the ant mask slipped off his face, coming to rest ten yards below at the feet of the bacchants. Several raised their eyes and saw his pale face illuminated by that immense moon, a clay-colored face that was the reflection of all the faces around. That awakened the fury in them. It was never known who was the first to pick up a cudgel and break the mask of the person next to him, but it turned out to be a contagious motion and very shortly everyone was brandishing a club and they were whacking each other right and left, breaking masks and defending their own. Maybe because each wanted to be the only one, the Sorcerer, not knowing that the real Sorcerer had fallen into a mystical ecstasy which was so really, so truly like a catatonic stupor.

At dawn, not a single mask remained, although there were a lot of masks of blood, faces of scabs and green welts and eyes like purée and all manner of disfigurations. And he as if absent, up there, not even able to enjoy the spectacle.

I told him so, I told him so, the Egret sobbed when the light of day permitted the private planes to take off and they were finally alone. I told him so, the Machi soup disagreed with him. The Machi got her revenge. Come back, Master, come back, don't let the witch swallow you inside out.

Come back, come back, I'm your Egret, your dog. I'm your aide, if you want, I'm your wolf, come back. And he shook him hard, trying to revive him.

"It's no use. Only he has the power to revive others, and he's the one who's out of commission now."

"Shut up, you squaw, you witch. He's never out of commission. He must be sunk in meditation."

"I'm going to call the doctor."

"Don't even think of it, you witch. You'll do some calling, all right, calling the other squaws, that string of idlers and good-for-nothings, so they can come and help me get him down from here. We'll bring him inside the pyramid, even if it isn't finished. He'll be cooler there, he won't get sunstroke there, he won't dehydrate. Besides, he says the bad vibrations won't reach him inside the pyramid. The perfect pyramidal form protects him. I hope he's right, inside. Because outside it's something else."

They tried to move him and he was rigid in a sitting position. Statuary. One of the maidens got the idea of running a pair of staves through the legs of the throne to carry him on their shoulders like that. It was his first gestatorial chair. Luckily, none of those present knew the tradition, and no one thought to feel his testicles. What a wild surprise the maidens would have had. Three balls. A trinity in the crotch.

The Lord and Master's swoon lasted two nights and the two days that went with them, but the days don't count in such cases. When it's night for him it's night for everybody, and the maidens took turns lying by his side to give him warmth and keep that ever so venerated body from catching a cold. The Egret couldn't stay by the Master's side because weeping would overcome him immediately, and the Master not only began to grow cold again but got wet all over. The Egret, therefore, would walk back and forth on his long heron legs, trying to think, trying to find a solution or an antidote.

He thought about the mushrooms, but he didn't have the heart to go back to the Tacurú, much less go in through the long corridors to the rock-salt cavern, where the Machi's ghost would surely be waiting for him. He thought and he thought, without results as usual, and he finally decided to put on one of the Master's masks that had remained intact, to see if he became inspired.

With the mask on, he looked in the mirror. There was never a lack of mirrors in the Master's domains. He looked at himself in the mirror and finally had an intelligent reflection. He then sat down on the Master's throne, which had been left empty. He arranged the Master's red velvet cape around him, then he decided to put on the Master's iridescent tights, and he was now complete. Not in the ant outfit, but in the Master's outfit. In the Master's face, trying for a more hoarse, unknown voice, which could be the voice of the Master.

"Maidens, maidens, come immediately, I need to whip you for a while."

And the maidens came quickly, because they had nothing else to do and because they were wandering aimlessly around and wanted a little fun.

The Egret in his red raiment began to undress them

with the Lizard's Tail, trying to catch a *tipoi* tunic with the long tongue of the whip, trying to snare a petticoat and pull it off.

The maidens laughed and helped a little, to give him pleasure. He's got the Master's face and he's not the Master, they sang to him, provoking him, enchanted that he wasn't the Master, that he was much more youthful and much less cruel.

And they went about undressing and opening their legs and tempting him, to the point where he had taken off his tights and his underpants and was wearing only the cape and the Master's mask and was perhaps on the verge of attaining what he had never attained before.

That was more powerful than all swoons put together. The real Master awoke with a leap and yelled at him. "What are you doing, you wretch? Do you think you can take my place like that? Death to the traitor, death to the dog."

"Master, I gave you back life!"

"You gave me back shit. Now take off the mask and come over here, we've got things to do."

If the witchdoc had died, I would have been left without a novel. But what a relief it would have been, what a relief.

Now I can keep on writing, that is, I can keep on disregarding my other duties without too much guilt, attending only to the more peremptory priorities. Even though I wouldn't like to play duck, going into the water without getting wet. Once at the dance, I'll dance, if I can, as much as I can.

Yesterday I went to see the ambassador. It seems he can finally offer asylum to the lawyer couple I recommended. All for the best, since the poor souls were on the point of falling into the claws of the cops. And the ambassador, what an interesting fellow he is. That's another story I ought to be writing. I wonder why fiction and reality get so intertwined in me, or at least in my writing, why I can't keep them separate. Everything mingles, the threads tangle, they wrap around my feet and tie me up. I like the ambassador and that gets me mixed up, too, why mix matters that are more or less emotional with these others which are matters of life and death. As if the emotional ones weren't matters of life and death too, or, rather, choosing life when everything is on the brink of the other thing.

Getting back to our witchdoc, I must say that he has recovered consciousness—or whatever it's called in such cases—and with it, all his power of destruction, and so is back to his old tricks. And I have to go on telling what I know or what I think I know in that regard, in spite of the fact that he'll still have an advantage over me there, not only because he knows more but because he invents things better. Damn him.

For that very reason I've decided without further delay to get rid of the little iron devil and all the rest of the magical paraphernalia, following my guide's sensible advice. The little devil with his trident and his lance, Eshú and his tools, with such an enchanting smile, so seductive with his pointed metal horns and almost horizontal prick. Eshú's prick almost horizontal? Yes, ma'am. The gentleman who was so kind as to make me a gift of it felt it was no compliment at all to bring me an Eshú with a fallen prick. One at a right angle, rather, that

points to the ground. That's what all metal representa-
tions of Eshú are like, you have to admit, but not mine,
because my knight-errant gentleman intended to change
that, straighten out the sex organ, giving it an erection, as
they say. But that's another story.

The present story can be wrapped up in a paper bag.
That's where I'm putting Eshú for the moment (bye-bye,
love), along with the peyote necklaces from the market in
Sonora, a few tablets from the witches' market in La Paz
on the Calle Linares, the love amulets (for all the luck
they've brought me) and the money amulets (I can say
the same) and a couple of *figas*, a male garlic with a red
ribbon, some deer eyes (seeds). Those other seeds that
the ambassador gave me aren't included. They're sea
tomatoes, one is female and the other male, and when you
put them in a glass of water the female floats and the
male sinks, something that usually happens to males in a
glass of water.

Talismans amulets charms tablets devil and his
armament necklaces of doubtful origin little sugar skulls
all in a paper bag and in another the bottle of dry cane
liquor that I was to buy for this solemn occasion.

My friend Julia, so perfect and punctual, will come
for me at a quarter to six in the afternoon and drive me to
carry out my assignment.

"On Friday, just before the sun goes down, do you
understand, my child? before nightfall, during sunset.
Take your little devil and the other magical objects to the
woods and hide them in the underbrush. Then take a
bottle of cane liquor and pour out half of it, making a
circle around the offering. And leave the open bottle
there, repeating all the while that you're doing this to pay
for your imprudence in having harbored evil elements in
your home, understand?"

Those were the instructions and I understand them

so well that as soon as Julia arrives we go off in her car to the woods near the airport, the only ones in the area.

After driving for half an hour, at the point where the highway is about to cross into the dangerous and guarded precincts of the international airport, we make a right turn and go along a route that's certain to take us into the woods. The sun is quite low, a few timid pink tones are beginning to invade the sky, when suddenly the car gives a shudder and a red light on the dashboard goes on.

"It can't be," Julia says. "It seems the fan belt's broken, and I just had a new one put in."

And I sigh and remember the second part of the story of Eshú, the words of Christian, my captain from across the sea, when he gave it to me:

A beautiful woman cannot be given a gift of a little fallen-phallus devil, that's why I asked the ship's machinist to straighten this one out, fix the phallus to what it should be. The machinist liked the idea and went off to his forge roaring with laughter to give the cock a few hammer blows and raise it to its proper position. I went back to the bridge and was up there when all of a sudden the ship lurched as if we'd run aground and the machinist showed up in a rage. Here, he shouted at me, take your shitty devil, he blew up my auxiliary boiler, which had been working perfectly, I'd just finished adjusting the pressure gauges. And he gave me back the Eshú and refused to hear another word about it, so here it is, for you, at half-mast, you might say, but it's the intention that counts, isn't it?

I decide not to tell Julia that part of the story, so as not to dishearten her completely. Instead, I open the car door, determined to get rid of that bad-luck cargo as quickly as possible. I step to the ground and stop short. Right there, above my head, threatening as warnings like these can be under these circumstances, is a huge sign with the dark outline of a soldier aiming his rifle at me. And the warning reads:

MILITARY ZONE
NO PARKING   NO STOPPING

And the sun, obeying the sign, doesn't park, doesn't stop. It goes implacably on its way down toward the horizon, soon it will disappear and it will be too late for us.

"Mr. President, General, sir, forgive me for bringing up these problems, but I think they're interfering with our plan for National Reconstruction. This isn't serving our high and noble interests, nor is our sovereignty preserved this way or its historical continuity assured. That man has tricked us again. Our representatives and special envoys to the so-called Festival of the Pyramid, along with their distinguished wives, have returned from the north in a lamentable condition, some with their faces seriously beaten, with cuts and bruises."

"Have them make me a written report. How did the gory event take place?"

"Well, actually, it seems they beat each other up without anyone provoking them. But I can assure you, Mr. President, that all the blame can be placed on that evil character. He must have put something into the hors d'oeuvres, which were quite frugal, according to what I've been told. But it seems that he served a potion that aroused people to violence instead of maintaining and increasing—if possible—the unity of aims and the bonds of a healthy and cordial camaraderie."

"Of course, of course. I'm sorry that our cameramen

weren't allowed to be present at that little party. But if Lieutenant López has followed my instructions, we'll have some photographs of the lamentable episode very soon. I want to see them."

"I'm very sorry, General, but it seems that Lieutenant López had his camera confiscated."

"Lock him up! I don't want stupid assistants who can't follow my wishes. My orders, that is."

"At your command, Mr. President. And what are we to do about the man up north? Our officers are very unhappy."

"We won't do anything. What are you thinking of? We'll leave him alone, let him organize another festival. Let him invite us again. I'd like to go as an impartial observer. They seem to be amusing parties."

"Anything you say, General, sir."

"You're excused, Colonel. But first please draw the curtains and turn on the lights. I don't like this hour of uncertain clarity. It's lasted too long already. Wipe it out."

Come on, boys, let's pick up the pace a little. We're all exhausted, but look, you can already make out the towers of the Basilica in the distance. Come on, companions! We've got to get there before sunset, She won't forgive us if we arrive to inaugurate her new sanctuary in the dark. And, to make things worse, they close the Basilica at nightfall.

What rot. Look at the horizon, dog. Better yet, don't, don't look at it. This hour of the day makes me nervous. It's as if something were opening up there in the background, between earth and sky. The pinks getting more and more intense don't bother me, I rather like them; I like it when the sun's disk turns red, flattens out, and loses its gaudy playing-card look. But at this terrible moment, look, no, don't look, it can drive you mad, it's like a horrible mouth, a woman's opening that wants to swallow you up, there in the back, with a greenish, unique glow; imagine that green in the midst of soft little pinks and blues, a green that's out of place, threatening, like the Machi's mouth. This is happening to me because I didn't keep her in my stomach, this is happening to me because I vomited her up with all my strength, tossed her up toward the sky. Now the Machi is challenging me with her mouth or whatever it might be, gigantic, green, and the sun like a tongue that goes on licking.

I didn't feel much like getting out of the car facing a sign like that, and very slowly we continue on in search of a telephone before the car falls apart on us completely. We have to get help from the Auto Club, move quickly; if we don't, Eshú will keep on with his tricks. We reach the gate of the army camp and Julia rather imprudently gets out of the car. I hear the click of the safety catches on the machine guns as they're released, I see the five guards move into combat position. Good God! Our armed forces in action. I open my door and get out too, my hands conspicuously away from my body, but my dignity intact. I smile as best I can, I shout, "Telephone, we're looking for a telephone to get a mechanic" (not a bullet in the belly). "Our car's broken down; fan belt, we think."

"There's no telephone here. Drive slowly down to the police post, and don't make any suspicious movements."

"Can we turn around here?"

"Affirmative," they answer, more relaxed now, but following us with their eyes just the same, and maybe with spyglasses from the turrets, and Julia, that madwoman, proposes that I get out a few yards from there.

"Run out and throw your little devil away before it's too late. It's his fault. He doesn't want us to get rid of him, and the sun is going down fast. In fifteen minutes it'll be too late. And then who can say if we can avoid another run-in like this one."

"And who will save me now? I get out right in front of the camp with that rather suspicious bag and a bottle that could easily be a Molotov cocktail. I get everything ready in the bushes across there, and one of the guards in the towers shoots me down. If I'm lucky; if not, they take me away for interrogation, as they call it."

We finally get to the police post, explain our dramatic situation. They let us call the Auto Club, they chat with us, the AC doesn't arrive, and the sun is going down, down, the light is getting dim, sunset, really, and I decide to gamble everything because I'm half out of my head, because a person says she doesn't believe and then just look at her.

I go back to the car with some kind of excuse. Julia, who got the message, stays in the guard post to distract the two policemen: I want to call again, where did I put the card, what a drag, and I hope my car won't be ruined, and things like that. Poor little helpless woman, and the policemen are solicitous. In the meantime, inside the car, I surreptitiously empty my handbag and I put the devil and the rest of the objects in it, I get out of the car like a person going off to pee in the underbrush there (as if my bladder were capable of functioning), I throw away the purse, I go back to the car, paranoia takes hold of me and I go back into the bushes to empty the contents of the purse and pick it up in case some clue was left. I look for the bottle, at any moment I expect a bullet to smash into my back, I expect a mouthful of blood. But no, not this time. I empty the liquor a mile a minute and get back in the car as brother sun finishes his visible course. Mechanical help is approaching in the distance, Julia returns with a forced smile, the policemen think what a nice lady, my heart starts up again, my diaphragm starts up again, and I can breathe once more because I am rid of Eshú now.

The illumination

At 8 p.m. the machines unlocked themselves by their own power and were able to go on printing. An inexplicable breakdown that not even Funes himself had been able to pinpoint, much less fix. And if old Funes couldn't, no one else at *The Voice of the Town of Capivarí* could. Old Funes had seen the birth of the machinery of that newspaper, he had reared it and, one might almost say, nourished it with his own secretions. A lot of sweat at least. And now, because of that integration, the old man had the coloring of linotype and the cough of a rotary press. Skinny, indeed, he usually went unnoticed, moving with the same rather clock-like movement as the machines. Whole days would pass without anyone's noticing his presence, but at the sublime moment of a breakdown Funes was indispensable. Was, had been, will be?— because the present tense couldn't be employed on this particular Friday. All his science had been of no use in the face of the generalized demise of the machines. Even Don Justino Alchurrón, publisher of the paper, had tried to encourage him, something that gave an even greater dimension to his failure.

After much effort and many attempts, old Funes— terrified by that world of paralyzed machines, which wasn't his world at all—withdrew to the darkest corner, having decided to merge forever with the burlap and tow impregnated with grease and printer's ink. Everybody forgot about him, upset as they were, and nobody thought to wake him and congratulate him when finally, at eight o'clock that evening, the machines came to life all by themselves and everything apparently returned to normal.

The Voice of the Town of Capivarí went on printing all night long, and it was the issue that had the greatest success throughout the region. The issue of Saturday, August 1, when everybody was in the general store of the town of Capivarí fulfilling his duty of consuming the ritual cane liquor with rue which would preserve him from illness for the rest of the year.

The newspaper reached them a little late, but with succulent news. Nobody wanted to be left without his copy—as a memento, they said—and that's why, when the Sorcerer's men arrived to seize it, they were unable to confiscate a single one.

The Capivarians, delighted. The age-old stagnation of the little town was finally being stirred up, and others, not themselves, were finally receiving the whacks distributed throughout the region. Scandalous Masked Ball! Histrionic Bacchanal! Such headlines for a humble newspaper that until then had concerned itself only with agricultural problems. A far-reaching event was finally upsetting the boozy calm of siesta time, an event with dark implications, but so very stimulating. And on the day of cane liquor and rue: one glass on an empty stomach and any good Christian is protected. One small glass, or let's say two, or several, and by noontime spirits were high and reprisals were planned. The great imitation. The parody.

"Are we lesser people, don't we know how to swing clubs? Don't we know how to take blows?—some confused little drunk shouted, and everybody chorused no, they weren't a lesser people, yes, they knew how to give and receive whacks—receive, most of all. And they were in agreement with the whole plan.

Schoolmaster Cernuda offered his school desks to build the pyramid, and by the end of the afternoon it was finished off with fruit crates. For cudgels they would use rolled-up newspapers, the peasants weren't so stupid as to go about injuring each other, and the gabble and enthusiasm reached its height when the owner of the general store dusted off three bags of masks, leftovers from past carnivals. A great idea, the carnival masks: the face of any monster might well be the true effigy of the Sorcerer, and it was better that way, there was less repetition.

Don Justino Alchurrón, mayor of the town of Capivarí as well as publisher of the newspaper, watched the preparations framed in the window of his residence on the square. He felt himself overflowing with pride. That mysterious note from an anonymous correspondent, which had arrived by messenger and which he had hesitated so much to publish, was now opening the gates of heaven for him. No one in all Capivarí and its surrounding countryside would forget the festival that was spontaneously being prepared, the fruit of popular fervor. Thanks to what had been published in his newspaper, to which no one had paid much attention until then in spite of its twenty years of devoted service to the community. The newspaper announced farm auctions, gave advice on the making of soap, advertised products to combat tobacco and corn blights, predicted the weather, and busied itself with other matters of small import. On that memorable day, however, the newspaper had unleashed a popular celebration that could become a custom, perhaps, and with the passage of years would turn into a traditional fiesta, the Great Folklore Festival of Capivarí that would attract thousands of tourists from the four corners of the nation and maybe even from neighboring countries. And they would all carry away souvenirs: braided lassos, whips, cattle counters in braids of four with silver circlets, local handicrafts all, wrapped in pages from the newspaper that from then on would be a real daily, a proper morning paper read by everyone. The Annual Festival of Capivarí with polka and *chamamé* contests. Famous musicians would be invited, accordion and harp players would come from more prosperous localities, a brewery would be established, Capivarí would come to know splendor. And he, Don Justino Alchurrón, would finally display on his person a mayoral sash and the newspaper would have a proper building, no more of that dark shed. There would be fireworks.

The Capivarians, less ambitious, were ready to have fun that night, and that was enough. Or maybe not. They would tell stories and more stories of that night to their children and to their children's children and anyone within earshot for the rest of their lives.

Everyone so busy: the men putting the pyramid together, going from house to house and hut to hut getting candles and gathering all available drinking supplies, the women taking bags apart and sewing burlap capes for everyone. The children were trying to manufacture more masks in case there weren't enough to go around, and the three village idiots were chewing away on hard carob pods, spitting them afterwards into the jars, along with plenty of saliva to accelerate the fermentation of the brew.

Schoolmaster Cernuda was the one who decided that the festival should be celebrated in honor of someone. Not any patron saint, but that most noble and self-effacing reporter who had risked life and reputation in attending that pernicious party in order to write his clarifying chronicle.

A small delegation set out for Don Justino Alchurrón's house and knocked on the door with all the solemnity the circumstances required. "We need to know the name of the hero of the day in order to pay him homage. We want you to tell us who the chronicler of that provocative event was."

And Don Justino Alchurrón, suddenly yanked out of his reveries, didn't even have time to put together a more plausible story and released the truth, which smacked of the fantastic in every way. "If I only knew who it was, if I only knew. I would promote him immediately to star reporter, make him doctor honoris causa, anything. But it's not possible for me to do that. The article came to me in a sealed envelope, handed me personally by a horseman dressed all in black, riding a dark horse. He didn't look like a gaucho, in spite of his broad-brimmed hat, but more like a musketeer. I don't know. He asked for me and gave me the envelope personally, without dismounting, almost without a word."

"And you didn't ask him what his name was."

"Of course I asked him. He said his name was Mascaró. But after reading the contents of the envelope I thought he was fooling me with the name."

Cernuda the schoolteacher decided no, Mascaró was the appropriate name, and he proposed dedicating the festival to him in absentia.

At dusk, the pyramid was almost ready. The only thing missing was the representation of the Sorcerer, now called Red Ant. No one wanted to take on himself such an irreverence, so Schoolmaster Cernuda got hold of some ancient Indian chronicles and directed the fashioning of the figure, making an adaptation here and there in line with local taste and possibilities.

"And at the beginning of the festival, at nightfall, they turned to making the figure of the Idol in human form, with a human face and all the appurtenances of a man.

"And this they did in the form of a human body made entirely from seeds of . . . [Well, there's no need to give everything literally. Put in sunflower seeds.] They placed him on a framework of rods and fastened him with thorns, put thorns on him to keep him steady.

"Once he was fashioned thus, they adorned him with feathers and gave the face their own features. They put on his stone mosaic ears [Well, we can skip the turquoises] in serpentine shape and from his turquoise ears hung a ring of thorns [One does what one can]. It's made of gold [ahem!], it's in the form of toes, it's put together like toes [with the feet].

"The bridge of the nose made of gold [Well, let's use our imagination. Children, go get some of that paper that chocolate candy comes in], with smooth stones. A ring of thorns hangs from the nose too, with lines perpendicular to the face. This facial decoration of transverse lines was blue [Let's make that crimson] and yellow in color. Over the head they put the magical headdress of feathers from a hummingbird [or a hen]. Then they placed a decoration of yellow parrot feathers around the neck [Some people like ornithological details!], from which hang tapering fringes, like the shocks of hair boys have. His cape, too, fashioned from nettle leaves, dyed black [That's easy], and, in five places, clumps of delicate feathers from an eagle [O.K.?].

"He is wrapped in a robe painted with skull and bones. On the torso he wears a vest painted with disjointed human members—all of it covered over with craniums, ears, hearts, intestines, thoraxes, teats, hands, feet.

157

"On his back, borne like a burden, is his blood-colored flag. This blood-colored flag is nothing but paper. [So much the better!] It's dyed red, as if dyed with blood. He holds a sacrificial flint as a crowning touch, and this, too, is only paper. It's also flecked with blood color."

"Don't tell me now that this doesn't look good. Just like the other one."

When they finished the image, which was somewhere between the terrifying and the ridiculous, the Capivarians, with the schoolteacher at their head, decided that it would be in no way a sacred festival. The festival that had got started hours before, probably with the appearance of *The Voice of the Town of Capivari*, was a festival of self-affirmation and therefore immensely free.

Several of them carried the effigy on a litter and with extreme care began to scale the pyramid made of benches, boards, boxes, branches. Part of it crumbled, the pyramid half disintegrated on one side, but they reached the summit safe and sound and deposited their burden there, surrounded by candles so all could see it.

"Do you think they're worshipping me?" asked the Sorcerer, again established in his headquarters at the Tacurú.

And the spy who had run to tell him about the latest happenings in the not too distant town of Capivarí answered without hesitation: "I have no doubt about it, Master. What else could they be doing?"

The Capivarians, far removed from that frame of mind, with the effigy atop the squat pseudo-pyramid, began the dance and followed it with a drunken spree. Don Justino Alchurrón didn't feel like getting involved in the festivities, but he gave his wife, along with his three daughters and the maid, permission to station themselves in the windows of the house, wearing colored dominoes. It was a way of showing their support without becoming completely involved, the perfect way of fulfilling his double function of mayor and journalist: up front, where the news happens, and at the same time in the rear to protect his people.

On two occasions he ventured among the dancers on the square and was able to admire up close the magnificence of the pyramid with its colorful figure on top. Both times, however, he had to return quickly to his house because everyone insisted that he drink some of that repulsive half-fermented local brew, and he wasn't one to disappoint his people.

Back in his house, Don Justino Alchurrón felt relieved and happily took up his dreaming again. The walls were lit with the reflection of Roman candles and flares that burst from time to time out in the square. The festivities would last all through Sunday, certainly, and he was beginning to wonder in what state the Capivarians would go to work on that following morning, stuffed with memories. A minor preoccupation, no doubt about it. So many beautiful things would come out of the festival afterwards, so many birth certificates—because it was common knowledge that the Capivarians were enjoying themselves in every possible way—so many weddings, perhaps; the mayor's office would take on an unusual liveliness and he would be able to devote himself to his favorite activities: registering, noting, writing, classifying, filing. The commissioner would also be able to fulfill his duties, life would begin its cycle again in the town of Capivarí.

An intense glow yanked Don Justino Alchurrón out of his dreams. And he heard his daughters' somewhat contradictory cries: "Papa, come look. Papa, save us, do something. Help, Papa, look how divine. Papa, it's wonderful, they've gone mad. How frightening, how fantastic."

Don Justino Alchurrón ran to the window and caught the bonfire at its moment of maximum splendor. It's not known whether in the spirit of purification or out of sheer fun. But someone had set fire to the wood and everything was now burning festively. Flames that reached the sky, to which Don Justino Alchurrón likewise raised his arms, but no one paid him the slightest attention. Everyone was enthralled with the flames, except schoolmaster Cernuda, who was lamenting the loss of his school desks, although he did admire the gigantic torch that was now consuming the image of the Sorcerer.

"What a world!" he proclaimed. "How much good must be sacrificed in order to consume evil. And how much beauty is given off by the sacrifice. How much illumination."

I know for sure that the wrath of the witchdoc, the self-called Lord of the Black Lagoon, made itself felt almost immediately. A glow that exceeded his? When had anyone ever seen such disrespect?

But I'm too busy with other difficulties to get concerned over the fate of the Capivarians. A sturdy people, capable of defending themselves all alone, protected from earliest infancy by capybara oil, which is so good for curing a cough and fending off the evil eye. Iconoclasts always manage to save themselves, that's why the ones who worry me now are the others, the worshippers, the blinded people who already number in the hundreds of thousands. They not only worry me, they also worry the Sorcerer, it seems, and that's good: they've escaped his clutches. They've joined the cult of the Dead Woman, which has much greater reaches. And that's why the Sorcerer has spread his nets and why his influence is already being felt in the Capital.

It's been only a few months since I started the biography, and how the man has grown; he's left his retreat in the false anthill and with all speed has set in motion a plot that takes in all sectors. I did what I could, I threw away my poor little devil and all the accessories and now I'm only waiting for the moment.

Navoni and I have started up our romance again. Things like these bring people closer together: when the ship is sinking, everybody embraces. A good embrace, Navoni's, I love him and I love the people of Capivarí because they don't compromise. They're each pure, in their own way: those who know without wanting to, and Navoni, who wants to know at all costs. And, as it happens, neither one nor the others think of themselves as owning the truth. They just do their best.

Now they're going to put the blame on Navoni and me for the fury that's been unleashed by our conspiracies. Especially on me, who brought the Caboclo de Mar into the struggle. It's easy to say: Let sleeping dogs lie, things like that, the laws of cause and effect, like that. Easy to say. But I'm not buying that blame business. They say the witchdoc resumed his activities because I began to write his biography, I woke the dog up, I stirred up the quiet clear waters of the black lagoons and the rot came up from the bottom . . . As if the rot hadn't been there from the beginning, as if that dog and his subdog hadn't been moving about in their sleep all the time, unleashing nightmares.

It's true that the witchdoc has grown, has become larger during these months in which I've been writing. He's woven a vast net and now he's everywhere, but it's not my work; rather, this unfolding of forces complicates the biography enormously for me. Now he's everywhere and I have to follow him through the most shadowy ways and byways. He's extended his domains, he's absolute master of the Kingdom of the Black Lagoon, mapped out by him and constantly enlarged by him. An expansionist like few others, and he leaves me no time to concern myself with the ambassador or with my friends in asylum, who now number eleven. They've tripled the guard in front of the embassy and the sentries allow themselves all manner of excesses: with their bayonets, they turn the pristine mattresses that arrive for the new guests into sieves. Searching for weapons, they say, for drugs, secret documents, whatever, so that they end up ruining everything; they inspect purchases from the market to such an extent that no delivery boy wants to run the risk of losing a whole day in the inspection. A good theme for a novel. But Red Ant won't let me, no, he insists that I concentrate my full attention on him, and for that same reason he doesn't worry too much about the worshippers of the Dead Woman, who no longer pay any attention to him. Did they ever pay any attention to him, did they ever know about him?

On the night of our sleeplessness, the worshippers reached the Basilica and filled it up. Who would have thought so: with the few relics of the Dead Woman that were left, they arrived on their knees, dragging themselves along. Now the Dead Woman has a visible shrine in the Basilica, on the surface of the earth.

And when Sunday arrived, thousands and thousands of people poured in. And thousands more came daily, to the point of filling fields that extended along the banks of the river surrounding the Basilica. A court of miracles, with all the cripples, invalids, amputees, blind, lame, and castrated who abound in these times and these latitudes.

The prior of the Basilica stays in the shadows and hasn't wanted to show his face, not even on the last Sunday evening, when word had got around and all five government TV stations appeared to cover the story. Live and direct. It was hard for the mobile units to make their way through the crowd that filled the central square and the streets all around. In a corner of the square a priest was waving a hyssop, blessing the cars, which went by at the speed of a walk, and collecting the 200 pesos established as the entrance fee. The main avenue was blocked off by the legless, who proceeded on their little carts. The armless carried candles in their mouths and dripped wax on the heads of those advancing slowly before them on their knees.

We all saw them on our TV screens and we felt our hearts beating with popular fervor; it was a little sticky, dangerous. The sexton kept showing his face, speaking in the name of the high dignitaries of the Church:

"No, madam, it is forbidden to enter the Basilica with a lighted candle. You can imagine what the floor would be like if everybody did that. You're not the one who has to clean it up, are you? No, madam. It doesn't matter if the Committee of Dames of Charity of the Holy Deceased offers its services to clean up every night. It's not that, you have to understand. It's because of the fire hazard. Yes, madam, yes. You can donate a candle, what's important for the Deceased is the gesture, and so much the better if the candle is virgin. Put your candle in the box. No, not that one, that's the big box for offerings; in that smaller box. We'll see to it that the candles are all melted down and with the wax we'll make the votive lights that will burn in the name of all the faithful, morning, noon, and night. Of course, madam, there will be a lot of candles left over, especially the larger ones, the prettiest ones, yes. We've thought of everything, and that's why we've opened a resale booth. With the money from that, we'll be able to keep the Basilica, the House of the Deceased, in perfect shape."

There were some protests:

"We brought a lot of gold and silver offerings. I don't see them anywhere, only the brass ones."

"Naturally, sir. The valuable ones go into the safe. We don't want our holy place to be a source of temptation. Besides, there's a plan to melt down all the precious metals to manufacture an enormous bell with a silver— argentine, that is—sound that will ring out like none other, for the glory of our Dead Lady."

The Sorcerer didn't let himself be moved by the improbable argentine pealing of a bell that would never come into existence. And from his kingdom, which seemed so remote from secular things, he demanded his tithe. He had mobilized the people so that they would take up the cult again and plunge into action and defend him, and the people had only fallen on their knees, forgetting about the enemy. Oh, well. If the people didn't want to move, make them pay for it. He knew quite well on whom to pour out his wrath, against whom to invest that money: the inhabitants of Capivarí, who had done the impossible to merit his thunderbolt of justice.

The Voice

The situation is growing clearer. It was getting extremely uncomfortable for me, that business of having a subterranean, ubiquitous enemy, in my image and likeness. Now I've got the enemy more within reach, in my gunsight you might say, a crossbow's shot away, and I can conduct the operation from my pyramidal heights and observe the results with my powerful binoculars.

Were they trying to make fun of me by imitating the festival? They'll soon see who laughs last.

As a first step, expropriate that two-bit newsletter, the cause of all the trouble. And I'll be doing them a favor: the printed word is the worst kind of poison and must be kept in responsible hands. Now that I've finally managed to organize my parallel army, I'll give the order for the arrest of the owner of that rag.

"House arrest, Master?"

"How could you even think of such nonsense, parallel Colonel? That business was for the other newspaper owner. Coarse concessions that those who only have nominal power might grant. The powerful, the omnipotent, like me, we never forgive. Let them crush that stinking little publisher in Capivarí, let him be puréed into mush. I'm not going to let him enjoy his home, where they tell me he has an orchidarium, a large cage of toucans, and three daughters in bloom. You're crazy. Make him disappear for me, and keep the house, the orchids, the toucans, and the daughters for me. I'll know what to do with them all. And especially keep the newspaper for me."

"Sir, excuse me, but Don Justino Alchurrón is a highly respected man. Besides, he's the mayor of Capivarí."

"So much the better. I am the only respectable person here. We'll annex Capivarí into the Kingdom of the Black Lagoon, we'll declare ourselves independent. The Capivarians don't deserve such good fortune; they're mere insurrectionists. Or maybe they do deserve it, for trying to emulate me. They've done the correct thing. They couldn't have a better model, even if they were a bit careless with the details."

"Excuse me, sir, but Capivarí doesn't want to be annexed. They're all roused up by the disappearance of their mayor. We planted a suicide note, but nobody paid any attention to it. They say he was abducted by the forces of evil, imagine that. It's true that our men were a little careless: they left one of the mayor's hands behind in the barn where the interrogation took place. No confession could be wrung out of him: the interrogatee stuck to his account of the rider in black who handed him the article. A rider in black who, according to the statement, said his name was Mascaró and who rode off at a gallop. He can't be found, Master. As for the interrogatee, my boys finished the job. But discontent reigns in Capivarí."

I don't give a shit if the people of Capivarí don't want to be annexed. As if the wishes of the Capivarians were of any importance. The time has come to enlarge my domains, and the annexation of the northeastern zone seems the next logical step. As far as I'm concerned, it's an accomplished fact already, though I wouldn't want to proceed in too brusque a fashion. I won't send my armed forces to make them bow down as a powerful person lacking imagination would. No. I want the people of Capivarí to admire and worship me. I will be implacable and splendid, I will force them to surrender of their own free will. I will act with method. With patience. Everything in its time and I in all times, Lord of Eternities.

"Look, pretty doggy, I'm going away until the new moon, but don't howl, no. Come let me pat that pretty little head. That's it, that's it. And now, aide, enough clowning around. I want you to listen carefully. I don't think that the internal enemy will attack during my absence, no, it's not the right moment. But I'm going to entrust you with two vital missions. The first will be the making of the cradle—yes, a cradle, don't interrupt; the second, the publication of the first issue of the newspaper under its new star—that's the word! And enough of that long and insipid name. It will no longer be called *The Voice of the Town of Capivarí* but *The Voice*, concise and sharp. Later I'll give you precise instructions for this first issue. But before anything else, a warning: Keep a close watch on the completion of the decoration of the inside of the pyramid, see that the proportions are followed exactly and that it's perfectly pyramidal. And sleep there every night. All alone. No man or woman or dog or rat or spider or bat or ant can sleep with you. I'm going to leave you my seal while I'm gone. The destruction that is wished for me could fall on your head if you don't protect yourself as you should."

Without his seal and without any worries, the Sorcerer boarded the Beechcraft. He had it land near the *quimbanda* sacred terrain, on the other side of the broad river, and he set out as one going to the ceremony. But at a bend in the cleared path, precisely opposite the tree that lowered its strangulation roots onto its brother tree, he veered north, making his way through vines and gigantic leaves. No black magic this time, this time he needed something much more overwhelming and immediate, for what he sought was to demolish a town so prone to mockery.

Meanwhile, the aide, handsome as he was and feeling quite powerful with the Master's seal hanging from his neck, gave himself body and soul to the making of the cradle. He could take his time, the Lord and Master had told him, and it made no difference to him from where, from whom, or how or when the newborn would come. Just making the most beautiful of cradles, a means of participating in the birth by carving the womb.

That same dawn he ordered the felling of trees until the woodsmen came upon a rosewood and an incense tree.

"We're cutters of ordinary timber, sir. How will we recognize such rare wood?"

"By the scent, you wretches. Cut down all the big trees, and when a fallen giant gives off an incomparable aroma, cry out with joy, I'll recognize that cry from here. Then bring me those logs, only those. But the aroma has to be all-encompassing and total, like nothing you poor boobs have ever smelled up till now."

And since before he'd become a grenadier he'd been a cabinetmaker in his father's carpenter shop, the Egret began to sketch out the motifs he would carve on the cradle. First he designed some large angels for the head, with garlands of roses that went all around and met at the foot in a huge cluster. Then he thought the business of angels wasn't the best, given the circumstances, and opted instead for an exceedingly complex design of animals and plants, vines and creepers, a cornucopia over-flowing with fruit, to recall that distant crate the Master had once mentioned to him. And over the head of the improbable future infant, something to hold mosquito netting that would hang from a thin carved branch and would be a Thousandmen flower made of wood.

He decided that the cradle deserved all his energies and he had three newspapermen brought from the Capital to fill the positions that had remained mysteriously vacant on *The Voice of the Town of Capivarí*, now *The Voice*, renovations and remodeling due to change in ownership. The Lord and Master had left precise instructions for the first issue in that new series that would no longer deal with rural matters but with the occult. *The Voice* would come to be the voice of the Master, his tribune of doctrine, and he already had the first editorial set up in type, inexplicably signed Red Ant. "The Best Enemy Is a Dead Enemy" was the title of the piece, and Red Ant showed that he had a thorough knowledge of his subject. Farther on, in the centerfold, the poster: Wanted, dead or alive, more dead than alive, Mascaró. And underneath, a composite of the rider in black, based on the confessions of Don Justino Alchurrón, R.I.P. AMPLE REWARD.

A few marriageable young women in Capivarí carefully detached the centerfold of the newspaper and tacked it up facing their beds. In order to recognize Mascaró in case we run into him in the marketplace, they explained. We could use the reward, some added, although the clarification was unnecessary. They kept Saint Anthony close by but hidden, and one must admit that the rider in the composite had a certain air about him. The artist who had sketched it had added a touch here and a touch there, giving him a great deal of charm. It was the last composite he ever did in his life.

The Sorcerer, unconcerned with those avatars, had

already set off his flare signals and his men in Zone 3 had gone to pick him up in the jeep.

"Master isn't planning to go to the sacred terrain on this trip?"

"No. I've got more urgent matters to attend to up north."

"Pardon me for voicing an opinion, but I think the Master's life has been so hectic that the Master could use a good purification ceremony."

"You people can do it for me this very night; we'll continue our trip tomorrow. The plane, with its valuable cargo, has gone to Zone 7 and will return to pick me up in thirty-six hours. I have to have everything ready by then. There are arrangements I have to make with the men at the dam."

"All the way to the dam? It's going to be a long and tiring trip by land. You should have stayed on the plane."

"It's not your place to suggest anything to me. I know when to move by air and when to crouch in the bushes like a jaguar. I need you people for transportation, and then you'd better forget you ever saw me."

The purification ceremony turned out to be a very simple but intense one. 730-Wrinkles, who had been called in especially, knew how to carry it off with an excess of zeal. She passed the egg of a black hen all over his body, singing incantations, asking that the egg absorb all the evil that his body carried. Afterwards, with very precise movements, she broke the egg over a glass of spring water. When the yolk came in contact with the water, a mushroom of smoke grew and enwrapped all of them for a few seconds. The liquid in the glass held by 730-Wrinkles began to boil with great bubbles, exhaling a pestilential odor of brimstone, of a thousand rotten eggs,

171

and grew darker and darker until it became completely black.

The Sorcerer burst out laughing, twisting with laughter, shaking and trembling in the midst of the tears that leaped from his eyes, and it was an uncontrollable laugh, pouring out as from a broken dike, a dam turning loose its contents of laughter, and the laughter sweeping away everything in its path.

"Look, you old witch, look what you've done to me. What a mess you've made. If it were up to you, you would have drawn out all the evil, you would have left me stark naked. Luckily, the evil I have in me is inexhaustible and what you pulled out only tickled me. Look at the ravages; you're sensational, old woman, I'm going to take you home with me so we can put on this show again."

"I'm sorry, sir, but I won't be going with you. I won't cross the border. I happen to know how the sorceresses you carry off with you end up."

"It'll be different with you, old woman. And I can take you even if you don't want to go, so it would be better if you came willingly, wouldn't it?"

"No. You might be able to take me, but it's not best for you. It's not good for you at all."

"Get out of here, you old witch. Don't threaten me, or I'll have you thrown to the dogs. Now get out of here, beat it, I've got much more pressing business to attend to.

"And let's get going now, right away, let's go, move it. We've got to be on our way before dawn. We'll push on hard all day, I want to get there before sundown."

To think it was I who got them the permits to build that dam—I negotiated with the three countries, I mobilized my resources—and now that I need a tiny favor from them, I have to do all this playacting and put up with all these annoyances. Not that I dislike playacting, quite the contrary. But there are problems I'd rather solve with a simple radio message, taking care that people in the Capital don't find out about it, and without giving up my modus operandi because of it.

I've got the African mask of *ndakó gboyá* and I stroke it as we proceed through the jungle. The red earth is tinting everything, everything around us stained blood-red, and it ought to please me but it doesn't. The mask, of course, can't be stained: I take care of it with all my love and with a large plastic bag. I've made a few local adaptations on it, now it's the *ndakó gboyá guazú*, and it's not just a long pouch of white material, now it displays two large sky-blue stripes.

It's a mask and it's not a mask, like everything that belongs to me. It consists of a narrow cloth cylinder ten feet long which I hold over my head with a long rod and with which I invest myself. I dance with the cylinder, I stretch it and fold it at will, *my* will, so as to rouse up all the powers of the *ndakó gboyá*, which are my powers.

No one can resist this apparition, much less the poor fellows at the dam. And if the *gboyá* fails—nothing can ever be considered infallible—the four men who are traveling with me know some persuasive arguments, and a machine gun is an irrefutable argument.

On the way, we stop to take a piss and I'm moved by the romanticism that sweeps over me sometimes and lends color to my less picturesque deeds. There, within reach of my hand, is the vine with beautiful fleshy flowers, full of suggestion. The *mburucuyá*, the passion flower with Christ's crown of thorns and the three nails. They say that you mustn't cut the flower of the *mburucuyá* because it will make the Saviour bleed again. I don't believe in such nonsense, the botanical superstitions of the poor. I'm the only Savior here and I cut the two largest flowers to put on my mask in place of eyes, and I cut all the others I can reach and I piss on them, so they'll learn. And because of that, we travel on quite a bit more vigorously, but still without exchanging a word.

We arrived at dusk. And I terrified them, but not sufficiently. It's three in the morning and I still haven't convinced them. These men at the dam are very stubborn.

So they don't want to close the sluices? So they need a joint order from the three governments? So they don't care about the sublime destiny of a little town, so they don't want to dry up a broad region, don't want to destroy the crops of a whole province, don't want cattle to die of thirst, and things like that? Poor fellows, how considerate, right? But I didn't come all the way up here to let myself be softened by their compassion—I've got my own reservoir. I came to cut off the supply of water to Capivarí, and it doesn't make much difference whether I get it by slashing a few throats. What do you think, fatty? You're in charge here, fatty, what do you think of our playing a little? You tell me to stop teasing you, that you want to go to bed? But you're drunk, fatty. You just close off the sluices for me when I tell you, or I'm afraid the sleep you'll be having will be the sleep of the just. The eternal sleep. If you take my meaning.

The boys brought the pots of honey, so get undressed, fatty, we're going to daub you all over. What for? So the bears can come and lick you, you'll see how they tickle, how you're going to laugh, you won't have a frightened face anymore. Bears like honey a lot. Are you going to tell me that there aren't any bears around here? Well, then, ants like honey, too. And I like ants, I'm in the

174

habit of giving them little gifts like this. There are fire ants hereabouts, nice little girls, I particularly like to be on their good side. Fatty-spread-with-honey should turn out to be a feast for them. I'm going to serve it to them for breakfast. Orderly little girls, ants: they get up very early and eat and eat and eat until they leave bare bones. Shiny white. Even though I won't increase the flood of the river of blood this way, I'll have other little pleasures. You'll see. Seeing is a figure of speech, of course. I think eyes are a favorite delicacy for ants, and you have such a sweet gaze, we're going to save ourselves about two little spoonfuls of honey. And don't shit in your pants, will you! The ants don't like that. I don't either. Come on, boys, a little more honey here, and don't hit him so much, the meat gets tough from the blows and my little ants will complain.

There are means and there are means. Intelligence is there to help you find the appropriate means for each situation. For example, this fat engineer won't ever forget me now, and I can be sure he won't tell on me either, though that doesn't worry me. A couple of my men from Zone 3 will stay at the dam to keep an eye on the engineer and make sure that on the appointed day and hour my orders to close the sluices are carried out. I'll be in the center of the square in Capivarí—at the exact point where my statue is to be erected—and I'll predict the disaster. I'll besiege them with thirst. If they don't give in quickly, they'll burst. I can annex the village with or without inhabitants, with or without trees, animals, birds. The toucans and the orchids of Justino Alchurrón's can go to hell. His daughters can go to hell. Although I can irrigate the latter with my own personal waters.

It's good you're back, my Master, sir, adored one. Your instructions have been followed to the letter. I'm making the cradle as you told me to, but I'd rather not show it to you yet. I want it to be a surprise. The first issue of *The Voice* has appeared. It sold out immediately, a great success. A whole lot of ads have come in, here they are, in proper order:

I make absent ones return. I undo evil spells.
Doña Elpidia, Apartado Postal 1072, Chihua-
hua, Mexico

LOVE HOPE REBIRTH
Wear
or
give
the BIOMAGNETIC MAGNACROSS
the jewel of happiness

FRIENDSHIP POWER SUCCESS

FREE talisman "The Secret of Happiness"
If you are a person of good faith and a be-
liever in supernatural powers, write me and
you will receive this talisman with all instructions for its use. I send it to you free because
of the spiritual mission I must fulfill, so that
you may obtain good luck in everything and
get ahead in your business and love affairs.
Mr. Herrera, P.O. Box 14/166, Capital

FANTASTIC!!!

Special announcement completely guaranteed

Make yourself invisible with a ring, be a mil-
lionaire in one day or win your loved one with
one prayer; with another you will win the lot-
tery; get out of jail, cure yourself of any illness; also drive off enemies and obtain
anything you desire. With our special prayers.
Send 1.900 pesos immediately. RECA, Inc.
P.O. Box 29, La Ciénaga

"Vest-pocket warlocks! Marketplace magicians! Do they think they can overshadow me? To the stake with all these fakers, burn them alive. Ordeal! We'll impose trials by ordeal to get rid of them. Anything else?"

"Yes, Master. There was a strange communication, Master, someone who said his name was Porcia, or Porquia, or Porchia. A certain Antonio. He insisted that he holds the copyright for all these names: *Voices, Voice, The Voice, Voicing*, that you can't use any of them—I'm sorry, Master, I'm only quoting him—for your infamous slander sheet. That if you go on publishing *The Voice*, it will cost you dearly."

"Don't make me laugh, sweetie pie. Don't make me laugh, because I laughed too much back there and now I feel like something different."

You're going to help me, aren't you, little aide? to engender my son with Estrella. You just make the cradle, it's an act of faith, the only thing you can offer. I'll attend to the technical details. You'll soon see, little aide, how well it's going to turn out for me, how beautiful the child will be. And you'll be the godfather.

And my Dead Woman the godmother. No doubt about it. If the Generaliss had been alive, he would have been the godfather, he'd earned it, but these are other times and a handsome aide is the best godfather imaginable. Especially if he comes all decked out in black, from head to toe, with a broad-brimmed hat, riding a black horse.

What am I thinking? What's all this? I'm assailed by images that don't belong to me; it must be lack of sleep, fatigue. Keep on rubbing, massaging me, aide Egret, and don't let nightmares coil around my daydreams.

Don't allow it, Egret

Don't allow it, Estrella

Don't allow it, E . . . my Dead Woman, rather. Your name must never be spoken. But please don't allow it either. In that way I'm protected by the Triple E.

Sublime Protection.

Navoni comes and says, Spread the word. No more reading *The Gazette*, *The News*, *The Nation*, none of those newspapers. No. We have to read *The Voice*.

You're kidding me, I answer him. The witchdoc's rag? It doesn't carry a single piece of news.

Of course, he insists. But neither do the others, if you think about it. And at least *The Voice* doesn't pretend to carry news. It carries other things. The time has come for us to learn to read between the lines.

All right, I accept; because I believe in Navoni and even more because I believe in the virtue of reading between the lines.

I'm not going to say that the thing is slipping out of my hands, that would be unthinkable. My hands are tentacular, I am Shiva, nothing escapes me, I clutch everything with my five fingers and the one extra finger as a bonus. But I can't deny the fact that the circulation of *The Voice* is growing, a fact that simultaneously makes me proud and worries me. And the misprints that get through—I've hired the best proofreaders but to no avail, the mistakes appear every so often, like cancer. I've printed an errata sheet to drive them away:

ERRATA

For:	*Read:*
always	sometimes
sometimes	never
never	——

Well, then, how should it read when through a typographical error it says

Nothing: the greatness of the great
or
Nobody is the light of himself, not even the sun?

The value of *never* should be the value of *nobody* and of *nothing*. That's how it should be read so as to gain full knowledge of my person.

Fuck it! This biography is getting out of hand. The witchdoc is taking on a life of his own, and I can't take that lightly. National events are becoming too serious for anyone to sit down and describe magic rites. Much less sponsor them. I haven't felt at all calm lately.

We've managed to get more people into asylum at the embassy, but I'm afraid they'll be the last. So many people are being persecuted, so many raids. Now threats from the Triple E are arriving, who can tell what lurks behind that formula, and there's the danger that my friend the ambassador will be recalled. The Foreign Office of his country can order his return as a reprisal because the local government won't issue safe-conduct passes for the people in asylum. I don't know what to do. I read *The Voice* and it makes me sick to my stomach. I'd like to go to bed for a long time, disappear under the covers, but bed isn't safe at all. In my immobility I would be in dread that they'd break down the door and come take me away.

I move, I keep on writing, with growing disillusionment and with a certain disgust. Disgust even with myself, for believing that literature can save us, for doubting that literature can save us, all that bullshit.

How calm I feel as I get ready for the taking of Capivarí. I concentrate on the speech I'll deliver to them tomorrow, at 11 a.m. to be exact, a speech that will last precisely an hour, because with my first word the sluices of the dam will be closed and exactly an hour later, bang! not a drop of water in the Capivarian canals. The town dried up by the astringent magic of my words.

An hour of perfect, polished discourse, which I foresee as absolutely useless, and that's what pleases me most: it's part of my plan. Those good, rebellious Capivarians will surrender only when the threat takes on substance and when not a thimbleful of liquid circulates through their irrigation channels. But before that, I'll have flooded them with words. I'll have made them feel my power.

People of Capivarí, annex! I'll exhort them, knowing all the while the scant effect such an imposing threat will have on them, people who have never been appealed to by any authority. Only a palpable danger will make them see reason and demonstrate clearly the sublime possibility I'm offering them of belonging to the Kingdom of the Black Lagoon. How much work you face when you are dealing with rustics with no concept of greatness. People of Capivarí! I will call them with all the strength of my lungs, even though they don't deserve such an appeal, such respect. And loudspeakers, wisely placed at certain intervals, will multiply the intensity of my words and disseminate the echo far and wide.

In the meantime, while I wait for tomorrow morning, I repeat, How calm I feel! How calm! The pounding of my aide's hammer as he carves the cradle produces this relaxation in me. He doesn't want me to see the cradle, and I prefer not to see it, until the moment comes: who knows what kind of cradle it will be, for who knows what kind of child.

I think seriously, while the hammer pounds and I grow drowsy, about the son who is coming. My beloved Estrella, in her divine, unbroken sphericity, will be unable to nurse him, and that's another problem that we have to face together. I can't allow anything impure to enter the organism of that creature who will belong to me completely: anything engendered by me will be born by me and nourished by me. I won't accept any foreign in-

tervention, no external help. This son will be the son of
my exclusive person, because Estrella is me. This son: my
continuance, my essence.

Biting the hand that feeds him. That phrase suddenly came to me, just like that, in my drowsiness, and I
hope with all my heart that it refers to me and not to my
future son, and especially not in relation to the one who is
ennobling himself now with the propitiatory act of building the cradle for me. He's using a hard wood, carving it
with hammer and chisel, and the rhythmic tapping rocks
me and reminds me of other carpenters. The woodpecker,
that is, back there in the jungle when, after visiting the ex-
teacher—oh, so much a teacher then!—I tried to return
home and couldn't find my way. I, thirteen years old,
those florescences, having learned so many things from
the teachers, sensing so many more things I would come
to know later, bearing the heavy burden of that knowledge and trying to return to the place where I was born,
on this side of the river, with the feeling in any case that
there is no returning home, there is never any return
home.
    I crouched hiding in the underbrush when I heard
voices, because, though I was already well into that benign forest between the barrens and the inlets, I had just
heard men's voices and men are never benign. I took
refuge in the broad hollow trunk of a tree, an enormous,
yawning mouth that was there as if waiting for me, and
above my head on that tree a woodpecker was hammering to make his nest, which would be his cradle. Luckily,
the woodpecker was pecking loudly and the men couldn't
hear the sound of the branch I had broken to get to my
hiding place. There were a lot of them, ten men at least,
all armed with shotguns, escorting one lone man, gagged,

hands tied. When they were almost in front of my tree, they added a blindfold and stood him right there in that clearing in the woods. They tied his feet like those of a hobbled horse, and without too much order or arrangement shot him out of hand.

I liked the corpse, it looked like a roast all trussed up with string. Tied so it wouldn't run, wouldn't move about, wouldn't speak, wouldn't see. None of it of any use now. I stayed in the hollow of my tree for about three days, eating fruit and watching the corpse. I stayed there to study how the man was slipping away little by little from all those unnecessary bonds, slipping away piece by piece in the belly of every predatory animal that came near. Gnawed at first by a rather greedy wildcat, then by rats, carrion hawks, buzzards, and most of all by those worms inside him which sounded like a sawmill in the night.

On the third day—I think it was the third day—two hunters came to the place and discovered him. They started to search him and one said to the other: "Hey, look at this protective fetish. Look at this little image of Saint Death. And the man had a slot on his forehead, the mark. Let's go, let's leave things as they are. We shouldn't touch him. He's evil. He's the one who got Eulalia the herb woman with child ten years ago or more. Could he have come back looking for the papoose after so long a time? I wonder what brought him back and who killed him."

Since I had no answer to any of those questions, I came out of my hiding place when the hunters were far off. And never again did I want to go back home. What for?

The one who came back to find his death and I: the one who is here to give life. Now thinking only about my son. That man, nothing to do with me: I had no reason to avenge him. But I went through the world avenging so many other affronts, so many abuses. My own and those of others, because abuses must be paid for even if you committed them yourself. All the more reason if you committed them.

The hammer pounds and pounds and I don't know if a cradle pounded on so much will be any good, but it's going to be a very beautiful cradle, like everything made by the Egret's hands. He brings a warmth into all this, making it with his own hands, and the rhythm rocks me to sleep. I sway in my old fruit crate and I'm small again —I'm enormous now; time doesn't matter to me, or size. I want to be the one I was before and at the same time be the one of today, the one of always.

The one of tomorrow will talk his head off and convince no one. The rush of my words will have its effect when the water is cut off. Another new abuse avenged by the abuser himself. I like this possibility of turning the coin, showing heads and tails simultaneously. I am Möbius's strip, Klein's bottle, Pascal's sphere, Red Ant's antenna. I move about in an ever so flat space because there are no obstacles whatever for me, neither mountain nor gully; I am in all places and in none. I am what I am not and also am, I can even be kind, splendid, and magnanimous. This is precisely what I shall show the coarse, irreverent Capivarians tomorrow. I am the Lord and Master and I can permit myself the luxury of forgiving them, after having cut off their water, after having them experience thirst and fright. That's already decided. They'll boo me at first, they won't believe my threats until their water runs out, but then they'll finally believe in my words and will believe it's too late. I'll forgive them then, after a great act of contrition they'll have to perform in the public square. They will humble themselves and cry for mercy, they will confess their sins, their evil thoughts, and I, who don't give a shit for all that, will appear magnanimous. With a sovereign gesture I will give them back their water. That amniotic fluid.

I will have myself called Magnificent Lord then. Father of Waters. Splendorous Master of the Black Lagoon and of Capivarí of the Seven Currents. Because they will have more water than ever, I'll flood them with water, and they, who were always sparing with their irrigation, knowing only how to grow corn, will have, thanks to me, rice paddies. Their land will form an enormous lagoon. I will enlarge my domains.

Navoni came to see me that night. Baby, he said, I think we're going to need you. It was around eleven o'clock, I'd been trying to write in spite of everything, trying to imagine what the Sorcerer could be plotting at that hour. I'd hit upon the idea of a father; no matter how great a witch doctor he was, that business of having been born from himself, right? nothing but the man's fantasy, dreams of self-sufficiency. But what part could a father play at such an advanced point in the story? I was bewildered. I received Navoni with joy, however, blessing the interruption, but not falling completely into his trap: need me, what for?

"Don't tell me you want me to get more people into the embassy. That's become impossible, I'm afraid. They've doubled the guard by the gates. And the ambassador, when he's not lying awake thinking the moment has come to break off diplomatic relations, can't sleep because every car that approaches at night might belong to the paramilitary come to storm the embassy and grab the people in asylum. Poor man, that's no life. I can't ask him for more."

"No, baby, don't get upset, I'm not here to ask for anything that concrete. It's something a little more esoteric, the kind of thing you like. Now that you've gotten rid of the little devil that had you all tied up, you can act with complete freedom, no? Look, all I want is for you to kill the witchdoc in your biographical novel, your novelized biography, or whatever it is you are writing. I don't think I can ask you to make the government fall, I'm afraid, but at least kill the witchdoc, eh, girl? so we can get that ghost off our backs, and one of these days the whole thing will blow up in sympathy."

"Sympathy?"

"Yes. Like bullets that go off by themselves sometimes, simply because another bullet was fired miles away. A somewhat loud sympathy, let's say."

He managed to arouse all my tenderness; in sympathy, of course. This guy who's so rational, pragmatic, look what he's coming out with now. I felt very close to him, so close that we ended up in bed. A very good location, a very good formula, although not very stable, let's call it volatile, when our friend Navoni is involved, driven as he is by duties that go beyond mere happiness.

After making love—and there I have no reason to complain, it was always perfect with Navoni—I think I put my foot in my mouth. With a little thread of a voice, it didn't occur to me to say anything better (as if it had been necessary to say anything in any case) than: This triumph I dedicate to the town of Capivarí, which is probably listening to me.

It must have been around three in the morning by

then, the town of Capivarí and all its inhabitants asleep, sound asleep, Olympically unaware of my imagined radio broadcast. But our enchanting hero—enchanting when in a horizontal position, verticality (and perhaps even verticalism) hardens him—leaped up as if remembering a mission that couldn't be postponed. Which was still half flattering. It led me to think that maybe, out of great good luck, he'd forgotten for a few, oh, so brief hours the aforementioned mission for something more substantive.

"I've got to run, my Curly Lady. Duty calls. But don't disturb yourself, stay nice and warm in bed. Or better yet, do disturb yourself, take a peek out the window when I leave, to see if I'm being followed. Take a good look, but be careful, eh? They mustn't find out what apartment I'm coming from. I'm going to stand on the corner a while as if looking for a taxi, then I'll walk a few blocks and call you from a phone booth. And you tell me if you saw anyone suspicious. And don't worry, I always use the stairs to go up and down. Don't worry. I love you. I'll protect you."

Some protection, I said to myself, some protection coming from someone who needs it most. The Great Protector got dressed in a hurry, his nerves on edge. He buttoned his shirt clumsily, leaving one tail out like a broken wing, forgot to zip up his pants, maybe in homage to what he himself had been in other times; a short half hour ago, we might say.

Beside the lamppost on the corner across from my window, Navoni pauses calmly to light a cigarette. I can

188

still see him. I can still see, too—and that's what puts our lives on the brink of doubt, sliding off into terror—the shadow that might have been just a shadow, moving a few feet away.

When the telephone finally rings, I try the impossible to regain my calm and come up with a code. "Ricardito, I'm glad you called. Mama's still quite bad. I'm terribly worried, you'd better come."

"Impossible, are you crazy? I'm too far away."

"But Mama's bad, very bad."

"Are you quite sure? I don't think so, did you take her temperature correctly?"

"Yes, I guess so. It looks as if she's failing. But I couldn't read the thermometer too well, it was very hazy and dark."

"Let's see, let me see . . . Look, the best thing is for me not to go to work at the factory today, the other watchman can take my shift. I'm going to walk around a little to shrug off this anxiety, and I'll call you at six sharp. If I can't get through, call the doctor right away and tell him."

"Wait, I'll come over."

"Good Lord, how can you even think of going out. Are you going to leave Mama alone? It would be too dangerous."

"It might be, but I'd feel calmer."

"It's not that serious, don't worry. Mama's had a lot of attacks like this before, and she always comes out of them. She's a strong old woman. Remember, I'll call you at six. Love and kisses."

Bullshit! I almost shout as I hang up, and I feel like kicking the telephone, just because I can't kick Alfredo. Just imagine: a strong old woman, and he's talking about himself. And he makes me wait until six o'clock, as if I hadn't waited enough already, and I'm to think of a lawyer in case he can't call at six o'clock. A lawyer, quick.

And I think of Carlos, but no, he's a marked man. Jorge Silva has to be eliminated, too. And Chochó and Perla; so many who'd give their lives to help Alfredo Navoni, and now they've been barred. Worse than if they'd lost their licenses. They're shadows too, now, shadows, but so different from the one that at this very moment might be tailing Alfredo, though with luck it might only be the shadow of my own fear.

Saint Death

On the Altar of the Finger there's a small dark chest, locked and attached to one of the natural columns by a thick chain. What's hidden in that chest is a secret to everyone, even to the Lord and Master, who has done a good job of forgetting its contents. A lot of forgetting when it suits him, a lot of mysteries relegated to the folds of a memory that's so doubled over onto itself, so full of furls. He's even forgotten about the people he had ordered to succumb on the altars of the Dead Woman. Those anonymous and faraway people who didn't know how to respect his orders no longer interest him, now he's only interested in those closer and more manageable people, the Capivarians. To hell with the others. And it's precisely there where they have their solace, having succumbed to idolatry, the greatest of delights.

The poor things drool as they creep on their knees along the streets near the Basilica in search of a small miracle. They're left without knees, with stumps, they put all their money in the alms boxes of the church and, mutilated and despoiled, at last they believe themselves to be brothers of the ones despoiled by the central power.

There is a certain homogeneity in the people of the Capital now, which makes them indistinguishable, monotonous. Only these rebels of Capivarí deserve his attention, and deserve for the Lord and Master to refresh his memory through them.

So up to the Altar of the Finger he goes, to the chest he goes, to hear the sound of broken chains, because he must cleave them with a sledgehammer to free the contents of the chest, the secret and forgotten contents.

All he finds in the chest are a spent bullet and a small skeleton, carved from a bone, presumably human. These items with no apparent significance are laden with significance. They are a protective fetish and an image of Saint Death. Talismans that will open the gates of Capivarí for him when the floodgates are closed.

Amen.

Dawn comes with the sound of the telephone, at six o'clock sharp, because these things have to be mathematical for them to work as they're supposed to. Punctuality is the best palliative for anguish. And a phone call is a relief like few others.

"Everything under control, everything okay. I'm afraid that business about Mama's illness was a false alarm, there weren't any symptoms, and I didn't go to work because of it and they were waiting for me to do a rather important job. But don't feel that it's your fault, beautiful. Now you can get back to your things, forget about Mama's illness, she's not in any danger at all, get back to your novel. And don't forget to get rid of the hero, eh? I think it would be the best way to be sure of a real success in the bookstores. A blockbuster, let's say."

"I'll do what I can."

"That's the way to talk. I'll call you when I have a free moment. I'm enchanted by interludes with you. I kiss your left eyelid."

"Should I take that as a warning to close my eyes?"

Lordly, with his two talismans hanging from his neck in a small green pouch—the inherited talismans are two, three are the ones that hang farther down on him by his own right. Lordly, and feeling himself complete master of his powers, he sets out on that luminous morning for Capivarí, where his spokesmen have been announcing his arrival since sunup. They are men skilled in the use of a convincing word, those spokesmen, and on all sides they proclaim the high honor it will be for the town of Capivarí to hear the Voice for the first and only time.

A thundering voice, terrifying as it rose up over the flat roofs and the few small trees of Capivarí, spreading out beyond the sad telegraph poles. The Sorcerer-orator began his speech in a slow but impressive way. He was prepared to make it long: during his sleepless night he had rehearsed a threatening but simple tirade—for those simple people.

"People of Capivarí," he harangued, encompassing

them all, and sure that not a soul in that town—thanks to the loudspeakers—would fail to hear him. "People of Capivarí," he repeated, more strongly now, "I know that you are unconquerable and that's why I like you; but I'm going to make you bow down your heads. I know that you're not going to give in willingly, that you don't want to be annexed to my Kingdom of the Black Lagoon."

And the Capivarians, clustered in the small square that was really a vacant lot where they usually played soccer, began to gather in small groups, consulting each other, whispering among themselves and passing the word along until they all began shouting in unison:

Black-la-goon
Black-la-goon

And they shouted yes, yes, we want to be annexed, an-nex-a-tion, and they began to leap and wave their arms with great enthusiasm and sang, Master, Master, how great you are, and the women ran to get their pots and pans and came out beating on them with their lids like cymbals, and the ball ran into the net and goooal! they all shouted yes, they wanted to be annexed to the Kingdom of the Black Lagoon and place themselves in the hands of the Master—Master of Capivarí now, and all the problems he would be able to solve.

And that was how they cut off the poor Sorcerer's speech, leaving him perplexed for a few moments. He recovered his control much more rapidly than any mortal under similar circumstances would have done, and whispered for his aide to try making contact with his men in Zone 3. They should prevent the closing of the dam's floodgates at all costs. And he proceeded with his speech, his tone changed now, showing the positive aspect of what he had intended to set forth as a curse.

As he spoke, he reflected: The water's going to ebb now, there won't be time for the men in Zone 3 to run to the dam to countermand the order. The water must be ebbing by now, and what am I going to say?

Never never never have I lacked means and there's no reason why these misfortunes should happen to me at my most glorious moment.

I was alone on the balcony for the first time—although it was only a platform made of planks—alone all alone facing the people, and the people of Capivarí were acclaiming me. They shouldn't be defrauded. Not then, at least.

I promise, I promise (promises have always gone with the wind in the end) that you will never lack for water, my children, my protected ones. If water doesn't reach you by an earthly route—something that could happen, earthly events don't merit much of my trust—water will fall from heaven for you. Miracles like this don't fail when I am involved: the celestial is my working area, I asserted, sneaking a look at the horizon, where a few dark clouds seemed to be forming. I could see them and they couldn't, I was elevated as was fitting and they only had eyes for me, as was fitting. But the clouds began to break up after a while, they were just another vain promise among so many others.

For that reason, at the exact moment in which I reckoned there would be a dearth of water, I shouted:

"Now we shall hold back the natural course of things, we shall reverse the currents, we shall make a change of liquids on these lands so that everything, very shortly, will find a more splendid and deeper channel."

Master, Master, they shouted, and they sang How Great You Are and leaped about and danced with a rarely

195

seen merriment, which carried me back to other times, times that prefigured these and opened the path of light for me.

The women with their pots used as drums, and anybody who doesn't leap about is a traitor; so much energy released, so much enthusiasm.

I promised them a monumental soccer match in which the Capivarí Juniors would be champions. I promised them an international witch doctors' convention, with invitations extended to all *babalaos*, all *ialorixás*, cabalists, spiritualists, *paleros*, astrologers, *oriates*, *osainaistas*, *ifas*, mentalists, *ilalochas*, shamans, curers, conjurers; those who predict by means of tarot, *diloggun*, *okuele*, *obi*; those who practice obeah, white tables and black tables, the *n'kaci n'kici*, herbalists, *vaudoists* and voodooists; seraphists and trance mediums, ensnarers and liers-in-wait. All. Absolutely all: the strength will be with us when the scattered light is brought together again, when the waters are sweetened and once more flow as they used to. They will come to join us together again as friends who have been separated for centuries.

Capivarí will be the Capital of Magic. Which, with a simple slide, will be transformed into the Capital. Magical Capital.

So much talking and invoking—with dissimulation —waiting for the miracle in reverse that would be produced when the waters were cut off. I promised to transfer to that same square—the only one in town, a poor orphan —the Main Altar of the Finger, without making clear which finger I was referring to or how many. I spoke to them of my childhood, of Sixfingers, of the village idiot, of the birds, the ants, and the capybaras—their emblem. I promised to send them a totem pole made by the very hands of my aide the artist-carver, I promised and I promised, and since the waters turned out not to be cut off, I cut off the flow of my words, my verbal torrent, and said to myself I'll make the people in Zone 3 pay for such disobedience.

No, I'm afraid I haven't got the strength to kill the witchdoc. I grasp my pen, on the point of doing it, and crack! up rise other themes that capture my attention, and the Sorcerer continues there, alive and kicking, as full of spark as ever.

It must be because of that sympathy business Navoni mentioned, and not precisely because of any kind of sympathy a person might feel toward a monster. Quite the contrary. Something related to sympathetic magic, rather: on paper, I suppress the witchdoc with a stroke of the pen, and that ever so simple act ricochets and brings repercussions for Alfredo, for me. No, I can't. And Alfredo hasn't called me since that unhappy morning, and I wonder where he can be wandering and if something has happened to him. There I go, hanging on the telephone for a guy again. I'd sworn to myself no, never again— although these circumstances are quite different, and I can even forgive myself the anxiety and accept it. I feel like going to the ambassador and asking for his help, but I can't, I'm afraid the help I'd ask for would have nothing to do with the political situation, and those other questions are better forgotten for now. I'm alone, meanwhile, waiting for a call. The witchdoc is alone in the midst of his horror, too. Maybe I do feel a little sympathy for him, after all: he's our reverse face, the dark side of our struggle. The arouser. I couldn't kill him if I wanted to, and I hate him for that reason, too. Where could Alfredo have gone?

I have my obsessions, I have my fear that drags me along. I've been woven into a network of fears, they cross back and forth over my head, they close me in like an enormous web spun by a spider in the reeds, black and precise, malefically beautiful. This net of fears, this geometric pattern, I go on weaving it too without knowing why, without understanding it. I would like to decipher a small end of it at least, a point in the web, so as to go along unwinding the infernal plot, but I'm not permitted that either. Some of my dearest friends have been killed, others are incapacitated or imprisoned, others—Navoni!—are running all kinds of risks, and here I am messing around, talking about a spiderweb that entraps me, putting myself into poetic images. The worst thing is that I can glimpse it so clearly, something woven by clusters of black spiders, crouching in wait for their prey, a broad, mile-wide web with us as the prey, and the spiders too.

I've been waiting for word from Navoni for four days. I'm no longer even waiting for his embrace, just to know that he's safe. *The Voice* that arrived in the Capital at noon today—they're bringing it in by plane now—told about the witchdoc's speech and the annexation of Capivarí to the Kingdom of the Black Lagoon. What rubbish. We've lost.

Kill the witchdoc in my writing? Impossible. The witchdoc isn't alive because of me, and I might just be alive because of the witchdoc. He's my real antagonist.

But I should try, as far as I can, to kill the military, who use him as a justification, as a shield.

I read *The Voice* in the hope I'll learn something about Navoni through that so very very indirect route. So he's promised them a soccer championship on an international level? How original. Nobody for one instant would doubt the victory of his team, the Capivarí Juniors, it would be a sporting event without too many surprises. That international congress of magic sounds more interesting. Who knows, maybe with a little luck somebody will come to us who can outdo the Sorcerer. That would be his real defeat, on his own ground.

> In the black corner we have the Lord of Night, who appears before us today in the mask of an ant. In the white corner we have the Caboclo de Mar, unmasked. It will be a fight to the finish, with limitless rounds, and no quarter. The victor must win by a clear knockout. Or we've all had it. Ladies and gentlemen, the gong has sounded.

> The crowd roars.

I ask for a moment of silence. A moment of silence to recover the thread of reality and not get lost in wishful thinking. The open confrontation hasn't begun yet, who knows if it ever will. And the other consideration: the real danger doesn't come from this rather farcical character, the witchdoc, the Sorcerer, the picturesque sadist, our homegrown Rasputin. Those who hold power here in the Capital are the real threat. But we always tend to look at the mask, and the mask belongs to the witchdoc. By destroying the mask, we hope to put an end to the men hiding behind it. The ones who are closing in on Navoni along with so many others, the ones who keep us in suspense and won't let me write in peace, the ones who don't know this last word, the ones who only nourish and promote the river of blood with our collective blood.

We will not make use of the taking of Capivarí as a means of pressuring the military regime, but rather to protest our situation and the government's indifference to our demands.

The Lord of the Black Lagoon and Capivarí of the Seven Currents does not plan to follow a policy of leadership, power, or hegemony beyond his domains or accept the same from others. He only aspires to the good course of bilateral relations between our kingdom and the now encompassing country.

We must keep alive the flame of indestructible cohesion between our two nations, who possess similar ideals for the defeat of subversive terrorism and ideological colonialisms.

The Tacurú has taken on a truly festive air. Never before had so many votive lamps been lighted there. The Tac is being ennobled in direct proportion to the high office now exercised by its Lord and Master. The latter is now Emperor of the Black Lagoon and Capivarí, the former is his central seat, summer palace, and government house all in one.

Machi's death has brought about great changes. The beds of hallucinogenic mushrooms have been transferred to other caves of lesser importance—the mushrooms no longer irradiate their green light, they were extinguished when their mistress was extinguished—and the splendorous cathedral-cavern of rock salt has been transformed into the throne room. It deserves it for being opulent and iridescent, bejeweled and precious. The long access corridors to the room are now reserved for the exclusive use of the inhabitants of the Palace; the others, the rude messengers from the outside world, must enter the room with a shove that is surprising—for them.

It is most desirable for them to reach the environs of the Tacurú at noon, when the sun beats down most fiercely on the barren desolation of the surface. A voice offstage then orders the visitor to stand on a precise spot, exactly in the center of the cabalistic pentacle sketched on the ground, and the startled visitor falls down a chute that takes him suddenly to a spot exactly in front of the throne in the rock-salt cathedral.

The Sorcerer is there, always there when visitors come, spotlighted by a natural beam in the best Delphic manner. And the new arrival, on seeing him all in red on the golden throne, in the midst of translucent and multicolored walls, stands there with his mouth agape. Speechless.

But that doesn't happen with schoolmaster Cernuda, no, not with him, Master Cernuda is never at a loss for words. And the word is

Sublime!

Sublime in every sense of the word: exalted, eminent, grand, also volatile. Passing directly from the solid state to the ethereal, an expression of desire that schoolmaster Cernuda managed to verbalize in the most subtle manner, without bringing on the

Master's wrath, as if flattering him. And in that vein he continued on with his dithyramb:

"O Master of Masters, Magnificent Lord, the people of Capivarí, your people, our people, have conferred upon me the very high honor of being named Special Envoy to Your Eminence. Here I stand, entrusted with the most noble mission of presenting you with this parchment richly illuminated by our very best vernacular artists. On it appear the drum and the whip as main emblems: we believe that the cultural and folkloric values of our region are our greatest wealth, and we are sure that Your Lordship understands that and will know how to safeguard them. And through them safeguard the values of local tradition that we know our Excellent Master holds in such high esteem, so we have decided to form our first *pato* team—an eminently national sport—for which we would require that the divine grace of our Chief Executive procure for us a troop of thoroughbred horses. As you well know, our humble country folk only ride humble native horses, useful only for the coarsest agrarian chores, and it would be inconceivable that New Capivarí, under the patronage and protection of such a High Magistrate, should not have the very best troop for its gallant *pato* team, a matched troop!

"Furthermore, Sublimity of Sublimities, we think that our old and worn-out electric generator won't have the capacity to carry out the High Mission now required of it; to wit, illuminating Your Majesty's presence and also illuminating the sporting jousts that will be celebrated in Your honor.

"But that is nothing, O Worthy One. The people of Capivarí know that Your Grace will have the streets paved, will have a sewer system installed, will not limit the new airmail service to the exclusive use of Your esteemed journal.

"We have taken very much into account, Excellent Sublime and Adored Master, the undeserved promises that you made to us a week and a half ago in your Unforgettable Oration. Nothing will gladden our hearts more than a Main Altar and a totem pole commemorating the glory of our Lord and Master. But does the Lord and Master think that the poverty-stricken little square of Capivarí, nothing but a vacant lot, is the worthy recipient of such sublime gifts? We don't think so, Magnanimous Lord. Therefore, we humbly suggest that before making such a great offering it would be proper and fitting to restore the square. Plant trees, set up flowerpots, a bandstand perhaps. And build a playground there, because, as we never grow tired of saying, the children of today will be your most loving subjects tomorrow, and that eventuality fills us with pride.

"Let us not forget, Master: in New Capivarí the children are the only privileged ones. They will conjugate verbs in the future tense, in their hands is the new Powerful Capivarí. And we must turn our attention to them, Most Revered One, creating, for example, a new school. A real school, not the shed we've been using till now. A school that will warm Your Excellency's soul, that will be like a most beautiful and rare flower in the lapel of your spirit; I can see it now, consisting of a kindergarten and primary and secondary levels, connected to the Ministry of Education of our sister Republic, from which we have separated but with which we still maintain bonds of fraternal friendship.

"On another occasion, O Magister Illuminatissimus, we will take up the question of running water and the reduction of the agricultural and livestock taxes. For now I will be content to plant these problems in Your most noble spirit, certain as we are that they will be attended to, O Great among the Great."

Is it possible that the witchdoc lost his shrewdness with that assault of praises? Had so much exaggeration gone to his head? Who is casting the first stone, who is being deceived? Perhaps only he—he's the only one who can allow himself to be. He, the boss, the Master, lord of drums, *capo* of Capivarí, omnipotent, omniscient. He allowed himself the luxury of letting himself be rocked with flattery, listening to schoolmaster Cernuda to the end and, with a gesture of magnanimity that did him honor, attending to certain requests, adding, of course, his own touch of (local) color.

"Make a note, aide, make a note. Improvements for my Capital: ask the rustlers for horses to make up the *pato* team. Yellow shirts with purple stripes for the soccer team, and the creation of the Ant Boxing Club. I like husky men, I'm a great patron of sports that ennoble the human being and take his mind off other less pleasant concerns.

"Wipe out the rest of the requests with a stroke of the pen. They are unconstitutional."

Now I'm going back to my pyramid and I don't want to be bothered. I'm not in for anyone, I will be given over entirely to my lucubrations, only they can interrupt my voluntary encloisterment this afternoon. Come, daydreams, speak to me of Capivarí my Capital, which I shall turn into a lake city as a double vengeance—and vengeance is the unmistakable mark of my passage. Those who didn't close the sluice gates up there that memorable day, doing me, without knowing it, the greatest of favors, will now have to open them wide, yawning sluices, overflowing waters, coursing waters to flood the fields of Capivarí, extending my lagoons.

Let the Capivarians raise their houses up on stilts so they can sway, cradled by the waters. Death, death, and more death to whatever doesn't seek refuge in the long-legged houses, to whatsoever tries to circulate on land, to anything that wishes to live without my permission.

The others will come, too. Lunatics. The Dead Woman's worshippers with their secret intention of attacking the fortress; they will drown in my waters. They have succumbed to alien veneration, and I don't dream of helping them. On a certain occasion I sent them the message of the Finger, asking for some logistical support, and they, lost in the iconography of the Finger, deviated from my purpose. Therefore, death, too, to the former adorers, they're ever so numerous, they'll feed my carnivorous animals and the wolf I carry inside. The adorers will come, I can see it quite clearly, up to the shores of the New Lagoon, begging my forgiveness, and I will forbid them access to the sacred city. They will be eaten by my piranhas, by my crocodiles.

Capivarí the Holy, purified by the waters, raised up on sacred stilts that I will bless one by one. And only the just will be saved, the ones not associated with that bonfire game that was meant to consume me. Ha-ha-ha, and ha, and ha, meant to consume me with fire, me, who am the living flame. That's why I only dress in red now, so they'll recognize me. And multitudes will come from the former Capital and try to acclaim me now that my greatness has returned to the surface and is again evident to all. And I will give myself that ever-satisfying pleasure: I'll crush them without mercy, they'll only see the sacred city as a mirage.

They'll contemplate the city mirrored in the waters, infinitely ennobled and beautiful, and they'll die at its edge—on the side of its rim—knowing that never ever will they be able to reach it, not even after death. Because I shall make a magic ring for Capivarí to protect it from ghosts and/or apparitions, and the only ones who'll be able to reach it will be the ones I choose and at the moment I choose. Let's say before or after death, let's say swimming, in a boat, or walking amphibiously along the bottom of my new lagoon. And those eternal water birds who transform themselves into a sharp object like an arrow will dive to fish for their prey and will peck at their skulls.

I like pecked skulls. I like to see the brains fly when someone's head is blasted by a gunshot. Not by me. I never carry weapons, I only load them from time to time in order to do honor to the old saying. You have to respect popular wisdom, and I'm not deceiving myself: I'm the devil, too, and I have to attend to the duties that tradition imposes on me, such as loading weapons. Overwhelming work, it has to be admitted; that's why many times I only instigate and delegate. Power attracts me like few other things in the world, but I have no desire whatever for the obligations that power imposes. That's why I've decided to interrupt—until I issue a new order—all contact with the government of what used to be my country before my separatist dreams became reality.

Today I'm going backwards, I'm going to recover the person I was twenty years ago, during the life of the

Generaliss, when he and no one but he knew about my powers and had a monopoly over them. A good formula for me while he was who he was and I was his secret co-pilot. Until he began to decline and I decided that he no longer deserved the exclusive use of my powers. Didn't he name me his unofficial successor? And rightly so. I am always a successor, with or without appointment: I'm the one who comes afterwards and who is always successful.

> I'm the one who
> paints the grapes
> and unpaints them
> once again.

I'm the one who has always been, and if folk singers don't sing about me more, it can't be for lack of merit on my part. It must be out of fear. I do inspire fear, and I say that with pride; fear is the purest feeling a human being can experience, because it stops him from acting sanely and obliges him to be himself. Fear dignifies far more than love.

That woman also dignified, the Dead Woman, because she spread fear throughout, and she also felt it and consoled us. She was our only consolation. Not the other one. The Intruder, neither fear nor consolation nor anything, only a great emptiness. But I was her friend, I tried to instill in her some of the Dead Woman's strength, and for twenty-seven nights the Intruder slept with the embalmed corpse under the bed.

If she didn't capture all the luminosity that emanated from the Dead Woman, it certainly wasn't through any lack of enthusiasm on my part. I encouraged her as much as possible and even held her hand at times when the Generaliss was sleeping. With the Generaliss awake, things were different, and his laughter sometimes gave me cramps of anger. Until I decided to bounce his laugh back at him: I turned myself into a screen and every laugh directed at me reflected off me and hit him, like a boomerang. He only lasted two months on his feet and then fell into bed forever. "It's no good laughing at the Sorcerer" were almost his last words, and I forgave him then. Of course, I didn't forgive him completely.

"Mr. President, pardon the boldness, but things are going from bad to worse. We here, trying to impose our model on the world, embarked on the great project of National Reconstruction capable of leading our nation to the fulfillment of its highest aspirations, and along comes that clown to create an independent kingdom in the heart of our country, paying no attention to all our appeals for unity. I don't think the maneuver is as innocent as it appears at first sight, I'll warrant that the man is an agent of foreign penetration. Everyone is aware, for example, of the imperialist megalomania of our neighbors to the northeast. I'm sure the apparent clownishness of the Kingdom of the Black Lagoon is in response to a plan, one that might not turn out to be beneficial to us at all."

"You're wrong as usual, Rear Admiral. If there's any maneuver, it's a diversionary one that might well serve our ends. Who's watching our governmental activities at this moment? On one side, the fanatics at the Basilica are attracting large crowds, and that's all the people are thinking about. On the other side, the foreign press is occupied with the Sorcerer and isn't thinking about us. Our hands are free for action. It's impossible to ask for better tangential circumstances."

Ten days, or can it be fifteen or seven, since I've heard from Navoni. Time becomes gummy and hard to grasp, as if I were in prison. I've got to start measuring it with contraptions, clocks, calendars, those items of grief; I no longer feel it passing in me, I know nothing of days or nights, I only know of separation, a great culture broth of separation, confused hours marked only by waiting.

I did something: I wrote a little more about the witchdoc without even being able to declare him ill. A physical illness, of course, because he's been psychologically sick from childhood. I know, because of the ant business: only the innocent and the mad escape the fury of the invertebrate world.

What else did I do? I went to see the Caboclo de Mar so he could talk to me about Navoni, and he told me that everything was in order, the man was in no danger at present, he was doing his thing, but it's best for me to keep away from him, he has more pressing passions than love. Because of which, instead of staying away, I began to search for him frantically. Where are these passions more pressing than love, why won't he infect me a little? When love appears, it makes everything so restricted, the focus of attention becomes limited and we don't allow ourselves the slightest deviation. To console myself, I say: Maybe it's not a question of love, there's another feeling behind that search, another anxiety is lying in wait. I began to roam the streets after that indistinguishable and coveted prey and finally I joined a pilgrimage heading for the Basilica. I did the last part in all humility and I reached the altar of the Dead Woman on foot in an attempt to decipher some message.

But, what an idea! Only I could have thought of that, stupefied as I am by anxiety. I've known it all along. Miracles don't exist, not even communication or faith exists. It's a complete fraud, relics are fakes, indulgences are sold. As always, as at all shrines in the world.

Does Navoni believe in the Dead Woman? Navoni believes in a people's strength that would have to be channeled, as he always proclaims, though I don't always pay attention. And then I accuse him of being naïve. And look at me now, at the foot of the shrine, with the urge to kick away the poor cripples, as if I, too, didn't know the power of faith. As if I weren't thinking that maybe, behind all this, though never right on the edge, but rather going along with the current, something might be realized someday.

All of which gave me the idea for the ad. A message in *The Voice* calling Alfredo. Saying something like: Come back little Angel Now, we need you. Luisa. He'll recognize the initials and will reply somehow. Reading between the lines is the key. Just in case, I look through the classified ads, under the unheard-of heading "Acknowledgments—13B."

PERSONAL Acknowledgments	13B
Ceferino Namuncurá. Thank you greatly. P.T.N.	
Holy Ghost. Thank you D.R.	
Thanks God and H. Ghost. R.S.	
Thanks God and H. Ghost S.S.	
Thanks H. Ghost & Cef. Nam. R.S.	
Thanks God and H. Ghost C.G.P.	
Thank you Holy Ghost Joe.	
Thank You Holy Ghost L.M.L.	

Thank you Holy Ghost G.K.
Thank you Holy Ghost N.S.M.
Thank you Holy Ghost V.L.
Thank you Holy Ghost E.B.O.
Thank you Holy Ghost E.S.
Thank you Holy Ghost C.B.
Thank you Holy Ghost O.S.
Thank you Holy Ghost C.L.
Thank you Holy Ghost Inés
Thank you Holy Ghost A.L.M.
Thank you Holy Ghost Nenuca.
Thank you Holy Ghost J.W.
Thank you Holy Ghost M.G.
Thank you Holy Ghost C.L.
Thank you Holy Ghost M.G.F.
THank you Holy Ghost R.G.S.
Thank you Holy Ghost G.M.
Thank you Holy Ghost A.G.
Thank you Holy Ghost A.D.O.
Thank you Holy Ghost E.H.
Thank You Holy Ghost Tito
Thank you Holy Ghost A.G.
Thank you Holy Ghost A.B.
Thank you Holy Ghost J.A.F.
Thank you Holy Ghost C.L.
Thank you Holy Ghost Juan.
Thank you Holy Ghost M.G.H.
Thank you Holy Ghost A.M.
Thank you Holy Ghost M.E.E.
Thank you Holy Ghost Beto
Thank you Holy Ghost S.M.
Thank you Holy Ghost Otilia
Thank you Holy Ghost N.S.
Thank you Holy Ghost DiDi
Thank you Holy Ghost E.C.
THANK you Holy Ghost E.C.
THANK you Holy Ghost R.F.D.
Thank you Holy Ghost Q.K.
THank you San Martín de Porres for the grace driven. Elba
Thank you God and Ceferino for everything. Celda & Fanny

Thanks? for what? in times like these? And to the Holy Ghost, no less, flighty little bird, as someone called it, ungraspable impossibility of hope.

> The esteemed public is requested to remain completely silent. Our aerialist will undertake a test of extreme danger and only with maximum concentration will he be able to attain his French Somersat! The best in the World!!

Somer*sat*? A typo like the grace *driven* to Doña Elba on the previous page? *Sat,* and the word *world* capitalized, and why French? We have to read between the lines, between the letters, around boxes, anything to find Navoni, and I think that maybe this is a message for me, of course, he had the same idea and got the jump on me. That's why I run out in search of a copy of last Saturday's *Le Monde* (the best in the World!).

I search and I search and I can't find one anywhere. Not at any of the newsstands where sometimes, with luck, they sell them, or at Air France, or at the French Bank, or at the Alliance Française. Nor—a last, rather stupid resort—at the Navifrance maritime agency. Nowhere. There must be some reason, I tell myself, as I head for the Casa Visigodo, where you can find anything. Old Tomás knows me, he knows I'm not just looking for it casually.

"Why Saturday's *Le Monde*?"

"For the serial. If I'm left never knowing if the widow killed her husband or not, I'll die. I can't stand the suspense. I'll pay anything."

"All right. I'll get it for you, but I'm warning you, it's going to be expensive. That issue was seized by customs."

That was how I spent my last few pesos on a hunch, and right I was. Because the newspaper had a more than unexpected single photo: a press conference by three hooded figures displaying, in turn, a second photo.

I recognize Navoni, not just by his build and his bearing, but by the stamp of his genius: those hoods that look like white masks have a lot to do with what is going on. The only thing I don't understand is how they could have got hold of the photograph they're showing, which looks like a framed enlargement. Not too clear, the second photo, taken in poor light, surreptitiously, that's obvious. But there's no doubt that it's the witchdoc in his crystal palace. And he looks just the same as he did twenty years ago, damn it.

Keeper of Pain, Keeper of Fear

A great thing, torture: fierce and fanged. On the other hand, those who manage (managed) to squirm out of our hands are toothless. We withhold their most vital parts, we will give ourselves over to the pleasure of dismemberment, and, what's even better, we'll lick our fingers. Yes, sir, fingers—our own, and even someone else's, especially someone else's; we'll suck and we'll suck until we leave them thin, until the flesh is consumed and our jaws are completely cramped.

Unable to articulate words now, unable to dedicate ourselves to any mastication at all, unable—and that's the most atrocious thing of all—to release a scream. Best of all is the absence of motive, and we have no reason to raise our voices or ask for help. Therefore, we must scream, blend our screams with those of others, overcome them, drown them out.

Who will open his mouth? Who, who will be prepared to let fly a shriek? With swollen jaws from so much sucking around (mucking around). With swollen jaws, puffed up, the shriek is still ours. All ours.

And our cry is a cry of triumph. Never permitting ourselves to slip into pain or fear. Or, rather, yes: permitting ourselves everything because, come what may, neither pain nor fear ever affects us, ever catches up with us or suffices. Because we are—I am—the only one capable of provoking them, as Keeper of pain and of fear.

Fear and pain, pain and fear: I'm used to imposing

them on others to keep them in line. Let others go along with the feelings I have brought on them. Let them go on, for I remain on guard against these contaminations. Unharmed. Unpolluted.

I drag others down to death to keep death far from me. Rending others means freezing the moment. Death as a prolongation of my fingers, that is, not impregnating me. Death that doesn't concern me when I produce it, doesn't touch me. I manipulate death, I guide it to my will and she respects me and doesn't touch me.

They, the ones all whitened, masked and hooded, challenging cowards who hide themselves, have managed to take a certain picture of my person at a rather intimate moment, which means that they not only have invaded my redoubt but have gotten closer to me than is advisable. There is evidently a traitor among the many people who surround me now. It might be amusing to put the squeeze on all of them, one by one or in a bunch, to make them sing, in the certainty that I would find the guilty party in the blink of an eye (or maybe in the tearing of an eyelid). But what do I care about that? Catching a photographer, a cheap spy, unmask one or two or three, now, when the masks have been multiplied to such an extent.

The stakes are different now, the values in play are different, if we can talk about values in relation to the purest cowardice.

With cowardice in play, I opt to remain on this side of the line I draw, and it's a circular line that goes around me.

I protect myself in a magic circle that for the present has the diameter of this room of mine, my pyramid. It's an expandable circle. I'll go on expanding my circle, and since I tend toward the straight line—as my actions have proven—the curve of my protective circle will follow the horizon and will faithfully respect the curvature of the earth.

On the one side will be me, framed by some latitude of my choosing, and on the other the mortals over whom I will exercise my gift of death in such a way as to halt my own deterioration.

All of them are masks.

Looking at me from across the street through the eyeholes in the masks to protect themselves. My glow could blind them, and blind victims are less victim-like. For this reason, only the ones I point out will lose their sight, and only when I stipulate.

I want them to see me, I want them to smell me, and at the same time I want to see them, touch them, smell on them that stench of terror that they ooze and that's acrid and biting like the smell of wild beasts. The smell of fear in others stimulates and excites me. People of Capivarí who don't fear me, I will bring on you subtle torments so as to be able to smell you in the air. I will sniff at night, I will stroll through the solitary and dark streets of my Capivarí—there will be a curfew—and from inside the houses the emanations will reach me.

A river of blood will flow.

A river of blood will flow that has already begun to form, and floating along that river brought on by me, I will go as far as the Capital, and I will stroll by night through the solitary and dark streets. There will be a curfew. There will be everything that I practiced in Capivarí, and much more, because I will stroll through the streets of the Capital imposing the silence and the stasis that I need around me in order to extend myself onto the world. A gag in one hand, a blindfold in the other, in the other handcuffs, in the other a whip, in the other a hobble and several feet of rope to tie them all up. My innumerable hands full and my countless arms and all my feet dancing. While I laugh at them.

That's why I shout, and to the rhythm of their shrieks of pain I will shout with fury. With joy sometimes; always with a healthy indignation that is born of my hatred.

Snapshots of me. What can they do with photographs of me? Can they point at my image with a finger, stick pins in it? What else can be done with a photo? And I, indestructible as always. Reshaping myself.

I am no longer the Egret. No longer wolf or dog; I am a woodpecker now, carpenter bird, craftsman of the miracle. A necessary transmogrification if the pregnancy is to be fulfilled. My partaking of the birth (let him take charge of hatred—that's what he knows how to do best—I shall pour myself into love). I'm carving wings for the cradle, I'm also going to carve a child. Just in case, the child. The wood is alive and I caress it. The Master will know how to breathe into it the spirit that it lacks. There are ways and ways of coming into this world, and if I carve the child I will be able to give it the softness of some of my traits and make it somewhat benign. The Master mustn't know. Tock, tock, let him think just the cradle. I sandpaper and I polish and every so often I give a few hammer blows to one side in order to cover up the silence of love. I sandpaper—I practically don't use any gouges—a polished little child all made of blond, opalescent wood. The cheeks of this wooden child are as if throbbing, and the Master mustn't know about this, my current carving. I want to contribute to the birth. Something of me in the Child: the work of my hands—my caresses.

Behind the second mask, which is a white hood with painted eyes, I recognize Alfredo, but behind the image of the witchdoc, so mask-like, can there exist some possibility of recognition? As if that mattered. All that matters—now—is to know whether Alfredo Navoni is still alive or whether he's been lost to us in this mockery.

I can hear the hammer hitting the chisel, and it's as if I could see the wood chips flying like bone splinters. Shavings on the floor, curled ringlets of wood, because the Egret is on the other side of the wall, making the cradle. For that son so completely mine. The Egret can only offer me a fruit crate; the fruit tree and the fruit will be me, fruit originating only in me.

What more? A fantasy that sometimes comes over me as I listen to the hammering: they're erecting a scaffold. A guillotine by the very door of my dwelling so that the heads will roll over to my feet and entertain me. They'll come to wink at me, the heads. They'll come—maybe—to propose a pact. I'm not dreaming about any compromises. Heads all hooded, all of them, covered heads, all by themselves, hooded, and not with an executioner's hood, but a white hood with painted eyes put there by their own free will. The only free will possible: that of covering shameful parts.

Those sons of bitches photographed me with my face showing. Only I am permitted the insolence of seeing myself just as I am. They use masks, they use hoods: devices for disguise that more than anything else give them away. Those who appear there with their faces covered are anybody are everybody and as a result everybody turns out to be my enemy. It's better to strike out blindly but to strike with fury than to try to guess who's behind the masks.

No. I think that for the moment it suits us to abstain. We'll celebrate the next ceremony behind closed doors, if only to cleanse ourselves. Evil can be contagious, but we're advancing in our commitment. The circle of rejection is closing in around the man of the Black Lagoon. He intended to bring about a popular uprising and only managed to revive a faith. He's grabbed off a town, and its inhabitants don't take him at all seriously. It seems that our Umbanda rituals are producing results. But we have to go on acting with extreme care. And leave time to do its work, too. Time, which this man tries Olympically to disdain, is going to be his real enemy in the end.

All I've got left is this poorly printed photo with the black granules imposed by the reality of a newspaper. A photo that is and isn't Navoni, showing the other photo that is clearly the witchdoc, his true effigy at last, at last the mug of the Sorcerer. What the devil do I care. Devil is the exact word. The face of the subject of my biography is given to me by Navoni, and Navoni isn't here. Where is he hiding? and what can he be hiding from me? I don't care anymore about the one whose face is uncovered, I care about the other one, the one covered up, who I know is Alfredo and who hasn't shown up.

I'm tempted to go and look up the witchdoc in person and put myself at his service. Become his ghost writer. If he's really writing his novel and I'm trying to do his biography with the few facts that come my way, why not combine his knowledge and my literary talents and achieve the true work that could well be this very same book? I've had it up to here with not being part of the story, and even more so with having had the only character in it who matters to me slip through my hands. Belonging. What if Navoni had left his seed in me when he went away? There's no precaution possible when a person clings so tight to the other being and clings so tight to life. Our child will be called Faith, and that's precisely what we lack.

"We don't have to let ourselves be confused by the occasion, Mr. President, we have to think fundamentally about the long haul. A lot has been invested in this Process, it's cost a lot of blood and a lot of lives, we're not going to abandon it easily now that we're so close to reaching our objectives. That's why I insist we should keep a very close watch on our man, as you call him. I doubt this mobilization of the Black Lagoon is just another bit of foolishness. We have to take into consideration the great expanses of water, it could be an invasion route."

"Let's not fall into the same paranoia that we're trying to implant around us, Rear Admiral."

"We shouldn't feel so secure, Mr. President. You can see already how it's been slowly escalating, coming to the surface: from the supposed anthill he climbed up to the pyramid, a height from where he permitted himself to toy with the town of Capivarí as if it were a puppet show. The Kingdom of the Black Lagoon—it was useful to our projects at first, and in a very limited territory he was exposed to the eyes of public opinion, isolated from us. A separatist isn't an accomplice. It suited our plans, agreed. But now he's carried the thing too far: showing his face in the foreign press is a subtle maneuver that must be tied in with inadmissible ends."

"It's better that he's shown his face. In that way the people won't go on believing that he's invisible and all-powerful. Now they know he's only flesh and blood, and quite a bit older."

"Not all that older, don't forget that more than twenty years have passed since his last public appearance. I think he's got something up his sleeve."

"In the picture he appears in his undershirt."

"For that very reason: nothing here, nothing there, and pow! one of these days the dove will spring out of the top hat. The dove, Mr. President! Do you realize what that would mean?"

I always go forward, forward always. Behind, all that's left—I've already said so—is my center of pleasure and a memory here and there that can't begin to disturb me. I always look on high, even though in the famous picture I seem to be looking down a little and it isn't very flattering. Who among those around me could have been the traitor? Not the Egret, I can hear him hammering and polishing and chiseling without cease, and he only stops when I send for him to take care of my most urgent urgencies. The ones I allow myself between one means of protection and another.

I've given orders that all photographic equipment found in my domains and the surrounding countryside be confiscated, although I'm aware of the futility of that operation. Just as they can focus in on me with a 2.8 lens, they can do it as easily with a telescopic gunsight. It doesn't worry me. I despise weapons and I despise poisons. Photography is a more subtle means of assassination; with photos they can work magic on me, and they've got my pictures. Now I have to concentrate on a countermeasure with mirrors.

PEOPLE OF CAPIVARÍ
TURN IN YOUR MIRRORS

I had that proclamation issued and there were no exceptions. The barber especially kicked and screamed, alleging that it would ruin his business, and how right he was. I sent two trucks to pick up the whole cargo, all the mirrors that is, absolutely all, from the three-paned ones on bureaus down to the tiny ones in women's compacts. All all, all all all all all all mirrors, even the rearview mirrors in the few cars they drive around there and the ones on tractors. I need all the mirrors, not a single one must be missing.

It caused more surprise than the matter of the cameras. It brought on a hazy, undefined fear, that business of requisitioning mirrors. And I'm glad: sowing an inexplicable fear is another one of my designs, a secondary one for now, the main one being the programming of the offensive.

They have one or two or ten or more images of me, that's all. I have in my possession *all* the others. I re-encounter myself with every step I take, I recognize myself and call myself by name. Calling myself by name with every step so as not to be dispersed, not to lose my identity, which is so much mine. The miracle of my identity will not remain in their hands, limited to those few hazy views of me in black and white. Only I know how to call myself by name, know how to be me and know how to become me. They don't even know what I really call myself, what my true name is.

With the mirrors of Capivarí, I'm covering the inside of my pyramid. Wisely spread out on the four triangular walls up to the vertex. And not in a smooth mirrored surface, but mirrors placed in myriads of facets of different shapes, sizes, orientation, which succeed in doubling multiplying fragmenting my image by repeating it to satiety. And right in the center of the pyramid, on a plumb line from the vertex, is my bed. I lie down and contemplate myself, I move and in every tiniest corner of my pyramid I'm moving. Every one of my gestures here becomes infinite. I'm everywhere.

Only I can enter this chamber of mirrors, only my image surrounds me and remains there, stays on there even though I have gone off to roam around the confines of my domains (my demons). That's it. My demons helping me in the enterprise. My incubuses and my succubuses, my poltergeists; Azazel, Luzbel, Semiazas, Asmodeus, Ayphos, Azqueel, Uzuzel; my dybbuks, my *Pombero*. They look at me with my own eyes, my thousand eyes in this pyramid of me. Where I recharge my strength.

Sitting down to write when over there, almost beside you, only a step away, innocent people are being tortured, killed, and one writes as the only possible way to counterattack. Goddamnit, what irony, what futility. What pain, above all. If I could stop other hands by stopping my hand. If my paralysis were only a little contagious, but it isn't: I stop and the others go on implacably, poking around in corners, making people disappear, without respite, without any justification whatever, because that's what it's all about, maintaining terror and oppression, so no one will feel like raising his or her head. I wonder how far this government's hunger for repression will go, what gluttony they're acting in response to, what gland it can be that secretes this indiscriminate hate, how we can ever put a halt to this chemical discharge.

Messianic, eh? I, too, am turning messianic, and there's the real contagion, the Sorcerer's impregnation. He would like to dominate the world by putting his foot on it and crushing it whenever he chooses. He hopes— through action—to destroy at whim. And I, with such a passive form of action as writing, would like to stay his hand, put an end to his influence by lapsing into total passivity, perhaps even silence. Holding back the horror by not naming it, that might be it. Gag myself? No: a gag implies knowledge forcibly silenced, censorship. And now

I realize that I don't know anything, I can't know anything, and I was deceiving myself all the while I thought it necessary to keep memory alive as a weapon of defense and enlightenment. Now I fear it's just the opposite, I fear that to name is to give life.

If I fall silent now and cross over to the other shore, maybe Alfredo Navoni will be able to come to me without running any risk and bring me the knowledge to which I have no access here and now.

Yes sir. I plant the flag, I plant the pen, I plant the written word, and maybe all that will serve me as seed someday. I leave my country, to be able to breathe freely for a time, and if Navoni still loves me, let him look for me. I'll be where he won't run any risk at all. Nor will I, for the moment. Later on, we'll see.

Who finds paper finds a pen, who finds his voice finds ears, who seeks breaks away. Finding without searching? It could be so, and therefore, Red Ant Sorcerer, lord of the Tacurú, master of drums, high priest of the Finger, owner of *The Voice*, hoarder of mirrors, probable impregnator of your own ball, taster of blood, here I leave you free to your fate, and I hope it will be the worst of fates, the one you have earned for yourself.

In this simple ceremony I abandon the pen with which, in other simple ceremonies, I took note of you. So you see. We're alike: I, too, think I have influence over others. By being silent now, I think I can make you silent. By erasing myself from the map, I intend to erase you. Without my biography, it will be as if you had never had a life. So long, Sorcerer, *felice morte*.

THREE?

How well I feel today, surrounded by myself! How free—how complete. Today I already have another face, I'm no longer the one in that terrible infamous photo. I'm going to celebrate this change of skin by submerging myself once more in

MY DREAMS OF BLOOD

which doesn't keep me at all from submerging myself in blood. The important thing is that the vital liquid not cease flowing, nourish me forever, nourish me always, for I am the sun and I grow splendid with blood. A river of blood will flow. Instigated by me. The sluiceways that I shall open to flood Capivarí will in reality be the veins of my enemies, and I think I will be lucky and there will be a lot of veins. Not arteries. The blood comes bubbling out of arteries, and I want an unbroken, constant flow. A river of blood without leaps and starts, without whirlpools, a glassy, majestic river that will continually change its course to sweep away any dike of peace that might be interposed.

As if there were anyone left to raise barriers against me, to reject me with disgust as the Intruder rejected me on a certain occasion when I explained my great dream of blood to her:

She, sitting on the elevated dais as on a pedestal, in a different heaven. She, on a throne, dressed completely as a queen, a queen on the outside and a queen inside too, sipping (I would set things up, I would get her the drink). A flexible plastic tube, transparent, the kind used in transfusions, and I would have chosen the virgin so well for her! Pink-cheeked, splendid, I would have dressed her so beautifully in white! And the Intruder up on high, scarcely making any effort at suction, which wouldn't even have been noticed, and I calming the maiden with my caresses and inserting the tube in her jugular and the red liquid starting to flow, flowing on its transparent path now and climbing and climbing until it reaches the lips of the Intruder and she is no longer an intruder, dazzling now, her lips red, sipping and sipping as the virgin in my arms grows pale, ceases to be pure, ceases to be a virgin, is emptied out completely, drained by the one up there, who is now pure, the virgin, the queen, the one nourished on blood, the warm one, the

the

party's over because there isn't a drop of blood left in the maiden and I in my position as high priest kiss first the one below, the bloodless one, and then I climb the steps to the lofty pedestal of the one who has been duplicated for me now, has been filled by the other and who gives me a red kiss, licks me with blood, adores me, red salty warm, calming my deepest thirst

and don't cry, Estrella, don't moan, come here between my hands, let me cuddle you a little, accept my caresses, and ah! if I could only kiss you, if I could only reach you with my lips, then, indeed, I would bleed myself for you, like the pelican I would tear open my craw to feed you, lick you with my own blood. I would give you my most ardent kisses, Estrella. Estrellita mine. I love you just the same, even though I can't reach you with my kisses; even though you, in turn, never bleed. Just the same, I recognize your extreme femininity and I know that you are part of me and I shall make you a son, we will make a son, you and I, I and I. I'll make myself a son who will also be part of me and I shall call him *I*. A son with whom we shall go forth—I shall go forth—to dominate the world. I himself will go along opening the way for us, leave the rest to me.

Enough of pleasures, enough, of pleasures enough and enough now of the pleasures in which we have been wallowing up until now. I don't please myself anymore, I don't applaud myself: I stay nice and quiet in my little cradle, in my great bed, which is really a gigantic crate for the most beautiful fruit, very quiet, with my knees almost touching my mouth, cradling Estrella I remain, rocking to the rhythm of myself as I circulate through my inner currents without wasting an ounce of energy in vain daydreams (in vein daydreams). I stay there, locked into myself with Estrella in my precise center, cradling Estrella, both perfect, two in one like the perfect circle of Yin and Yang. Do you realize that, Estrella, pulpy little thing, peach Estrella, sweet, velvety, warm?

The time has come for action to be restrained, we won't move so much anymore, I shan't shake you in ceremonial dances for the time being. Locked into ourselves, recycling ourselves, nothing can affect us, not even the apparent indifference of the Central Government, which now pretends to disdain us and no longer sends emissaries. They want to isolate us, ignore us, not knowing that it's exactly what we're looking for. Our new separatism is a form of self-communion so we can make love as we like and fertilize ourselves. Estrella. Adored little ball, little ball of sweetness. I'm going to take you into the jungle and cut all the flowers for you. One of them will know how to awaken you and transmit my urges to you, another will teach you to open up. You're my flower, Estrella, and I will be your pollen, your pistil. But let's keep it a secret for now.

Egret, I shout, maidens, I shout, for them to help me bottle this love I feel for Estrella; don't let love escape through my pores, and never never let my seed spill. The moment has finally arrived. I have the centrifuge ready and the freezer is going. The hands of the Egret—somewhat callused now, from so much woodworking—are going to celebrate the back-and-forth ceremonies one more time, but now without waste. My semen will be collected in test tubes and will be centrifuged and frozen while it awaits the sublime moment. And then, freed of my male part, I shall be able to devote myself successfully to hormones and develop my other aspect, the feminine one. And in that way I shall engender I, and *I* himself will be born—be reborn—to support me in my/his/our enterprise.

The Indian maidens act as a backdrop for these solemnities. They are the chorus. They move stealthily there in the distance while I try to hit them with my darts. I use a golden blowgun because I want to wound them in a deluxe way. They contort with pain. I contort with pleasure, I don't know whether from the pain I inflict on them or from the deft manipulations of my aide in spite of the fact that I have forbidden him to use his tongue.

That is, he can't lick or say a word—only work with unction and be careful in gathering my sacred sperm. Thus, my virility remains on deposit in these test tubes that are like glass phalluses and I can go along letting myself be penetrated by the female principle. My whole person, my total person will come to be Estrella so I can give myself back my seed, reintegrate myself by giving origin to I, who will be not just a doubling but a totality, in him we shall be the three-in-one: I. I will pass from one to the other of my manifestations to reach I, and there are so many who think the I doesn't exist!

Love, love, I whisper to myself as I blow the darts through the long blowgun, and if I'm lucky I stick them into the maidens' vital parts. They're love darts, of course, darts that pierce their copper skin and, with a little bit of luck on my part, will find their channel in the blood torrent and sooner or later will reach the heart, bringing on death. I will keep an eye on the Indian maidens to await that sublime moment. Women cannot survive in the Palace when I shall be the only woman, goddess of fertility and death, Hecate and Pomona, Venus Coliade, Cuetlícue, Coyoalxaoqui.

A river of blood is already flowing and it's not exactly menstrual, contaminated blood.

Afterwards, now, that is, at any point in time that holds me without care for its being simply that, time, I will busy myself passing on to the level of forgetfulness. I will harvest forgetfulness, giving myself over to non-memory so those who try to tell my story will be unable to harm me. Not even in that minimal, tiny mosquito bite which, before, perhaps, could have harmed me.

I am floating, I am in the delightful emptiness of memory as in amniotic fluid. It's as if a hand has been stayed, as if someone has stopped writing about me. I am the pure future, now, emptied of my sperm, lightened in my two auxiliary balls, given over to nothing but Estrella's palpitation. A touch of estrogen for now, later on progesterone in massive doses. The recipe appeared in

The Voice, and although I don't know who commissioned that article, I do know that it's benefited me a hundred percent, and I'm not surprised. That's why I created that newspaper, and even though sometimes bits of nonsense appear, like

I almost haven't touched mud and I am mud.

or

Everything is like a river, the work of slopes.

or

What is paid for with our life is never dear.

I recognize that it's a matter of clumsy typographical errors that in no way cloud my good name or the respect I deserve. My readers know quite well that *nothing* is worth or can be worth or ever will be worth more than my life, and they also know that my river pays no heed to watersheds and flows where I decide, for the simple reason that it flows with blood.

As for mud, I have my reserves. I, who've learned to read between the lines in my newspaper, I, the recipient of its full message, have mixed feelings regarding this pronouncement. I certainly have touched mud, but I'm not mud for a very good reason. Quite the opposite, I'm what is prominent and dry, unless they mean primordial clay and then, yes, I am mud, I am the one who creates everything and out of which everything emerges. I shall show that even before I engender *I* himself.

In the meantime, let's have some blind workmen come and cover over my chamber of mirrors. It's already fulfilled its function of protecting my image. My image is different now, it's in full mutation, and no one will be able to attack this my new image: it will be the repository of all tenderness.

"Blind men, I said! blind from birth. I want my

chamber of mirrors to be covered over by skillful hands, not by the clumsy hands of people who were once used to seeing."

"Men blind from birth aren't to be found in this region, Master. Those blind at birth never reach adulthood here—who can save his tender life if he can't see vultures? Can a blind child see the pit viper that sneaks up and poisons him? Do you think, Master, that anyone without the sharpest sight could survive in these lands? All of us here are relatives of the lynx, we have extra-sharp eyes. Those of us who are left, I mean."

That's what the Indian maidens charged with getting the team together allege. The Egret, on the other hand, so sweet, imbued with my teachings, suggests:

"Let's pluck out the eyes of four of our Capivarí peasants. Some of them are skilled with the lasso, there are accomplished weavers of eight-folded braids like the Lizard's Tail. Some of them can clip horses with their eyes closed. Blinded, they'll be able to do a great job."

Today I'm in a generous mood, and besides, I need men who really know how to work in the dark. There mustn't be even a drop of light in my chamber of mirrors when strange presences enter. Mirrors that will hold only my image, mirrors that must not be broken or scratched but kept forever. If men blind from birth don't turn up, I'll find other solutions, I have no end of resources.

Waiting for the idea that will blossom very soon, I carefully follow the recipes that are unwittingly offered to me by my newspaper. There has just appeared, for example, an article on synthetic hormones. German scientists believe that synthetic hormones ingested by a mother produce offspring with a high degree of social aggressiveness. What good news! Not that there's any risk of a child of mine turning out too peaceful, but it's best to be absolutely sure. I've ordered several gross of di-

237

ethylstilbestrol ampules, DES to the initiate, and I've begun to inject myself with them. I rub some on Estrella so she will absorb the hormone through her pores and will in turn become aggressive, predisposed.

DES is my ally now, as is *Proginon Estradiol* too, another of the compounds that my newspaper offers me on a platter.

Somebody is going around giving the Sorcerer the answers and encouraging him in his enterprise, but he refuses to look into it. He likes subordinates, not accomplices, and this apparent ally who week after week goes along opening the doors to transformation for him is almost like a brother who knows and stimulates his secret. They are apparently scattered items that appear in *The Voice*, but he knows that they're directed personally and unmistakably at him. None of the three editors he has had brought in from the other capital, who only follow his directives, could have selected them. Or any other person who has access to the newspaper. Who, then? Some angel fallen from heaven or from hell with the sole aim of applauding his enterprise.

WAS KING TUTANKHAMEN
REALLY A MAN?

Were the Egyptian pharaohs kings, queens, or both at the same time?

Scientists the world over have been asking that ostensibly senseless question. Let one consider, for example, Tutankhamen and the three pharaohs who preceded him. Did they really possess the breasts with which the art of their period has so generously adorned them? Was Akhenaten—who appears in one work without genitals—abnormal at birth, castrated in battle, or is the statue unfinished?

These disturbing questions have arisen because at least the last four pharaohs of the eighteenth dynasty are depicted with effeminate traits. Some investigators have advanced medical hypotheses such as glandular disorders, but others allege that such disorders would not explain the androgynous quality of the four.

At the present time, scientists in Delaware claim that the pharaohs suffered from—or enjoyed—a hereditary condition that bestowed ample breasts and generous hips upon men. A condition that goes by the name of incomplete pseudohermaphroditism, type 1.

Properties of mud

I remember that phrase, which I had cast aside. *I have never touched mud and I am mud.* I think that's how it went, that's how it went, I'm sure. Generative and curative mud, and therefore I am mud and I can remodel myself as I see fit.

Not soft unctuous and fertile mud, not for now; that will come later. I'm gritty clay, the kind that Adam was molded out of, mud to begin over again.

In a certain corner of the black lagoons there is an auspicious clay-like zone. In the company of the Egret, he takes up boating again and goes in search of the silent sawmen who have spent the last months on a binge on an island. Strong booze at night and women at dawn—the sawmen are no longer what they used to be, and now when they see him arrive they do not lower their eyes as a sign of respect but light firecrackers to celebrate him. Because the Lord and Master never comes alone, the Lord and Master always brings new ideas that stimulate the imagination and enrich the festivities.

This time the Master gives them little reason for celebration and drives the women off. Out, witches, out, out, witches, he shouts at them furiously, and chases them off the island with lashes. They know how to swim, but it's a long distance to the mainland and if the wind doesn't take pity on them and bring them a floating island many will perish on the way. The Sorcerer pays no attention to such trifles. The four sawmen let him do it without defending the women—they're obedient men—and when he orders them to get into the canoe, they know it isn't to rescue those small dark heads that are getting lost in the distance.

The sun has already risen fully and the Sorcerer doesn't want to disturb the still air with the roar of an outboard motor. The long canoe is ideal: one sawman rowing in the stern and another in the bow, with the other two holding up the canopy. And the Egret at his feet, licking his soles.

The surface of the lagoon is one more mirror for him, but he's not thinking of the remodeling of the pyramid now. This lagoon is a polished mirror that, instead of reflecting, swallows his image. To transform it in the depths, to return it changed into another, this is the real reason for the trip.

The bright boat ride brings them to the resplendent zone of the ditch reeds. They're not tall rushes with the soul of a curtain, no. Here there are only low bulrushes that maintain a precise crystallized individuality. These rays of a brand-new sun that reach him at water level give the bulrushes a golden splendor and are the same rays that a little farther on will turn the crests of the cattails silver, a delicate sea of silver that waves in the breeze. And the Sorcerer, paying no attention whatever to the morning glow, accepts it with the natural air of one who knows he deserves much more than that.

it's a tanager
it's an *aguapeazú*
it's a little *pituhué* dove

it's an owner of the sun
a cardinal
a blackbird
an oriole, that nest

They might well be all those names and many more,
with the gaudiest feathers in the world; they will need
colors to shine, splendid songs. I shall sink myself into humility without colors and without song, I shall transform
myself into a bird that is very much ours: I will be the
ovenbird, I will cover myself with mud, my own nest
around me, enveloping me, my new form that the Egret
will know how to mold. Egret promoted from carpenter to
potter, Potter of God, my nest around me so I can bloom.

"What about the cradle, Master? It's almost finished."

"The cradle is for later, don't worry about it. And
don't call me Master. It's a name from the past now."

And I gave minute instructions so nothing would distract me during the ritual.

You can call me My Queen

He's standing in very transparent water that barely
reaches his ankles. The bottom doesn't stir, doesn't bub-
ble up or suck him in. It's a hieratic depth from which the
Egret is drawing handfuls of mud without roiling the
water at all. Mud that he deposits methodically on the
Sorcerer, daubing him, sculpting on him—first one, then
the other—a pair of beautiful teats with erect and ready
nipples. And with clay the Egret slowly models him
downward: generous hips that stand out and make the
waist narrow, little by little a prominent pubis that shows

off Estrella, covering the ones to either side. White-hot thighs, well-turned calves.

My Queen, the Egret sighs and tries to caress him— but that lump of clay, which is slowly drying, cracking, doesn't invite a caress. It invites wonder, yes, perplexity. And an ecstatic gaze.

"You like me, eh? I'm the sculpted figure of an *almost* complete woman because the water is my vassal. She not only reflects me, she defends me, too, did you notice? You haven't been able to go on modeling me. The whole calf, yes, almost down to the ankle, down to water level. And under the water I'm the one I've been all along. Never an idol with feet of clay, but quite the opposite: I'm clay with the feet of an idol, with my usual feet, firm feet to step over anyone who stands in my way. But tell me, how is it that you know so much about female bodies, you shitty little fag? And do you think you're the Creator now that you've modeled me out of mud like the other one? You'll soon see who gives the orders here."

And then and there the clay-covered Sorcerer expelled a terrific fart that made the waters tremble, fragmenting his image into a thousand pieces. And the poor bed of reeds—which, with the sun on high now, was no longer golden but mere overly dry straw—burned for days on end.

Counterdance and dance, ecstatic unrestraint, the sound of the drums, a few thin flutes—penetrating—

243

sharp fiddles the fiddlers rest against their plexuses to transmit the sounds of their insides to them. Everyone dances as they play their instruments, and the Sorcerer dances more than anyone, and all venerate the glow that comes to them from far away, from the waters that are on fire. The horizon doesn't change color, it's a constant burning sunset from morning till night, and even during the night, celebrated with the dance.

With the dance the Sorcerer is losing his mold of a woman, little by little pieces of dry clay are falling, pulling off his body hair and other virile roughnesses.

Like a chicken cooked in mud, the Sorcerer is slowly coming out of his shell, and what blooms now is his new and female pulp. His flesh has been learning something from the mold and has become juicy, hairless, tender, and his brimming breasts now point to the glow of the fire, and Estrella seems to reign in solitude.

Indian maidens, sawmen, and other serfs of the Tacurú and the Pyramid, all dance for that miraculous metamorphosis, and the Sorcerer dances more than anyone, leaps twists shakes his hips to get rid of the last traces of his shell, bringing back a waving of the pelvis unknown to him before.

An ancient memory is revived behind his present memory that is being erased. He dances to rid himself of past rubble and also because he knows that in the future he will dance no more, for a good while at least, until the birth of the son who will carry him to the great dance of the world, to conquest.

The raft dam of reeds goes on burning and the rushes burn, the cattails, the canebrakes, the bamboo, the beds of straw. So much the better. There'll be no more straw in the world now that I can't even touch myself.

From animals burned to a crisp comes a smell of meat roasted in its own skin that stimulates the appetite.

Fine. Today I will eat all I can and much more. I will vomit and eat and vomit until I'm weary. Later on, I'll watch my diet when the time for gestation is signaled. Soon.

The glow awakens what's asleep and something seems to be stretching in the jungle on the other side of the river beyond the frontier. The men of Zone 3 are peaceful because they still haven't received new orders regarding the floodgates of the dam and they can devote themselves, without any interference, to hunting and the other pleasures of the waiting. Because of this relaxation of discipline, they haven't even raised their eyes to detect the glow, nor have they lowered them enough to detect that something is slowly slipping away from them out of the camp like water through their fingers. With their eyes fixed on where they can place their bullets, the men of Zone 3 let slip away from them one, two, three four five six 730-Wrinkles. The old woman with powers.

Something is calling her to that very distant glimmer of fire, and she crawls through the jungle dampness, losing sight of it—because of the trees that close over her head—but in every one of her wrinkles she hears the crackling of the flaming straw.

This matter of appeals, calls. Others also perceive it in spite of the fact that they are quite safe after crossing more southerly boundaries. And they, too, decide to stick their noses in where perhaps they're being called. They are three: a corpulent man in white, another who seems to have become a part of his hood-like white mask, and a woman with curly black hair. They set out in a woodcutter's launch and head upriver, against the current.

In Capivarí there is a pause. The Central Government is combing the entire country for a certain fugitive leader. The name and description of Alfredo Navoni flood the radio and TV stations, as well as the newspapers, sometimes describing him as dressed all in black. No one in Capivarí takes any notice. Those events have nothing to do with the Kingdom of the Black Lagoon, and they don't appear in *The Voice*. The country, under general mobilization, can fall apart if it wants to: in Capivarí and in the neighborhood of the Tacurú and the Pyramid, dead calm reigns. The Sorcer is wrapped up in itself, machinating. Now neither man nor woman, nothing but transition, s/he can't be classified and new genders and new pronouns have to be invented. Not neuter ones, because there is nothing neuter about the Sorcer. Mutant pronouns are needed.

All the while, the Sorcer ponders the best way to nullify the mirrors on the inside of the pyramid without destroying the masculine image, which has remained inscribed there. Those mirrors contain the Sorcer when s/he was only he, and as long as they remain there, the Sorcer can't return to the pyramid, under threat of contamination. Nor can the Sorcer or anyone else be reflected again in those mirrors, which have to remain sanctified, held in a moment and a reflection. What can be done, then, so the Sorcer can return to the comfortable pyramidal womb? As always, the Sorcer comes up with the most perfect solution. The Tent!

A huge tent will be built, also pyramidal, which, set

up inside the chamber, will serve as a curtain. A magnificent white theater curtain for the grand finale: the birth.

What are the people of Capivarí up to, going about absentminded, not even making an offering? The days of selfishness are over. Now they will have to donate all the white cloth in their possession: mantillas for mass, lace-trimmed tablecloths, white Indian tunics if they have any (they don't deserve them), embroidered handkerchiefs, petticoats, white shirts. No sheets. By no means. Nothing that smells of sex, of a vaguely shared misfortune. Only the finest cloth, lacework, embroidery, trim, things made of the purest white, purified in the sun, which will serve to fend off these mirrors pregnant with images. And if the Sorcer is still feeling magnanimous—at this moment s/he is, but that might not last—there will be a donation from what was requisitioned from the former shrine of the Dead Woman: an altar cloth, a wedding gown from among the most faded, the ones the Sorcer doesn't wear.

The Capivarians will sew the different pieces of bright white cloth together—wearing dark glasses, so as not to be dazzled—and when the tent is finally ready, in the exact shape and measurements, a few chosen people will enter the pyramid in the deepest darkness and place it by feel, covering the walls of mirrors.

Another layer of Capivarian donations for this milfoil sanctuary. For the Thousandmen flower.

As far as the Sorcer is concerned (the ex-Sorcerer, the great mutant), there seems to be no separation between the word and the deed. As soon as they are mentioned, actions are put into practice. As with the verb *to swear*: it's enough for it to be uttered for the act to be formalized. The inhabitants of Capivarí and neighboring territories are therefore already sewing away in the broad and desolate town square. The women use silk thread, the men baling needles and twine to sew up flour sacks. Meantime, the Sorcer's men go up and down the streets, requisitioning everything that seems appropriate: from a bride's tulle to the smallest handkerchief embroidered with your hair if your hair is white, because in the fashioning of this white tent of purity not the slightest touch of disgust can be attached.

And Capivarí, in the silence of this shared compulsive sewing, is turning into the hub of the world. Forces are converging on the tiny town, now beginning to take on grandeur. It is now Cap. and not just of the rather indefinite Kingdom of the Black Lagoon. And all this even though the glow has gone out. The fire from the Great Master Fart has ended up consuming the straw patches that marked off the lagoons, and only a few sad floating islands were saved. The underwater roots did survive, though the barrage is still there. The paradise of the pit viper and the boa constrictor will return, but in the meantime vultures have turned into waterfowl and are diving to devour the toasted remains of the last swamp deer.

Weep, hunters of the marshes. No longer will you go out with your stepladders and plant them among the reeds to spot your prey from above. There are no more reeds and no more prey. The Lord of this region—now an indefinable *L*—has altered the ecological balance. As corresponds to its high and rather destructive thaumaturgical properties.

The lagoons are blacker, more tranquil than ever

248

because the wind no longer sways their blond tresses. The fugitives, on the other hand, are more restless than ever. They no longer have any place to hide, it's better for them to give up and give in to this kingdom of the Sorcer, who is upsetting everything.

They go to the Cap., the fugitives, the runaways, the ones fleeing the police and seeking the protection of the now-burned canebrakes. And silently they approach the main square (the only one) and sit in some rather inconspicuous corner and start sewing along with the others. They have nothing to fear. They've taken to the wilds for crimes that aren't condemned in this new kingdom where only disrespect to the *L* is cause for condemnation.

Reintegrated, then, useful to society once more, rapists, murderers, those sweet creatures sew prolifically on the pyramidal tent, and every so often they improvise a piece of embroidery. Like someone whistling under his breath.

Cap. is a magnet that attracts many.

Upriver comes the woodcutter's launch with the three mysterious characters. And through the jungle? More mysterious yet is the crawling that is becoming greenish, integrated. Amid trees growing inside or atop other trees, under gigantic leaves that serve as a roof when the rains are of long duration, 730-Wrinkles advances and, for no apparent reason, chooses to feed only on mushrooms.

In Capivarí the tent keeps on growing and taking shape, although a great many feet of cloth are still lacking.

A great many feet, and nice white cloth becoming

scarce. A certain fear arises. Schoolmaster Cernuda, who is in charge of the operation, sends an SOS to the Tacurú.

The Sorcer then strips the Indian maidens of their tunics. Strips the Egret, who, as his name indicates, is clad in white, and after some reflection consents to give away some of his own supply. A loaded dump truck goes to Capivarí and pours its contents out onto one side of the square. A cataract of white cloth that is received with jubilation.

Sewing is a way of praying. Praying is connecting the loose scraps of the Mystery with an invisible seam. The Capivarians pray with their hands, with the tender shuttle of the needles. In some way they're brothers and sisters of those downriver who are praying at the new Shrine of the Dead Woman, secretly asking for peace (while bullets fly in the south, while there are still sirens and raids and disappearances). In Capivarí, peace isn't even mentioned, it's a forbidden word, but the white stitching and the rivers of white cloth may be a way of attempting to absorb the river of blood that is flowing from the old prophecy.

An air of calm reigns in Capivarí for a moment at least. Until a newcomer, a very old, very wrinkled woman, sitting to one side of that wavy sea of white cloth, exclaims: "That's my wedding dress! I took it to the altar of the Dead Woman more than forty years ago, the old altar. What's it doing here?"

Miracles don't retreat, offerings advance in sanctity, they never return to the hands of the one who offered them. Anathema. Anathema.

And to think how they had cheered the arrival of the truck that brought them this unpleasantness from the Tacurú! Other items from the Shrine were being found by the old woman, and people began to raise a ruckus. What should they do, then, put the relics back into the remodeled Shrine or just sew them up into the tent ordered by the Sorcer, L of the Tacurú and the Pyramid, Pre-eminent Personage of the Black Lagoon?

"We're going to have to sew them in, that's all. We're running out of cloth, and the tent has to be finished as quickly as possible. Tremendous catastrophes will befall us if we don't hurry."

In spite of these well-founded fears, the old woman refuses to give up the items whose origin she knows. What once belonged to the Shrine of the Dead Woman must return, and there's nothing more to be said. But the old woman agrees to replace the cloth, inch for inch.

(They make a bundle, they put it in a plastic bag and send it downriver on a raft. They're sure that the followers of the Dead Woman will recover it at the mouth of the river and take it to the New Shrine, happy at regaining some of the emblems of yearned-for times gone by.)

730-Wrinkles then gets ready to keep her promise of replacing the cloth. Even though she sometimes lies—she had never even dreamed of getting married, why should she?—she will never defraud her people.

And while the others go on sewing very slowly so that their cloth and their hope will not give out all at once, the old woman goes to the tumbledown shed where a few linotype machines from *The Voice* lie abandoned. And once there, in the darkest corner, she rummages through the tow and not only pulls out the whitest fleece but also carries on a dialogue, and it's almost as if she were talking to herself. But she listens, listens, and to the rhythm of a very faint voice she goes along spinning the tow and then weaves it. She creates a goodly piece of cloth with a rather open but strong weave that will soon form part of the tent, bearing the words that had been exchanged in that ineffable encounter.

There are still some blank spaces. The transparent tulles and the lace edgings have been rejected by the Sorcer's men. It's not a tent to see through. The one they're sewing in Capivarí is a tent to hide things, to separate.

Only a few gaps before the work is finished. And the three strangers who have arrived in Capivarí, presumably by way of the river, gaze in amazement at the white cloak that covers the square and the neighboring corrals. They would like to be accepted and are doubtless going to make a contribution. The woman takes off her petticoat, the tall man hands over something white that's a cross between a hood and a mask. Schoolmaster Cernuda feels an inexplicable reverence as he accepts that last gift, and decides that all the openings must be sewn up so that it won't be rejected: three stitches for each eye, nine for the mouth, and the ears have to be closed, too. That's the motto for the time being. See not, hear not, speak not. Just wait.

Finally the heavyset man gets undressed in silence. He's garbed in white from head to toe, and one by one he donates his clothes. Avid hands take them from his hands and swiftly sew them onto the tent, before he changes his mind; they go along like that, filling in the gaps until the work is finished.

This tent has denuded many people. It has despoiled people like crazy. But there is only one truly naked person left, standing statuesque, almost a monument, in the center of the now white square of Capivarí. Like a snow-covered square, and he a copper statue, irreverent

naked

mast erect

Until the truck from the Tacurú arrives and takes away the tent, leaving him alone, inconspicuous now, blending in with the earth.

Blending in with the earth, the Caboclo de Mar? Yes. These are topsy-turvy times.

For that reason, it's no surprise either to learn of the other two peacefully sipping maté with schoolmaster Cernuda under the willows and chatting about essential things—the weather and the crops, calves, the black-faced sheep, good for swampy terrain—as if the tent had never been made. As if the fugitives had not volunteered to hang it up blindfolded.

The Sorcer immediately accepted their offer and left the task in their hands, in full confidence. Men outside the law who had spent the best years of their lives hiding in backwaters. Who better than they to cover up shine and to move in darkness? They didn't break a single one of the hundreds of thousands of mirrors, and finally on a certain day the Sorcer was able to return to the pyramidal nest, cloaked in white. Then they lighted all the oil lamps and it looked like the inside of a gigantic meringue, but the Sorcer recognized certain familiar reflections that escaped through the finest weave and was reminded of the bejeweled throne room—the cathedral of salt—or of certain parts of the lagoons at a particular hour of the day.

253

The white tent separates the old, more or less virile image of the Sorcer, deposited forever in the mirrors, from this new figure that takes delight in mutations and is beginning to demand its gift.

The hour has been sounded! The hour has been sounded, the Sorcer exclaims in a high-pitched voice, trying to assume completely the new role of receptive female.

The hour has been sounded

and the Sorcer hesitates between officiating at a grand ceremony or celebrating his auto-communion in the greatest intimacy. He opts for the latter, and the Egret, the sacristan, surrounds the Sorcer with incense. Naked now, the Egret, having donated his clothing to the construction of the cloth pyramid, can't get dressed again for a time without infringing on the laws of the Black Lagoon (laws as changeable as the waters themselves).

The Egret, naked now, sacristan of that ceremony, feels divine. He has finished his cradle, the ritual of wood. Now he begins the ritual of water. It will be his hand— and nothing else, more's the pity—that will officiate in the theocopulation.

The Sorcer so soft now, so caressable finally, smooth as s/he waits, all dressed in white, concentrating only on that sublime ball that the Egret thought was just a testicle but which, now he knows, has the name of Estrella.

Grown already, Estrella, star of the first magnitude, occupying all visible space and especially at ease in the other space, the invisible. Estrella is also like the earth, round, and wrinkled in places, and there she is, like the earth, ready to receive the seed.

He, the Egret, will officiate as sower, and even if the seed is not his own—he has already melted against his chest one of the test tubes in which the generative liquid

254

had been deposited—he is aware of the ineffable privilege of being present at such an event.

This is the third stage in the consummation of my marriage to Estrella, the Sorcer thinks, and so-called reality is already becoming dim and all s/he is pure consummation.

Meantime, the Egret is preparing elements that have the splendor of simplicity. A syringe for vaccinating cattle with a pressure jet, and the odorless, colorless, tasteless compound to which the ex-Sorcerer had devoted his attention more than a thousand years before. A liquid akin to distilled water, which had failed as a solvent of the uteri of others but which will now fulfill the new mission of softening Estrella and awakening her disposition.

Nothing happens at the sublime instant of the mingling of the sacred sperm with the liquid, it's a time of pure respect: not even a spark to break the heavy calm. And the spermatozoa must feel happy wriggling in the liquid, leaping about again, and their happiness can be smelled in the air as the sacristan prepares the liturgical instruments with unction.

The injection has been given. 20 cc. The Theocopulation. Now the Sorcer in the huge bed of the pyramid sleeps a well-deserved sleep among pillows, and the Egret, his hands empty but his heart overflowing, strolls through the twists and turns of the Tacurú, planning the building of a baby carriage.

I'll take him out for a stroll. I'll be his nursemaid. Let his motherfather teach him about duty, I'll have him touch pleasure with his own hand.

Transvestite, transsexual, sodomite, catamite Sorcerer, witchdoc, magician of mere hormonal transformations, necromant of confused gonads, warlock, no one even dares write about you anymore, who points at you now? Who looks at you, who follows you with one eye and handles you a little and sometimes tells about you, orally, because your story no longer even deserves to be written?

You're lucky always to find someone at your service, waiting for some obscure recompense that might well be your annihilation.

I am the fathermother neuron, the being in the White Pyramid repeats, and although s/he no longer says Mirror am I, look into me, the transparency will be found in my image which is in the purity of one who suspects and is, s/he takes the spell by the tail and insists and insists: my flatus is land and my lessened palpitations oceans and skies. I am the fathermother neuron

and soon I will be motherfatherchild and then no one will be able to come and take my place. There will be no more presidents, no more generals, isn't that just what so many people want? There will be me, only me and I, and I don't know whether I shall allow my son to be separated from me or whether I shall retain I himself forever in my innards.

Now I shall be my own son, as once I was my own father. And without the help of any woman, without the support of hostile powers. I will remain in this white cloister of mine for the ten lunations established by natural law—the only law I choose to respect from time to time. The Egret will be my feeding tube, he will nourish me from his mouth to my mouth, and every so often he will oversee a new inoculation to keep Estrella contented.

Estrella. Beginning to grow slowly but inexorably in the secret of the pyramid. And the Egret, who notices it, brings more and more food to the recumbent figure, giving it food that is already chewed so that the divine person will not waste energy. He puts the food into the other's mouth with his tongue, and it looks like a kiss. They are kisses. Of devotion to the Divinity, who must be kept lubricated and content.

Massages with precious oils, much kneading of the incipient breasts that will in due time grow to Estrella. The Egret attends to the Divinity without allowing himself a moment of rest. He rehearses his role of nursemaid and bathes and powders the Divinity, with special attention to that stomach so round that is swelling little by little, turning into a sun around which the planet Earth will spin.

Oils of the finest almonds, so that the skin of the sun will not break or develop stretch marks. A skin ever softer, more elastic, expanding more and more as it receives with fruition the new injections.

As Estrella grows, expectations grow in the Kingdom of the Black Lagoon, as well as in the nation that surrounds and includes it. The separation between one and the other is unclear, and on hearing that a military convoy is on its way to Capivarí, the three strangers disappear without a trace. There are two frontiers that can be crossed with some impunity in that part of the world, although one can never count on anything.

The Voice doesn't mention the advance, arrival, and subsequent departure of the military convoy, and the journalists, who no longer receive directives from the Tacurú, busy themselves writing about their respective fields of interest. As none of them is personally involved in the matters of magic they had been obliged to write about, the impact of the newspaper diminishes until it disappears, and little by little Capivarí recovers its rural calm. In spite of the military contingents that pass through the town with growing frequency, headed north. And later, headed south, coming back from their fruitless, mournful hunt.

And in Capivarí it is as if nothing is happening. Though the search is becoming a thorough affair. The remotest farmhouse is gone over with a fine-tooth comb, and interrogations are frequent and repeated. But nobody knows anything.

"We haven't seen any suspicious stranger, who would want to show up in this barren place? Not a sturdy man in white, or woman, either. Yes. We took a good look at their photographs. They keep showing them to us. We haven't got the slightest idea. You can hit us harder, if that makes you happy, what can we do, what do you want us to say?"

"Yes, we sewed up some white cloth. No, they weren't shrouds. No, nothing to do with politics. We didn't write anything on them."

"No. We're not worshippers of the Dead Woman. No, we didn't know that the cult had been declared illegal, but that doesn't concern us, we're far from all that."

"Yes, we know the ancient prophecy. 'A river of blood will flow, and then twenty years of peace will come.' I wonder what they mean by that business of a river of blood? And what kind of peace?"

"No. We're not separatists. All that nonsense about the Kingdom of the Black Lagoon is somebody's idea of a joke. Nobody consulted us."

"To vote? What's that?"

"Alfredo Navoni? This is the first time we've ever heard the name."

"Umbanda? Is that some kind of food?"

"A woman writer? Don't be funny, women don't know how to write."

During the interrogations, one lost his tongue, another lost three fingers. No one lost his patience. No one talked.

Where could the relics be, they wondered afterwards, if the shrine had been declared illegal? And where had the rebellion gone, if there was any of it left?

What about the old woman's bundle? You remember, the bridal clothes that she wouldn't let us sew into the tent. They've probably drifted down the river and are being worn now by some of the hundreds of corpses it seems they've tossed into the river, with their bellies opened up so they won't float. Or with lead weights on their feet if they were thrown alive out of a helicopter. Well, they at least died standing up.

"Hey, if the woman turns out to be a writer, the one with the curly hair, do you think we'll come out in a book?"

"I don't think we're going to come out in anything. We're not even coming out of this one."

Delirium

Why are the spiders coming to visit me? I didn't summon them to my white pyramid, and there they are, all black, all crouching, disgusting, to one side of the web of lace that's my web, woven for me, it's no spiderweb, it's webbing to entrap other bloodless monstrosities that wouldn't nourish spiders. What do the hairy things want of me? They want to leap on me and they fix their eyes on me, their four eyes, their ten eyes, their Idontknowhowmany spider eyes, they look at me and I close my own beautiful eyes, just the two of them, the ones that have their quite personal way of seeing, and even though I close my eyes, the spiders stay there, usurping my web. They look at me through my own closed eyelids, they scrutinize me, and I close my eyelids tighter and tighter until the spiders with eyes and legs and hair and everything disappear, but what doesn't go away, doesn't go away at all, is the cramp, the tugging in what was once my Estrella and is now my womb, rather low, I admit, but round, bulging, a womb that gives me cramps, and I know they're not birth pangs, I'm not giving birth yet, I stay here and I shout. No, I don't shout, even if I wanted to and even if no one can hear me, I don't shout, it's the son who's growing inside me that's kicking, and I have to allow that son to grow in the greatest silence. Not break it with a shout. This is the happy pain of procreation. The essential demiurgy.

I'm not going to laugh, either. A laugh of mine could break the mirrors hidden behind the lacework, and then the spiders will indeed appear, will become myriads of quicksilver spiders, devourers of ants. I don't want that.

I'm the only one around here who can devour ants, I kick open the anthills and I eat the larvae. Bright white, the little larvae, sticking to each other like that embroidery there on the left, why is the embroidery moving, who gave the larvae permission to come to life? I'm in my pyramid, my magnetic field, my circle, I'm in my total protection and not in the middle of the desolate countryside, why are the reeds quivering, then, why are they rocking? Stop moving, you're making me sick! stop moving! I tell them, you shitty threads, you devil's spittle, getting unstuck and floating in the air, carrying away the air, consuming it. It's the threads those rags were joined together with, who authorized them to sew with devil's spit? Where'd they get it from? I close my eyes and I can concentrate on the slow growth of my womb, bubbling. Air bubbles are growing in the almost liquid clay of my Estrella, and the bubbles are bursting, dismembering me. If I open my eyes I see arms and legs hanging from the vertex of my pyramid, they're not mine, therefore they drip that thick liquid onto my bed and I can't move, Estrella is like an anchor, a ballast, a lead ball to sink me, and the liquid is covering me, I'm drowning now. I'm drowning!

With my eyes closed, I drown more than with my eyes open. With my eyes open, I see a part of the tent where the weave is thinner and there, precisely there, the Machi's face appears as she sticks out her tongue and mocks me. Many are mocking me from the lacework, from the white cloth.

When the Egret comes in to feed me, they all hide, but they reappear afterwards amid more laughter. I don't want to ask the Egret to stay with me and hold my hand. The Dead Woman never asked for a hand, and she must be there feeding the ghosts, sending me those visions in order to form *I*. For him I must bear them and suck them in, incorporate them into my convulsed system. *I* himself must be warlike and fearless, from here on he must grow accustomed to facing reality and also the irrealities that become detached from reality like shavings.

All these visions belong totally and absolutely to me, I must recognize that. Recognize them. Accept them, swallow them. Some show up who want to grasp me, swallow me perhaps, and each hand has six fingers and another finger appears and finally I know: it's the seventh finger, the seventh seal. The Seal.

Do I know whose corpse that is, all tied with rope like a roast, which is being eaten by bright white worms, the brocade of a bridal gown? The thongs that bind it move the skeleton like a marionette. Saint Death isn't alien to me, everything belongs to me. The skeleton dances and I dance with him to the rhythm of the bright white threads, I dance and I contort, the fingers point at me, I'm dislocated in the dance

"Divinity, wake up, Divinity, wake up, you're dreaming and it might be bad for you. You're shaking too much. It might interrupt the gestation."

"Nothing's been interrupted by nothing and you're interrupting my sleep," I shout at the Egret, but under my breath I thank him. He brings me to the surface and then my pyramid appears just hung with white curtains that aren't terrifying at all.

The Egret is unaware of my torment, my delirium. He can only love me with hazy (lazy) purity, bathe me once again, caress me and anoint me. "It's getting bigger and more beautiful every day. It looks magnificent."

With his words and his attentions, the Egret drives off the horror, and then I begin to miss the horror. That's why I propose to him: "Why don't you bring in one of the younger maidens, put her up on the foot of my bed and lash her with the Lizard's Tail whip that provides so much pleasure?"

The poor fellow can't think of anything but the scandal: "Bring women into the sacred precincts? It would be sacrilege."

"All right, calm down, calm down. Bring in one of the fugitives who volunteered to re-cover the chamber. Now that they've got nothing else to do, they must be loitering about the Palace getting drunk."

"No, Divinity, please, let's not touch them, they're our best allies."

"And what do I want with allies? Don't question my orders. Pick out a good one, a healthy one, and give it to him hard until the blood flies. I want to spatter these overly immaculate walls with blood. They give off a glare."

Oh, my God, my God, the Egret sobs, tugging at my feet. My God, my God—and he knows that I've forbidden those imprecations—I took such care with the details, he sobs and sobs, I personally inspected the tent and at a spot where I found a tiny drop of blood because someone had pricked a finger I made them cut out the piece and sew it up again. I gave my whitest clothes—now I have to stain all that pureness.

And then, still sniffling: "If blood is what you need, Divinity, you can do what you want to with me. You can bite the hand that feeds you, you can bite the lips that give you food and suck out my blood."

"Go fuck yourself!"

But I should have done it in the end. Biting him and chewing him up. Only blood can erase these monsters that come back to claim me when the Egret goes and leaves me to my phantoms.

Seven inoculations have been given to Estrella, who is the size of a watermelon now, and the success of my project—I must confess—worries me. Now Estrella is going along marking the days for me, with her growing volume she shows me the passage of time, which I always disdained.

And the monsters who break away from the cloth to harass me take advantage of my new sensibility. And they're all creatures of my own harvest. I identify them one by one. I had that one's fingernails pulled out and then I had his hands cut off and now he's threatening me with the stumps as if they were fists. I myself put a mouse in that one's vagina so it would slowly gnaw at her and now there's that huge black hollow like a mouth that wants to devour me. I don't shout, I don't twist, I contemplate, recognize, and challenge them. Do they think I can't identify them, individualize them? Do they think I'm so indifferent? Even if they can't show me the results, I know quite well what punishments I've gone about inflicting, and to whom, and I remember down to the smallest detail the act of inflicting the punishment and to what point it was deserved.

But they don't even let me take delight in the memory. Quite the contrary. It's as if they'd wanted to give me back the attention paid, and I feel that it's me the torturers are now dismembering and I'm the one getting the electric shocks. Everything burns me, and even though I didn't want to cry out, didn't want to remember and enjoy myself, it's me it's me burning in torture to the point of flying into a thousand pieces, and this tent is closing in on me, tightening until it crushes me with its spit-covered rags that are like icy white clothes that triple the burning instead of easing it.

Egret, I shout, Egret, with my mouth open and at the top of my lungs, at the risk of shattering the mirrors and covering myself with a rain of quicksilver, and the tent, tiny, tiny now, becoming my shroud.

"Egret, faithful and efficient servant, the moment has arrived."

"Oh, oh, oh, the moment for birth, what shall we do? I'm so afraid! I'm going to boil some water, I'm going to get the cradle ready, I'm going to sterilize the diapers, I'm going to . . ."

"What birth, what birth! Stop that senseless fluttering. I still don't know whether I'm going to allow such a birth to occur or whether I'll keep my son inside me so we can be more complete."

"The womb will keep growing."

"Of course. I/we will keep growing, I'll be immeasurable."

No, the moment that has arrived is the one for restoring me to the world, I have to give my subjects back the happiness of looking at me. You have to organize everything, and quickly, because I want to be taken out of here as soon as possible and carried up to the top of the pyramid. They'll have to construct a majestic litter to raise me up to the top. Get help from the sawmen, the fugitives, everybody you've got on hand. When night falls, they'll light torches and enthrone me on cushions. I want the platform of my pyramid to be well adorned, because I shall reign there until further notice.

"General Durañona sends word that the process of Re—"

"No interruptions! The only process is this process of generation that I am involved in."

"But it so happens that production for the milit—"

"There's only one production: that of the Sublime Son."

"There is threat of a popular upris—"

"Uprising? The only thing rising up will be me when I feel like it, when I rise up on my feet above everybody."

Just because I'm stationed at my base camp for the moment, outsiders have no right whatever to come here and bother me. My Condition requires a most absolute calm, and these inconsiderate emissaries come to disturb it and talk to me about a popular uprising, when I can't even get my head to rise up.

And quite naturally. They're taking advantage because they find me at ground level and outside my pyramid, which was my protection and later on turned into my torture chamber.

My sloppy sacristan is taking longer than necessary in building the litter. He said it has to be solid and well balanced. The steps of the pyramid are too steep, as in a proper Aztec temple, and they'll have to carry me with infinite care because I, accustomed to flouting all laws, unhesitatingly respect the law of gravity.

267

I ascend on the shoulders of my four strong sawmen and I feel perfectly well. Locomotion by human blood has always been best for transportation, and if this isn't quick enough it doesn't matter, just the same I can ride slowly on manback. I am the burden that will always lie heavy on their shoulders.

Very slowly, step by step, one by one, and with effort, on the orders of my sacristan, who acts as coxswain. One, two, one, two, they go up with a tortoise-like rhythm, but with rhythm nevertheless, and I amuse myself contemplating Estrella, who is riding along in the open and is enormous now and brilliant in the setting sun. Little by little she is taking on pink tones and also a certain life of her own.

As they are about to get there, I shout to the rustics: "You may call me Your Highness. Now more than ever."

Because I'm on the summit once again, and they put me down ever so gently on the cushions at the top, under the canopy that the Egret had ordered built to surprise me. My clothing has been displaced more than was necessary to show off the now gigantic Estrella, and one of the rustics opens his mouth to ask his idiotic question, pointing with his startled finger: "What's that, Your Highness?"

"You really are moronic! It's my love cannula, what else? Everybody has it beneath the stomach, I have it on top. I'm different in that, too."

I've had the place decorated with feathers. Adornments and fronds of peacock feathers, fans made of feathers, cushions, an enormous plume from the best of aigrettes, the finest egret feathers, without having anyone feel he has been mentioned or take it as a personal matter. I haven't plucked anybody, although this is nothing but feathers and I feel angelical, graceful.

Hatching the philosopher's egg from which the Phoenix Bird, my son, will be born. The great egg grows and grows, I ought to be filled with pride, but the only thing that fills me, from sunup on, day after day, is boredom. Remaining motionless up here with thousands of eyes looking at me has become intolerable. Peacock feathers, yes, but still cocks and the eyes on the feathers observe me and I feel iridescent and motionless like them, varying only with the variations of the light. Hatching under an awning that covers the sky and even the flight of the cormorant, which looks like a vulture.

It's true that it also covers me from the flight of the vultures, and that can be an advantage. What I would like to see are the ducks passing in V-formation heading south, toward my target. But vultures, buzzards, bald-headed birds of prey, those evil creatures flying in concentric circles, making my egg the only target, those I prefer not to see. I know that they're up there, flying in avid circles closing in over my head. The awning separates me from them as if to protect me. I don't want the protection of rag! I'd like to fulminate them with a look, with the support of the myriad of eyes on the feathers, fatuous as they are. Let them serve me in some way.

Egret! Egret! come pull down the awning with your bill!

"You'll get sunstroke, Highness."

He says it puffing, panting from having had to climb up on the run. What crap, and I translate to myself: The egg's going to fry, the sweaty idiot thinks, it's going to cook in the sun. And he might just be right, that's why I keep a dignified silence, looking for a change in direction for my complaints. This is getting too boring now, I've got to bring on the ending.

"Look, staid aide, cancan maid, canine-made. Now you're going to change roles. You're going to put on your emissary suit and go to the Capital and tell them to come."

"To Capivarí, Divinity?"

"What do you mean, Capivarí! I'm playing no games. You're going to the real Capital, south, and you're going to gather together all the worshippers of the Dead Woman. They'll be glad to come because they've got nothing else to do, I've been told the Shrine has been outlawed again. They deserved it for being so passive. Go tell them that their true Illustrious Divinity, I in person, the one who first brought them together, am on the point of giving birth. Make clear to them that the birth will occur through my mediation and in my body. Thanks to me, all will be illuminated."

"As you command, Highness."

"You'll be sorry otherwise. And now let's be practical. Did the plane come as usual to take away the merchandise?"

"Of course, Divinity. That process hasn't changed, it functions like clockwork, like the cycle of seasons that we don't see here but which we know takes place in the south. I wonder what the weather's like, down there? What shall I wear?"

"Stop your foolishness, but put on something discreet. Don't attract attention. Especially, don't let anyone recognize you. You can board the Beechcraft, and have them drop you off as close to the Basilica as possible. I'm sure you'll find them all still there at the Shrine, contrite. Take them the Good News and tell them to come and adore me. And hurry. The great Advent is at hand."

The annunciation (the announcement)

Now I, the Egret, the staid aide, a dog made (the cancan maid?), converted into a messenger of the Divinity, with winged feet, stuck, rather, into this winged mechanical beast, am on my way to the Shrine to fulfill the most beautiful of commands. I am the angel of the annunciation now, now I am the star that will guide them to the place of the birth. On my return, I will climb up the pyramid with the cradle and will stand beside the Deity awaiting the sublime moment.

"I'm dropping you off as near as possible to the Shrine, but not too near. This area is closely watched, you're going to have to proceed with great caution if you don't want them to grab you. The situation is very tense. There are rumors of a plot, and the military are on war alert. They're not fooling around."

Fooling, I mumble, once on solid ground and walking toward the Shrine. If that imbecile of a pilot only knew. But there's no reason for him to know anything about anything, he's not the one who has to transmit the message, and that's why I prefer to keep quiet.

The pilot spoke of a plot, naturally. Everything must be in convulsions over the closeness of the Great Event, what a celebration when the News is announced! What joy!

I do advance with caution, though; this is no time to ignore the signs of destiny, as the Master would have said when he was Master and not Mistress. S/he uses more poetical but just as precise words now, and even from a distance reminds me to be careful. I can't allow myself the luxury of falling into an ambush and failing in my noble mission.

I'm insanely careful. I wait in a grove for nightfall and I advance in the darkness with my owl eyes. I have become a nyctalope to serve the cause, I've become as astute as a fox. I advance in the night with my new wolfish darkness, I've got something of the stealthy panther about me as I slink around the guards and pass close by without being spotted. Once on the grounds of the Basilica, I wait for dawn in a cave by the river and hold back the rooster in me that would have liked to celebrate the first light by giving out with a crow of joy.

When the sun is already lighting up the world well, I come out of my den to imitate it by bearing to the faithful my portion of the true light. All the people will be waiting for me, and when they receive my word they'll form caravans and arrange long pilgrimages to the squat pyramid of the Kingdom of the Black Lagoon. And at the precise moment the fireworks will go off. The sky will fill with lights. And all the people will be there to receive the child. My cradle shall be the craft in which we'll carry him downstream. We will all go singing along the banks of the river until we reach the spot where we will call a halt and salute the Shrine before entering the heart of the Capital, where the Main Square and, above all, Government House await us.

The first attack is a question. Where are the people? And as it is asked, that question externalizes all the horror and the lacerating deception. Where are the people, where? Because the square by the Shrine has been devastated. Not even a trace remains of the crowds who had congregated there once, there isn't even a miserable half-burned candle or a crushed beer can. The Egret practically weeps, unable to hide his disappointment, his misfortune. And he has no reason to hide them. There's not a soul there who can see him, nobody. Nobody at all.

More and more daring and desolate, the Egret goes on to the center of the square, amid the vast abandonment of the place that he had imagined as a Persian bazaar. It's as if the twin towers of the Basilica were coming down on top of him as he goes forward, trying to devour him. Yes, let the towers swallow me, let the earth swallow me. What won't swallow him is the Basilica itself, its doors closed, impenetrable.

Everything so dead. In the back of the entranceway, only a slim little cloud of dust is alive. Like a small pompon of smoke, it moves about, comes and goes, sometimes rising a little and at other times shrinking and growing dark.

For lack of any other stimulant, the frustrated messenger approaches cautiously so as to at least transmit his message to the little cloud. But when he is a few steps away the dust dissipates and in the middle of what had been the cloud a terribly wrinkled old woman with a broom in her hand appears. She has stopped sweeping for a moment and complains: "This has become a pigsty, you can't imagine. Luckily, they've forbidden the worship, but now I've got to clean and clean to get everything back in order."

"Crazy old woman. You don't understand anything about sacred disorder. Where has everyone gone?"

"I am everyone now, can't you see? Or do you think I swept them all away? They must have gone back home. The ones who could, of course. The others I'm afraid are carpeting the river, serving as food for the catfish, who'll eat any slop. On a certain afternoon the troops came as trumpets sounded the charge and they took away all they could. They took a lot of them away and we never saw them again. As usual."

"Why such fury?"

"How should I know. That's the way they are. One day they prohibited the worship of the Dead Woman— touch wood, they mustn't hear me say her name—and they gave absolute orders to break it up. But there wasn't time. They wiped out everything immediately, they even roughed up some priests. And they carried away all the relics."

"What shall we do now?"

"I have to go on sweeping."

"I'm not worried about you, you old crone, I'm worried about myself."

"All right, then. Follow the river back to where you came from. But go by water, they won't find you that way. The river is the zone of the dead, not of the living, they won't be looking for you there. But don't even think of sticking your nose into the Capital. There they'll make you disappear for sure."

Flying down in a small plane is quite different from finding oneself forced to row upriver against the current. Being called the Egret, a long-legged and somewhat aquatic bird, didn't make the adventure any easier for him. Days and days of rowing under the haughty sun, allowing himself to be devoured by mosquitoes, and then those nights, as if hanging from nothingness: falling asleep from fatigue in the boat docked in among the bushes along the shore, the protection of a very feeble nest. Until one afternoon, when he was on the point of surrendering to despair, he recognized the shore.

It wasn't so much recognition of the landscape—so identical, inextricably, in the last stretches of the journey. It was a perception in the distance of the activity of the shad fishermen, men from his parts, fishermen on horseback, in what other area of the globe could they have come to be? Only in a land where everything looks inverted yet is over-intelligent.

The shad fishermen drag their long nets into the river mounted on Percherons. The horses do the dragging, that is; the men direct them acrobatically, standing on their backs. And sometimes—if the horse has to swim—they grab it by the tail so as not to be kicked. In addition to that subtle maneuver, the horses know their trade better than any fisherman, and on reaching midstream, they fan out to spread the net. And then, with an enormous effort, they drag the net out of the river.

On this particular occasion, the dragging turned out to be harder than ever. Amid a myriad of shad, a man stood out, having left his boat to wriggle in with the swarm. He no longer had the strength to row or swim to shore.

A man tanned by the sun, like a huge fish, a golden fish in that throbbing tide of silver, the shoal of shad. Gilded by his days of rowing, covered over with silvery scales like sequins, the Egret felt he was the angel of the annunciation once more and recovered his strength. He demanded, making use of all manner of threats, that the shad fishermen turn over to him their only white Percheron, and without saddle or stirrups, he set off on his way at a steady pace. He would gallop to Capivarí, bearing a happiness of dangling feet, face to the wind, his skin golden and star-speckled. He would arrive and bring them together, he would harangue them, that mockery of a people, so that they would finally run like surrendering lions to the feet of the Childbearing Deity, the Chihuacóatl Quitzali, or whatever one calls it.

They are about to arrive, soon the Egret will deposit the people at my feet. They will be down below, as usual, they will lick the soles of my feet from a distance, and I can finally anticipate the splendor and recover my pride.

I can go back to total happiness and abandonment. I can rejoice in my capacity for completeness: complete I am, total. Father mother and son am I, and this my present passivity is not such—how could I have made the mistake of feeling bored? I am the internal birthgiving revolution. My fruit is growing in me. Estrella is already wholly integrated in my body. It is I on the inside and I on the outside. I who is growing and I my own being, my en-globement.

Under a canopy, atop my pyramid, I am everywhere simultaneously, and shortly I will flood the earth. I am the salt of life, for the very simple, magnificent fact of bearing a son. The happiness of a son. We shall praise the glory of the son which is my exclusive glory. We shall be immortal, ubiquitous, dazzling, merciless, ominous, dar-ing. Indivisible we shall be; I will be indivisible in all my capacity of division. Invincible.

With a cheerful tremor I'll go on with my gestation and one day we will rule the world. To rule the world is the only possible voluptuousness. The great cosmic or-gasm. The joy one feels in destroying others and the plea-sures of torture multiplied to infinity, now being born of me, in all ease, without the slightest effort, developing on its own. So naturally from me that it is already I, my son. My supreme joy. My arm, my weapon.

Glittering with silver scales, mounted on a moon-bearer, I go; singing to the setting sun the grandeur of my destiny, I go. A few miles from Capivarí I acknowledge the happiness I feel and will feel when I am received as an apparition. Fatigue has been banished from my muscles and my arms have forgotten all the rowing and only my thighs are tense and alert, holding me up on the haunches of this fiery steed that now, why? suddenly stops and draws back. I give it some kicks on the side—it almost bucks, for nothing in the world will it follow its path. And suddenly I hear the terrifying hissing and I see them—and my hair stands on end, I feel all my scales falling off, my teeth chattering from terror, it's an ineffable current that passes from my horse to my crotch and runs up my body.

Under the shadowless light of dusk I see them and for the first time I know true fright. It's the vipers' knot, the wheel of the world, spinning, pairing off, the rattlesnakes shaking their rattles, the coral snakes and their poison, the pit viper, the *curiyú* viper, all of them, I can't make them out, they're colors that mingle, tails and heads so much alike, and all copulating. The great wheel of copulation, spinning, fluttering to the sides. The viper, an animal with two phalluses. The envied one, the envious one, joined in a single mass, hissing, and my horse rears on his hind legs and I can no longer hold back, I let myself slip to the ground and I open my mouth so my scream of terror will flee from me and leave me deflated and without air.

It's a sign, there can be no doubt of it. The fireball of copulating vipers that spins around the world to announce misfortune.

And I, horseless now, stripping myself of my golden skin, without a tiny scale of decoration now, without the slightest twinkle, tearing myself apart, I run and stumble and run and fall again and get up, dragging myself as best I can, hurrying as best I can, because something very serious must be happening to my Divinity. There in the pyramid. The one I love needs me. My deity, my mother. My all.

He finally arrived. Covered with thorns and brambles. Lacerated, he crossed woods and barrens, jumped over anthill clumps, and, more dead than alive, reached the foot of the pyramid at daybreak.

And it was as if something else had broken at that very instant. There was a big bang and a crimson jet rose up in the air, spouting forth from the summit of the pyramid. And the thundering voice let itself be heard:

Even though my veins are vipers with red teeth, my blood shall not be any less whipped by a poisoned wind in the union of my remains!

And then nothing. Just a pale echo repeating *remains, mains, mains, mains, mains.*

The Egret collapsed at the foot of the pyramid.

Up above, on the platform of feathers and ruffles, something that had exploded began to bleed finitely. And a red line, like a string of ants, trickled down the steps one after another, and advanced, following the natural slope of the earth, cross-country, heading south. A red thread, alive, a long, thin little viper with its tail up high in the pyramid and its head moving toward the Capital, stretching out along the river, which was growing turbulent. Not the thread. Without changing thickness or texture, it advanced, swiftly, sometimes meandering, turning away before some unexpected obstacle, always heading south. Always forward. Mercurial, not allowing the earth to absorb a single drop. Slowly slowly heading south alongside the river, with a guidance all its own.

In the Capital, two people seated in the Main Square saw it arrive and were startled.

"Look," the woman with curly hair pointed out. "We should go tell you know who. Look, the famous river of blood has finally materialized. There it comes. With a little luck, the president will come out of Government House now, slip on the river of blood, crack his skull on the curb, and, oh glory! we'll know peace at last. The twenty years of peace promised by the prophecy."

The heavyset man in white shook his head. "I really doubt it. Tyrannies are not what they used to be. Now they have replacement parts. One president falls and another is ready to take over. There's no shortage of generals. And this little thread is certainly not the river of blood so often mentioned. If it were so, we would get not twenty years but under twenty *minutes* of peace."